LUCIENNE BOYCE has always b
era. In 2006 she gained an M
Open University specialising
2012 she published her first F
(SilverWood Books), an eightee
and the South Seas (which was awarded the Awesome Indies
Seal of Approval). Lucienne has been a member of the Historical
Novel Society since shortly after its foundation, has contributed
numerous articles, reviews and interviews to the Society, and
edited the HNS newsletter.

Lucienne also writes non-fiction and in 2013 published
The Bristol Suffragettes (SilverWood Books), a history of the local
suffragette movement. She is currently working on the second
Dan Foster Mystery. Lucienne was born in Wolverhampton
and now lives in Bristol, which is the setting and inspiration for
much of her work.

Want to know more?
Find Lucienne Boyce on Twitter: @LucienneWrite
You can also stay up-to-date by visiting her website at
lucienneboyce.com

BLOODIE BONES

LUCIENNE BOYCE

SilverWood

Published in 2015 by SilverWood Books

SilverWood Books Ltd
14 Small Street, Bristol, BS1 1DE
www.silverwoodbooks.co.uk

ISBN 978-1-78132-360-1 (paperback)
ISBN 978-1-78132-361-8 (ebook)

British Library Cataloguing in Publication Data
A CIP catalogue record for this book is available from
the British Library

Set in New Baskerville by SilverWood Books
Printed on responsibly sourced paper

BLOODIE BONES

Chapter One

Dan Foster rolled from beneath the hedge, his breath puffing on the cool morning air. He jumped lightly to his feet, wincing at the stiffness of his muscles. Uncomfortable place, the countryside. Uncomfortable and lonely. There was no traffic on the road beyond the hedge, where Dr Russell had dropped him last night after showing him the corpse, though here and there he saw smoke rising from chimneys. In a field a long way off, a farm worker was walking purposefully towards a tree-topped ridge, a black and white dog running around him.

Dan was cold, damp and hungry – all useful states for a man in his disguise. He had a long walk back to Barcombe, but he did not want to arrive too early in the day. Plenty of time to do some stretches and running on the spot to get his limbs moving.

As he exercised he reviewed the events of the last twenty-four hours. At this time yesterday he had been in the gymnasium, sparring with Noah, when a messenger boy had come from the office to say the Chief Magistrate needed him urgently. It was perhaps just as well for his pride – his wily old opponent was still nifty on his feet and handy with his punches, even with gloves on. There had been no time to go next door for a steam bath, and Dan had had to make do with a cold dousing in the shower before setting off from Cecil Street at a run, dodging the laden carts turning from the Strand down to the wharf.

He had reached Bow Street before any of the night patrols came in with their catch. Pre-rush, the gaoler lounged about, chatting with the cleaning woman. Dan went straight to

Sir William Addington's room, where he found the jowly old man waiting for him with a stranger. The man was expensively though darkly dressed, and drenched in scent sufficient to overcome the musty smell of wormy wood, dusty carpet and heaps of yellowing papers.

"Ah, Foster, sit down," Sir William said. "This is Mr Garvey. He's here on behalf of his client, Lord Oldfield."

Dan moved a pile of pink-tied documents to the floor and sat in the ancient leather chair. "What's the story?"

Garvey frowned at his directness. "I represent Lord Adam Oldfield of Barcombe in Somerset." He had a deep, gravelly voice and drew out each word as if he were charging by the syllable. "His Lordship has recently entered into his inheritance at Oldfield Hall, a fine mansion set in an estate of some two thousand acres, which includes prime woodland. Like his father before him, he's plagued by poachers. One of his first in a series of planned improvements was to enclose the woodland and deny the encroachers access to it. Unfortunately, this has resulted in a spate of illegal protests – fence breaking and so on – and it has not put a stop to the thieving. If anything, it's better organised than of old. Now it seems they've gone one step further. Last evening I received the message that Lord Oldfield's gamekeeper was murdered by poachers on Wednesday night."

Today was Friday. "Two nights ago," Dan said. "Any witnesses?"

Another frown. Garvey did not like being questioned. "I know no more than that and so can give you no further information about the crime. However, His Lordship has instructed me to go down to Barcombe immediately and bring a Principal Officer with me." He glanced at the magistrate. "Sir William tells me that you are the man for the job."

Sir William nodded. "You're to go down with Mr Garvey and infiltrate the gang responsible for the outrage. His Lordship is the local magistrate, so there'll be no problem with obtaining warrants when you need them."

Garvey stood up. "My carriage is waiting at my chambers in Lincoln's Inn. When can you be ready?"

"I'll join you within the hour," Dan answered, rising.

Sir William came round from behind his desk to escort Garvey out. When they had gone, Dan hurried downstairs to the clerks' room. He unhooked a key from the wall and opened the cupboard where he kept an overnight bag packed ready for such emergencies. He checked his supply of ball and powder, then rifled one of the desks for pen and paper and scribbled half a dozen lines to Caroline, telling her he would be out of town for a few days. He added a reminder of where his will was kept – the only part likely to interest his wife.

He spent more time over a second note to his sister-in-law, Eleanor. Caroline had complained so often about the hours he worked and the nights he spent away from home that, as soon as he had been able to afford it, he had taken a house in Russell Street large enough for Eleanor and his mother-in-law to move in with them. It was one less worry knowing they were there to keep an eye on Caroline.

Dan called the boy and sent him off with the notes, then pushed his way out to the street through the crowd of drunks and whores fighting and shouting around the gaoler's desk.

Garvey had had his private chaise brought up from his country house in Streatham, and four fresh horses were already in harness. The driver, a swaggering man in livery, was accompanied by a groom of sixteen. It was the boy's job to ride ahead and order a change of horses at each stage, and the man paid the turnpikes.

As soon as they were in the carriage, Garvey opened a case of documents and buried himself beneath a pile of deeds and maps, turning his papers over with crisp, irritable movements. The smell of his eau de cologne was cloying in the confined space. Dan pulled the glass down an inch or so until an angry 'tut' compelled him to raise it. A few miles outside London, Garvey told him to lift up his seat and take out the basket he would find there. They breakfasted on the contents, and very welcome they were: small beer, soft rolls, cheese, chicken, eggs, cake.

No expense was spared, since they were travelling out of Lord Oldfield's purse. They changed horses every few miles, and Garvey was always careful to ask for a receipt. They made good speed, but even so it was dark by the time they got to Barcombe, and Dan could make out very little of the country.

They drove through ornate iron gates and along a short drive to the front of Oldfield Hall. Lights glittered out of numerous windows. Dan put on his hat and pulled up his coat collar. A liveried butler led them into a small, green drawing room. It had curtains all the way to the floor, shiny wallpaper, and a pale carpet which Dan thought it a shame to walk on, but short of flying, there was nothing else for it. The room was full of furniture that did not seem up to the part: upholstered, spindly-legged chairs and fragile, polished tables covered with ornaments and vases of flowers. He glanced at the paintings on the walls, which were mostly of half-dressed men and women cavorting by unnatural-looking woods and lakes.

Lord Adam Oldfield sat alone, reading. He looked at Dan as he rose, letting his newspaper fall to the carpet. Dan recognised the latest issue of the *Sporting Magazine*, September 1796. It was open at the 'Champions of England' series. The article featured Tom Johnson. Dan had read it himself a day or two before. He stored the fact for the moment, in case it should be useful.

Lord Oldfield shook hands with Garvey. He motioned the lawyer to a chair. Dan was left standing, hat in hand.

"This is the Runner?" Lord Oldfield asked, resuming his seat.

"His name is Daniel Foster," Garvey replied.

Lord Oldfield acknowledged the information with a slight nod. Dan, reckoning his own age from the assumption that he had been thirteen when Noah had taken him in, put His Lordship at three or four years younger than himself, which would make him twenty-five or six. He had a trim, supple figure and a handsome face, full of pride, as was only to be expected in a man of his class. He was not at his ease, however. His pale blue eyes were troubled and his manner subdued. When Garvey invited him to describe recent events he hesitated, finding it difficult to begin his story.

"My gamekeeper, Josh Castle, was lured out of his cottage during the night and killed while a gang of poachers helped themselves to two of my deer. The animals were caught in nets, pole-axed, and butchered. We found nothing but the heads and skins. It was a professional job."

"Who found Castle and when, My Lord?" asked Dan.

Lord Oldfield did not look at Dan, but directed his answer to Garvey. "The first underkeeper, Caleb Witt, went to his cottage early yesterday morning to get his orders for the day. He found the door open, a half-eaten meal on the table, and no sign of Josh. While he waited outside, thinking Josh might be close by, he heard a dog howling. He followed the sound and found Josh with his dog beside him."

"Has the coroner been?"

"Yes, the inquest was here this morning. Unsurprisingly, he returned a verdict of murder," Lord Oldfield snapped at the lawyer, who was innocent of making the query.

"How was Castle killed?"

"You can go and look at the body, can't you?" Oldfield said fiercely, raising his eyes to Dan's face for the first time. Mastering himself, he turned back to Garvey. "He was beaten to death. I want the culprits hanged, Garvey. Do you think yon man can bring that about?"

"Sir William thinks so," Garvey answered.

Dan had been called worse things than 'yon man', but he found it hard to control his irritation.

"Where is the body?"

"We put him in the ice house," Lord Oldfield told the lawyer. "Dr Russell will assist. He examined Josh and gave evidence at the inquest. He is with Mother at the moment. This upset has brought on one of her nervous headaches."

He rose and rang the bell by the fireplace, rustling the newspaper with his foot.

"I saw Johnson's first fight," Dan said.

Lord Oldfield spun round, his face animated with sudden interest. "You did? Where? When?"

"It was at Blackheath in '81, versus Stephen Oliver. Yes," Dan added with a smile, "I saw Tom Johnson beat Death."

Lord Oldfield smiled too, getting the joke. Death was Steevy Oliver's nickname, given him on account of his pale face. "Do you recall anything of the fight?"

Dan had cause to remember that fight. He had been drawn to it by the crowds; the takings were always good from the Fancy. He had been trained by one of the best, a receiver called Weaver. The old devil sewed bells on his coat pockets, and the trick was to rob him without setting them off.

A bigger boy had taken exception to Dan encroaching on his territory and the two got into a fight. In keeping with the sporting occasion, a ring had formed around them while Dan took his beating. He would not cry quarter, though, even when the lout left him flat on his back. When he opened his good eye, there was a face grinning over him. Instinct had told him that was a moment to scramble and run, but the man pushed him back.

He dabbed painfully at the cut on Dan's forehead with a wet handkerchief. "You've got bottom, lad, I'll give you that. With a bit of training you could make a tasty fighter."

Dan croaked, "What the fuck do you mean, *bottom*?"

The man laughed. "And a foul mouth for a young 'un! Bottom is staying power. Endurance. Never mind. I'll explain another time. Can you stand up?"

And that was how Noah had lifted Dan out of the gutter, taken him to his boxing academy in Cecil Street, trained him to fight by scientific methods, and driven the savage out of him. But this was a tale Dan did not tell His Lordship; a tale he did not tell many. Instead, he answered Lord Oldfield's question about Johnson's performance.

"It was touch and go at first, My Lord. That is, Death did the touching and made the claret flow, though a veteran. But age soon told on him. Tom's manoeuvres were marvellous to watch. He'd look out for his opponent's weaknesses and go straight for them, the head especially. He was nothing showy, though he was cool in a fight. He stalled off Death that day, My Lord. I saw him a few years later fight Bristol man Bill Ward, in Berkshire."

"The championship fight!"

"It was not a good match. Ward took a doubler from Johnson in the first round, and realised he couldn't beat him except by tiring him out. So we were treated to a display of humbugging, with Ward dropping to his knees whenever Tom came near him. After an hour and a half of this, Ward cried foul and bolted."

Garvey gazed at the two men as if they were speaking in a foreign tongue, and an uncouth one at that. The butler, Ackland, came in for his orders and was sent to fetch Dr Russell. He soon returned with the doctor, a lantern and a key.

Leaving Garvey and his client looking over the documents the lawyer had brought with him, Dan followed the doctor across the hall and down the service stairs to a wide, flagged corridor which led to the kitchen. Larders, washrooms and offices opened off on each side. The place smelt of plentiful supplies: game, bread, cheese, beer. Dan heard servants moving about in the kitchen, the murmur of voices and clatter of dishes. He and the doctor passed cautiously through the open back door into a courtyard. They left this through a door in the wall. Dr Russell pointed out the stable block to the left, on a rise a little above the house. Lights shone out through an archway with a clock above it as the stable lads went about feeding and settling the animals for the night. Dan and Dr Russell crossed a dark stretch of lawn, passed through a gap cut in a yew hedge, and went down some steps to a small cylindrical building.

Russell opened the door with the huge key and they descended a wide stone staircase that followed the curve of the brickwork. The walls oozed icy water, and the iron railings felt cold enough to tear the skin off bare hands.

They reached the bottom of the building, which was several feet below the ground. The doctor opened his lantern and took a candle from a box on the wall. He used this to light the candles set in box about the chamber. They hissed and fizzled reluctantly, burning feebly in the damp air.

A circular stone counter ran around the wall, with crates of ice stored on and beneath it. There were also dishes of frozen, flavoured cream, covered with muslin. In the middle of the room was a marble slab used for cutting up the ice, with lidded buckets for carrying it to the house stacked between its massive stone legs. Josh Castle lay under a sheet on the slab. Pale pink water flowed along a channel around its edge and drained into a stone vessel.

The doctor pulled back the sheet to expose the naked corpse. In spite of the keeper's wounds, Dan saw that he had been a handsome man, golden-skinned and dark haired, with a well-shaped mouth which must have produced an engaging smile. He had a fine figure, vigorous and muscular, as Dan would expect in his line of work. Such a man would not have been easy to overcome if his assailant had faced him. But his attacker had not. He had felled Castle with a blow to the back of the head and then administered a beating so severe the arms, legs and ribs were broken.

"The corpse is not stiff," Dan said, laying the head back on the slab after examining the smashed skull.

"No," said Dr Russell. "The atmosphere of the ice house has delayed rigor mortis."

"Would the blow to his head have killed him?"

"Almost certainly."

"And the beating was given after death?"

The doctor nodded.

"Was the weapon found?"

Dr Russell crossed to the counter and came back with an iron bar. Dan took it from him. It was stained with a red that was not rust.

"It comes from one of the gates on the edge of the estate," Russell said, replacing it on the counter. "Such acts of vandalism have become frequent since the enclosure of Barcombe Wood. They also found this lying next to Castle."

He pointed to a form stretched out beside the bar. At first Dan took it for a second body. Stepping closer, he saw it was a crude scarecrow made of sacks and straw, with a rope around its neck. White lines had been daubed across the front of it to make a rough representation of a skeleton. The skull was crudely drawn: white circles for eyes, a dab of nose, a grinning grid of teeth. There was a piece of paper pinned to its chest. Dan removed it and held it close to the lantern. It had been torn from a larger sheet of thick, ivory-coloured letter paper, and misspelt words were scrawled on it in what looked like blood: '*Tirants Bwar Bloodie Bones.*'

The doctor had moved away and stood shivering at the feet of the corpse, his breath steaming.

Dan said, "Who, or what, is 'Bloodie Bones'?"

"Bloodie Bones is a bogeyman, and the name the poachers use. Her Ladyship tells me that a few weeks ago a similar note, wrapped around a stone, was thrown through a window in Oldfield Hall. It threatened arson and bloodshed. Days later a hayrick on the estate farm was set alight."

Dan picked up the noose. "The rope has been cleanly cut."

"Yes. The other end was hanging from the tree beneath which they found Castle. He must have been cutting it down when he was attacked."

"It must have looked like a hanging man in the dark."

The doctor said nothing to this. He stared morosely at the body. Dan put the note in his pocket.

"Was Castle armed, do you know?"

"His gun was brought in with the body. It had not been fired."

"I've seen enough."

Russell pulled the sheet over the gamekeeper. Between them they extinguished the candles, Russell took up the lantern, and they ascended the stone steps. The doctor carefully locked the building.

Chapter Two

Lord Oldfield and Garvey seemed startled by their return. His Lordship broke off in mid-sentence and the lawyer hastily rolled up the map they had been looking at. Lord Oldfield pointed to a tray of decanters and glasses on the side table and told them to help themselves to sherry. Dr Russell poured himself a liberal measure, but Dan said, "No, thank you."

"So, Foster," said Lord Oldfield, "what do you make of the crime?"

"It was a savage attack, My Lord," Dan answered, "with care taken to link it with recent protests about Barcombe Wood. I can't rule out the possibility, though, that the Bloodie Bones angle is just a ruse to deflect suspicion. We could be looking at the work of an outside gang, especially if this isn't how your local thieves normally operate."

"I see you're a man who likes to look beyond the obvious," growled Garvey. It was not a compliment.

Lord Oldfield shook his head. "No. I'm certain that our home-grown poachers are behind the Bloodie Bones outrages, and they murdered Josh. If you can rid me of them, you'll rid me of a host of troublemakers at the same time, which means that my plans – "

Garvey cleared his throat and Lord Oldfield checked himself.

"Well," Dan said, letting the gentlemen have their secret, "even if they weren't from around here, they must have had help from someone in the village. Do you have any suspicions who your home-grown poachers are?"

"All of them!" Lord Oldfield cried. "Every countryman is

a poacher if he gets the chance. Rabbits, pheasants' eggs, fish – they help themselves to whatever they can. It could have been any of them."

"Dr Russell tells me you had a letter signed 'Bloodie Bones' some weeks ago. Do you still have it?"

"It's in my office. Doctor, would you mind?"

Lord Oldfield told Russell where he would find the letter, and the doctor obligingly hurried off.

"I shall also need directions to the spot where Castle's body was found," Dan said.

"I can give you those, though you won't find anything. I had my men search the ground thoroughly."

"And I'm sure they missed nothing, but it is always useful to see the site of a murder."

Dr Russell returned with the letter. It was written on the back of a dog-eared receipt from the Angel Hotel, a coaching inn on Westgate Street in Bath. The receipt had not been used, so there was nothing to give a lead to whom it had belonged. Anyone from Barcombe could have picked it up: carriers, farmers, tradesmen, shoppers, pleasure-seekers.

'Remember the pore in distres,' it said, *'or els there will be blood and fier you may depend upon these lines to be trwe for we will sartainly do it. Bloodie Bones.'*

The note had nothing in common with the one Dan had taken from the scarecrow in the ice house, apart from bad spelling and poor handwriting. They differed in length and style, and there were no similarities between the paper used. There was not one person behind the notes; anyone and everyone acting out a grudge called himself Bloodie Bones.

"How will you find the killer?" Lord Oldfield asked.

"Not by going amongst them as a Bow Street officer." Dan picked up his bag. "Is there somewhere I can change?"

"Dr Russell can show you into the library."

"Then I need to make my way out of the village without being seen, so I can enter Barcombe tomorrow on the tramp."

"I can take you in my gig if you like," the doctor said.

"People are used to seeing me going about at odd times of the day and night on house calls."

"An offer I gladly accept."

The doctor waited outside the library while Dan exchanged his own clothes for dirty and threadbare corduroy breeches, coarse grubby stockings, a grimy shirt, tattered jacket, greasy hat and clumsy, thick-soled shoes. With the finishing touch of a night in the open and a hike back to Barcombe in the morning, even Eleanor would not have known him. She certainly would not have liked the rough fellow he had become.

He had worn worse: clothes so patched and thin it seemed only dirt held them together. Dressed like this, those days did not seem very far away. Going undercover was a going back, a reminder that it was always possible for a man to fall again. It was that constant, nagging anxiety that gave him his edge, kept him alert to danger. Battle ready, like in a fight. Every villain he brought low was a victory that took him further away from his past, drew him closer to money, promotion, security. A step further away from the gutter.

He hid the two Bloodie Bones notes in a concealed pocket in his portmanteau and packed his clothes, tipstaff and pistol on top of them. He wrapped a few pennies in a rag, threw his purse in with the rest, and pocketed his razor case. His razor and hone were good quality. A decent blade was something he had not been able to bring himself to do without, but he had fixed it in a cheap wooden handle and kept it in a battered box more suitable to a man of his supposed station.

"What arrangements will you make for reporting your progress to me?" Lord Oldfield asked when Dan and the doctor returned to the drawing room.

"There will be no reports. I will only contact you in an emergency or when the case has reached its crisis."

"We need to find somewhere safe where you can leave a message."

"No, I'll put nothing in writing."

"Then how will you get in touch with me?"

"I'll think of something when the time comes."

"Could I help?" the doctor asked. "Since I am often visiting Lady Oldfield, you could easily contrive to leave a message with me."

Dan considered the suggestion. "Very well. But do not expect to hear from me for some time, My Lord. Though it may seem to you that nothing is happening, be assured that will not be the case."

There was a muffled "Humph!" from Garvey.

His Lordship reluctantly accepted the arrangement and agreed to store Dan's things in his muniments room, to which only he had a key. Leaving Garvey to his maps and deeds, the other three hurried away. In order to minimise the danger of fire, the room where the estate documents were stored was at the end of the block opposite the kitchen, in a stone turret reached by a short spiral staircase. Lord Oldfield let Dan into the windowless chamber. He deposited his bag in a corner between two tall wooden cabinets. Lord Oldfield locked the door, whispered "Good luck", and left them.

All was quiet, but lights still burned in the kitchen. They got out without being seen, and Dan, keeping to the shadows, followed the doctor across the courtyard. He waited in the darkness under the wall while Russell went to fetch his gig. The stable boy's cheery "Goodnight" drifted down to him with the clatter and jingle of harness. A moment later the doctor emerged from beneath the clock arch. He drove slowly along the drive without stopping. Dan jumped up beside him and hunched down. They drove away from the Hall in silence.

Beyond the Hall gates, Russell pointed to the left. "That's Drover's Way. The keeper's cottage is down there."

The yellow light from the carriage shone briefly on a bracken-filled ditch and fence before the darkness of the forest swallowed it up. Dan would not have known there was a track there if it had not been pointed out to him.

At the end of the lane they turned onto the Bath Road. The

village lay behind them and, after passing one or two outlying cottages, the roadway was empty. They clopped along between dark hedges, looming trees and black fields.

Dan now had an opportunity to turn his attention to Dr Russell. The doctor was a pleasant-looking man of thirty or so who seemed at ease in his grand surroundings. When he spoke to Lord Oldfield he was polite but not fawning. Clearly he had confidence in himself and his skills, and had no need to toady to win favour. No doubt he also had a sympathetic manner with his aristocratic female patient, an attitude necessary for any practitioner who wished to make his way in the world.

"Have you been the Oldfields' family physician for long?" Dan asked.

"Since the night Lord Oldfield died, and I was only called on then because it was too far to send to Bath for Dr Kean. By the time the family did bring themselves to summon a mere country doctor, it was too late to do anything for the sufferer. His widow, however, was in a pitiable state, and I was able to be of such use to her that she has come to rely on me. It was a stroke of good fortune for me," he added candidly, "that will help to establish me in my career."

"How did the old Lord die?"

"He had a bad attack of gout. They tried all the usual treatments – warmed flannels and bandages of sheep's wool and oilskin around the foot, as well as administering pints of gruel and glasses of lemon juice and water. But none of it did any good to a constitution debilitated by long duration of the distemper. It was a nasty death." Russell was silent for a moment as he negotiated a corner. "Many in the village say that it was Bloodie Bones who killed him – gout is a disease of the joints, you know. Not one of the poachers, you understand, but the very ghoul himself. Some believe that Castle too was killed by a spectre."

"I think it very unlikely." Dan had no time for the hobgoblin business. He had seen too many real monsters.

Russell laughed. "I'm sure you do. But there's no logic in superstition. It doesn't occur to them that if Bloodie Bones was on their side, he wouldn't have killed the old man, and in the middle of Fence Month too."

"Fence Month?"

"June and July time, while Barcombe Wood is out of bounds for the deer-breeding season. The festival is an ancient ritual. Its purpose is to remind the lord of the manor of the people's time-honoured rights to hunt and cut wood there. A youth in dun leggings and tunic with antlers on his head represents the deer – it was Walter Halling this year. Bob Singleton on a hobby horse was the hunter. The role is usually his, for tradition dictates it should go to the village blacksmith. A matron dressed in green is meant to personify the vernal life force. That was Mrs Wicklow, who has blessed the world with an oaf called Abe. The mummers prance up to the wood with ribbons and bells, and the villagers trail after, blowing horns, waving rattles, banging drums. Afterwards there's a fair on the village green – pies and beer, jugglers and jesters, men on stilts, puppets – you've seen the sort of thing."

"Of course. We do have them in London." Dan had seen tooth drawers, giants and dwarves too. Once he saw a man remove a harelip from a two-year-old boy, but he did not know if the child survived the operation. Fairs had been a source of income to him all his life, though nowadays he went to catch the pickpockets, not to swell their numbers.

"Lord Oldfield died on the night of the stag dance. His son closed the fair the next day and, instead of reopening the wood as usual, brought in a gang of Irish labourers to fence it round. There's always been poaching in the wood. The old Lord turned a blind eye to it mostly, provided his deer were left alone. His son wants to build up the herd, and it's to preserve their peace that he keeps the people out. There's been a running battle between him and the village ever since, and now poor Josh Castle has fallen victim to their malice."

He brought the carriage to a halt beneath a canopy of

soughing leaves. "Of course, there's an end to the festival too, and no bad thing, for it usually ended in idleness and drunkenness...Is this far enough for you?"

Dan thanked him and climbed down. The doctor circled the vehicle around, gave a wave of his hand, and disappeared along the road back to Barcombe. Dan turned off the highway, climbed over a gate into a field, and settled down for the night under a hedge.

The farmworker with the black and white dog had disappeared into the trees by the time Dan finished his exercises. He ran his fingers through his hair, shook out a few leaves, picked the burrs off his jacket, put on his hat, and vaulted over the gate into the lane.

The church clock was striking eleven when he reached the outskirts of Barcombe, passing the top of the lane that led to Oldfield Hall. A little further on, he came to the village green on his right. On a rise above it stood two or three old houses, but most of the villagers lived in the cottages strung along the main thoroughfare. One of these housed the general store. Through the open door, Dan glimpsed a group of women gossiping with the shopkeeper, who was leaning across the counter on his folded arms while his apprentice ran back and forth, fetching goods to fill the women's baskets.

Dan followed the aroma of fresh bread to the baker's, where he was pleased to see the effectiveness of his get-up. After one look at him, the woman called her husband from the kitchen. He stood by with his arms folded over his floury apron while Dan bought a halfpenny loaf and asked if he could have a drink of water.

"Village pump is over the road," the woman said, examining the coin before pocketing it and adding darkly, "Next to the lock-up."

The tiny roundhouse did not look as if it had held any miscreants for some time. The bottom of the heavy wooden door had been gnawed by vermin, and its hinges and locks were rusty. If Dan had not been in Barcombe to find a murderous gang of poachers, he would have judged it a law-abiding place. As it was, it only confirmed his opinion that it was high time the old, inefficient parish system, where the ratepayers took it in turns to serve as constable, was done away with. These days most ratepayers hired substitutes to do the job for them, or paid the parish to employ someone at the lowest possible wages, which guaranteed that only incompetents and misfits would undertake police work.

The pump was in a stone shelter over a grating with the spring running beneath it. Dan drank from his cupped hands and looked about while he ate his bread. A back lane looped behind the high street, starting beside the bakery and emerging by the village inn. The houses on it were thatched and smaller than those on the main road. Beyond these, three or four grand residences of grey stone with slate roofs stood in their own grounds. Behind them the country rose to grass-topped slopes dotted with sheep and horses. The Stony River glinted in the valley below.

Through the open casement of the ivy-clad inn came a hubbub of shouting, booing and cheering. Chairs and tables scraped along the stone floor, feet pounded in the porch, and a crowd of farmworkers and labourers, their dogs barking at their heels, tumbled into the street.

A man in shirtsleeves, breeches and scuffed black pumps pranced at their head, punching the air with scarred fists and grimacing with theatrical menace. He was accompanied by another man carrying a bucket, sponge and a bladder of brandy. Dan recognised them immediately. Not that he knew them by name, but he knew what they were: an itinerant fighter and his manager, the sort who would pitch up in some small town or village, issue a challenge, promise a large purse for the winner, then sit back and count their takings. Dan supposed he should call them 'pugilists' for want of a better word, though they usually relied on brute strength and the gullibility of their opponents rather than skill.

Jabbering excitedly, the company thronged over to the pump. Dan stood aside to let the manager fill his bucket. When they moved off, he followed them back to the green. Here there was a great deal of fuss and flourish. The boxer stripped off his shirt and strutted about the circle the spectators had made around him – they did not trouble to erect a ring – snarling and flexing his biceps, shoulder and pectoral muscles. Dan would have been impressed if it had not been for the flabby stomach and saggy face.

The manager unfurled a poster and read out the terms of the challenge.

"Here," he cried, "stands Bold Ben Jones, whose reputation goes before him. I've trained this boy, gentlemen, since he was knee-high to a blade of grass, and I can tell you that in all my years I've never seen a better champion. Why, Lord Barrymore himself said as much! He's stood up to the Coachman, the Young Ruffian and George the Brewer."

It was not impossible, though improbable, that Bold Ben – probably one of a number of names he had owned to over the years – had stood up with the Coachman, the Ruffian and the Brewer. Dan doubted entirely, however, that Lord Barrymore ever had anything to do with him. The Earl had been dead three years. He had been known as 'Hellgate' by his friend, the Prince of Wales, or so Dan had heard from Officer John Townsend, who had the plum job of guarding the royal family. The name Hellgate summed up the man: a reckless prankster and gambler, fond of the stage, a bet, a horse race and a fight – the lower and nastier the better.

The manager pulled a jingling purse out of his pocket, though whether it contained coins was anyone's guess. "Here's two guineas for whoever can beat him!" Then he opened his book and began to take bets.

Standing next to Dan was a stocky, clean-shaven man in his early fifties, his hands in his breeches pockets and his long coat thrown open. He wore muddy gaiters and sturdy boots, and his rough-haired lurcher lay quietly at his feet. There was an air of authority about him, though his clothes were those of a working man. He watched his drunken friends gamble away their money with a tolerant eye.

"Where's this Jones from?" Dan asked him.

"All I know is that he's just come from Stonyton, where he beat all comers, every one a miner."

"A tough lot then."

The man laughed. "Very. But our man's no weakling. That's Bob Singleton."

Bob Singleton: the blacksmith who, Dr Russell said, had pranced about on a hobby horse in the Fence Month festival. He was muscular, with not an ounce of fat on him and fists that looked as if they could smash an anvil. The villagers were confident he would win and their bets were all on him.

Jones took up a fairly creditable stance, and they set to without the advantage of Broughton's, or any other, rules. Jones went on the attack at once, hopping out of harm's way whenever he made a hit. After a third blow landed on Singleton's temple, the blacksmith realised he would get nowhere staying on the defence and chased after Jones, swinging a series of hammer blows at him. They were ill-aimed and Jones easily defended himself, but they did demonstrate the strength of his opponent, especially when one or two accidentally hit home. The first round ended and Singleton retired to have the blood washed out of his eyes.

"A good fight," Dan's neighbour bawled in his ear above the cheering. "Nothing to tell 'em apart."

Dan silently agreed it was true that the two were evenly matched in size and strength, but it was not a good fight. Singleton was the fitter, and whenever his blows hit home they did the business, but with his right eye closed it was not often enough. Compared to Jones, he was clumsy too. The leveller was not long in coming.

A round later, the deflated crowd counted its losses, among which must be numbered its pride. Jones, who apart from bleeding knuckles was hardly touched, did a victory dance.

The manager led a round of applause for the vanquished, who was in no state to appreciate it, and shouted, "Any more comers, gentlemen?"

In the shuffling silence, Dan said, "I'll have a go."

Chapter Three

The manager grinned, already counting his winnings in his head. "What's your name, son?"

"Dan Fielding."

The villagers, whose hopes of seeing Ben bite the dust had been raised by a fresh challenge, groaned when Dan stepped forward. Their disappointment did not rattle him. He would have made the same judgement himself: that he did not stand much chance against the big fellow, who must have been seventeen to his twelve stone.

The man next to him clucked his tongue. "I wouldn't if I were you."

"I'm down to my last penny. I might as well try."

"Well, then. I'll mind your things for you. My name's Drake, by the way. Lucas Drake, Field Officer."

That explained Dan's sense that he was a man of position. In a village, the field officer was the most important of the parish officials. It was his job to enforce the regulations governing the use of the common land, and make sure no one took more than his entitlement by overstocking or grazing his beasts where he had no right. His decisions affected almost everyone, from the prosperous farmer turning out his herds to the poor man collecting firewood and berries. A corrupt man could easily win enemies, an honest one friends.

Dan shook hands with Drake and took to the field barefoot. Ben leered at him and stomped across the arena, fists up. Dan stood his ground but did not brace himself. He held his fists in an amateurish way, arms low and close to his body, which brought a contemptuous snigger from his opponent. He was rewarded for his lack of skill by a peg on the ear, the main force of which he deflected by ducking his head. The betting was already against him, and the crowd, feeling a little more cheerful about their prospects, was prepared to be sympathetic to a game loser. They 'oohed' and 'ahed' whenever he took a hit. He buzzed around the big man with a series of feeble, fly-flap blows, and managed to get through the first round without taking more than sufficient hits to make the thing look good.

Ben Jones began to relax, and when they came together again he dropped his defences. Dan landed one on his nose towards the end of the round, which, as Ben's manager was timekeeper, ended short immediately after. Ben retired to his corner, irritably blowing blood out of his nose. His manager squirted some brandy into his mouth and must have told him to hurry it up, for in round three he charged in to finish Dan off.

Dan dodged and went for Ben's eyes. Ben gave a roar of pain and rage as the blood started from above the socket. He was sweating and puffing, but for all his effort not a blow got through Dan's guard. There was no doubt who was in charge of the bout, and suddenly the odds were coming up in the challenger's favour. The manager began to look worried at the frantic change of bets. Dan decided he had shilly-shallied enough, and when Ben went on the throw – advancing his left leg ready for the attack – Dan put in a one-two and drubbed him to his knees.

David could not have been more popular when he felled Goliath. The villagers whooped and hollered as their money found its way back into their pockets. Even the baker, who had given his wife the slip, applauded the tramp he had glared at a short while ago.

"Very sly," Drake chuckled when Dan made his way back to him. His dog, infected by his master's good humour, danced around them, barking and wagging his tail. "You had us all fooled. Ho, there! Bring some water and a sponge for this man!"

Several containers of water appeared – pitchers, tankards, a broken cup – and in the absence of a sponge, a thin, aproned man threw a beery cloth to Dan, who wiped himself down and put on his shirt. Singleton, who had come back to life during the match, shoved the crowd aside, strode up to Dan, and knocked him sideways with a clap on the back.

"This man deserves a drink!" he yelled.

"Got to get the purse first," Dan said.

They all surged after him when he went over to the manager and held out his hand.

"Tain't a fair fight," the man grumbled. "You never said you was a fighter."

The villagers were having none of it and, wisely, the manager handed over a threadbare cloth bag.

"Wait a bit," Dan said. "This is short."

The manager glanced at Ben, but the big man was in no condition to intimidate anyone and there was no way out of it. He dug deep into his pockets and made up the prize money to the full amount. The people cheered, and Singleton grabbed Dan's arm and dragged him off to the Fox and Badger, leaving Bold Ben Jones and his manager to slink out of the village.

They piled into the bar, Drake carrying Dan's jacket and hat. The thin man in the apron darted behind the counter and shouted, "The beer's on me, boys!"

"Hey up, lads, Buller's giving summat away!" someone quipped.

A tankard passed through several willing hands before it reached Dan, who did not mind that half its contents was spilled in the passage. He only drank when his work demanded it, and then as little as he could get away with without exciting the suspicion that he had all his wits about him.

A man with a face like a startled rabbit, who had been watching the fight from one of the windows, came in for a good deal of teasing.

"Enjoy the match, Sam?"

"You can come out now it's all over!"

"Buller put your bets on for you, did he?"

The man protested in a squeaky voice, "I was keeping an eye on it all. I'd have broken the fight up if there'd been any public disorder."

"Aye, so you would!" they jeered.

"The constable?" Dan asked Drake.

Drake nodded. "Sam Ayres. Been constable for years."

No one believed that Ayres would have risked anything so unpopular as stopping the match, and having seen the state of the lock-up neither did Dan. However, the mood was too good to leave him out of the celebrations and he was served his beer with the rest.

After a while Ayres, Drake and most of the others drifted back to work, leaving Dan with Singleton and a few idlers.

"So, what are you going to do with your winnings?" Singleton asked.

"Live off them until I find work," Dan answered gloomily.

"What line are you in?"

"Anything. I hear there are mines at Stonyton. I might as well try there, though the idea of being underground makes me sick."

"I could do with some help in the forge until I've taken a new lad into the trade – the last one struck off for himself a few weeks back. It's not light work, I warn you, but you're stronger than you look. I can't pay much either, but I can offer you a roof over your head and your meals. What do you say?"

"I say 'Yes, please'."

"Good. Then let's try it for a week or two. As long as you're honest and pull your weight, we should get on."

They drained their glasses and walked along to the forge. It was at the edge of the village, opposite the church. Next to the graveyard was the rectory, a substantial, well-cared-for property behind a high wall. The road to Stonyton ran past the side of the church, disappearing over the top of Barcombe Heath, which was crowned with a few wind-deformed trees.

31

Singleton's cottage stood sideways to the main road. Its front door opened on to a yard between the forge, stable and outhouses. Mrs Singleton stood on the doorstep with her arms folded.

"You lost then," she said.

"I did, but here is the winner. He's come to work for us."

She took no notice of Dan. "I'd better look at that eye."

"Never mind the eye. Is there any lunch?"

"When is there never any lunch? Wash your hands before you come in. And take those dirty boots off."

It seemed a long time since Dan had breakfasted by the village pump and he was hungry after the fight. He devoured as much fresh bread, cheese and meat, with a home-made onion chutney of the highest savour, as was put in front of him – a great deal. When they had eaten, Mrs Singleton washed her husband's cut and applied a salve. It smelt evil, and Dan said so.

"It does," she agreed. "But it does a power of good. All Anna Halling's remedies do."

She went upstairs, and returned with a clean shirt to replace Singleton's blood-stained one.

"You're a town man, then?" she said to Dan, putting away her things.

"Yes, missus. London."

"Dirty place, London. What did you do there?"

"Lots of things. Hauled coal. Worked on the docks. Bit of building work."

"Learned to fight too?"

"Not really learned. Just picked up some things by watching."

"They have lots of fights in London?"

"Leave off with your daft questions, woman," Singleton snapped, emerging from his shirt. "Do they though, Dan?"

"Yes. Wimbledon Common, Tothill Fields, Lisson Green – there're lots of places to see a good match."

"Well, there aren't many fights around here," Mrs Singleton

said, in a 'and it will stay that way' tone.

They left her pummelling the stains out of her husband's linen and went to work. Singleton was the village farrier as well as blacksmith, and two horses stood outside the forge waiting to be shod. He gave Dan one of his leather aprons with a small knife and a wide rasp to put in the pockets until called for. While Singleton hammered out the first horseshoe, Dan kept the fire fuelled.

"Hold his head while I take off his old shoes," Singleton said.

Gingerly, Dan grabbed the harness dangling beneath the plough horse's massive teeth.

"You really are a town man," Singleton growled. "Here, grip it like this and stand to the side. He won't hurt you. He's a good 'un, ain't you, old Joe?"

Joe snorted agreement. Singleton ran his hand down the horse's leg and Joe helpfully lifted his foot. The smith cradled it in his lap, opened his pincers, and began to unclench the shoe nails.

"The thing to do here, Dan, is pull the nails out, nice and clean. You don't want to rip them off, else you'll take off horn with them, and when the horn is thin you'll be driving the new nail into the quick." He patted Joe. "We don't want that, eh, old man? Now, look at this."

Dan leaned down and stared at the bare hoof. "What am I looking for?"

"Broken nails. Loose horn. Looks all right to me. Hand me the rasp."

Joe shifted uneasily.

"It's all right, old man, just going to smooth it out a bit before I put the shoe on. That's the thing, Dan. Treat them kindly and have a care for their feet, and you'll get a lot more out of them. I'm just going to shave it lightly – like brushing more than shaving, see? You see this bit? That's the frog. Never touch that, mark me well. It's the most tender part, and if you expose it, it'll bleed or bruise." His hands worked deftly.

"Nine times out of ten, if a horse shies or stumbles, it's down to bad foot care. Have you ever travelled footsore, Dan? Then you'll know what I mean. It's the easiest way to waste a good horse. You'll notice what I don't do here."

Dan did not, but Singleton told him anyway.

"I don't put a notch in the hoof. It doesn't make the shoe fit better, it just dries out the horn and weakens the foot. Now for the shoe."

"It isn't red-hot anymore."

"No. Doesn't need to be, neither. How would you like to try on a red-hot boot?"

He showed Dan how many nails to use, how and where to drive them in, and how to remove the points with pincers. Dan had no idea how complicated and delicate a thing a hoof was, and Singleton's knowledge and skill impressed him. He had always thought of horses as ill-tempered and dangerous brutes, but now he realised that was probably due more to the way they were treated than any flaw in their temperament.

The other animal was a saddle horse, a well-behaved work-a-day hack, and after Joe Dan managed him quite well. When Singleton had done the shoeing, Dan applied the ointment which was put on to stop the hoof drying out. He wiped his hands on a filthy cloth while Singleton reckoned up the costs on a slate. They had just finished when a stocky man in smock and gaiters turned into the yard. He and the blacksmith shook hands, then he nodded at Dan.

"Is this your champion? Doesn't look like much."

"He's pretty tough, though. Come forward, Dan, and say 'Good day' to Mr Dunnage. So you heard about the fight?" Singleton asked, when Dan had touched his forelock to the prosperous-looking man.

"Ar." Dunnage ran his hand down Joe's legs, lifted his feet, and inspected the heavy shoes. "Looks in order."

"You knew it would be."

The farmer grunted. A careful man, but a fair one. He glanced at the chalked calculations and paid for the work there and then. The business done, he said in a low voice, "Are we still on?"

"Dan, start sweeping up," Singleton ordered. "You'll find a broom on the hook there."

Dan went back inside and watched them while he worked. He could not hear what they were saying, but Dunnage was fretting about something. Singleton said a few words. After that the farmer seemed a bit easier. "All right then," Dan heard him say, "I'm in."

They separated, and Dunnage gathered up Joe's halter. "See you at mine, Thursday night."

A few minutes after he had gone, a short man in coarse breeches, heavy riding boots, and carrying a riding whip strutted in to collect the other horse. There were no handshakes and no chit-chat. No money changed hands either as Singleton brought the horse's tack out, helped to saddle him, and led him to the stone mounting block by the gate.

"You'll put it on His Lordship's account?" said the rider, settling comfortably into the saddle.

"Of course."

The man spurred his horse and rode away.

"Who was that?" Dan asked.

"Edward Mudge, Lord Oldfield's steward. You make sure you keep out of his way – him and all His Lordship's men."

"I haven't any plans to make friends with 'em."

"Good man. Ah, the wife is calling us in. Time to eat."

They washed at the pump in the yard and went indoors. Dan was hungry again and gulped down the food, hot this time, plentiful and filling. When they had eaten, Mrs Singleton cleared away the dishes and sent Dan to fetch some water.

"I'm off to the Fox," said Singleton when he got back. "Coming, Dan?"

Mrs Singleton, who had settled herself by the fire, looked up from her knitting. "I'll leave you some blankets in the smithy, Dan. You can make up your bed there."

She did not expect a man in his situation to protest, nor

did he, and not only because of the part he was playing. For someone who had lived among the brick kilns of Notting Hill, a warm smithy with clean straw, a roof overhead, and good eating counted as fine lodgings.

They were terrible places, the brickfields, where people starved, sickened and died – the ones who didn't make prey of their fellows. True, there had been warm ash to curl up in, stacks of drying bricks to shelter behind, glowing kilns to creep close to – but only in the mornings when the adults and older children had given up their prime positions and wandered into the streets of London to spend the day begging and stealing. There would be only a few moments' warmth before the workmen arrived, picking their way with curses over the empty gin bottles and human waste, grabbing bits of broken brick to throw at Dan and the other children to drive them away. The men were as black as the mud they worked in, their language as filthy as the smells the burning bricks made.

It was while there that Dan had been taken to Weaver by one of the boys he sent out to trawl the streets for stray children, luring them in with promises of food and shelter. Some of them he sold to the brothels – girls and boys. Others he sold into a sort of slavery as labourers in factories and workshops. Some, like Dan, turned him a profit by thieving.

It had been Noah's idea for Dan to join the Runners, put into the old man's head by one of the night patrolmen who was a regular at the gymnasium. Dan had no other plans for his future apart from taking over the gym one day, and he was content to go along with whatever pleased Noah. It was only meant as something to bring him in a bit of money in the meantime, and he continued helping out in the gym when he was not on duty. No man relied on the patrol for his income; they all had daytime jobs.

Dan had been surprised by how much he enjoyed the work and the pleasure he got out of putting a rope around the necks of the Weavers of this world. He began to ask for extra duty, and his enthusiasm had not gone unnoticed. It was nine years since he had joined and two years since he had been promoted to Principal Officer.

He never found Weaver, who had probably died in some hovel or gin cellar somewhere. Dan hoped it had been nasty: syphilis with all its pains and deformities, or a knife in the guts and a long-drawn-out bleeding.

Chapter Four

The Fox and Badger was crowded. Dan had been introduced to many of the drinkers at lunchtime, but some faces were new to him. They were clustered around a table where Lucas Drake and a pale, plump man who smelt of soap and dry tea were in the middle of an argument. The man's hair was cropped short and he wore a brown jacket with large buttons and a carelessly tied white scarf. It was a look Dan had seen sported by radicals in town a few years ago.

Drake struggled to make himself heard above the company's jeers and hisses. "All I'm saying is that His Lordship has rights too, and if you want to assert your own, trespassing on his is no way to go about it."

This provoked loud groans. The pallid man winked at his supporters. "And that's the way a man of the old regime would talk, but times are changing, Drake. People aren't prepared to obey laws that aren't fair and just."

"Who's the speech-monger?" Dan asked Singleton.

"Travell, runs the village shop. Has a school there too, which sticks nicely in the parson's craw. His Reverence doesn't think it part of the natural order of things for ploughmen's sons to be able to read."

Dan remembered the glimpse he had caught of the shopkeeper earlier, leaning over his counter. Talk like this in a London tavern or coffee house had been known to get a man arrested, but Dan had heard enough heated conversations in public houses to know not to take them too seriously. It was what a man did that mattered. Was Travell capable of matching action to words? The reference to trespass was interesting, but it was not clear whether Drake was actually accusing Travell of going on Lord Oldfield's land. Travell neither denied nor admitted it, though there were a lot of knowing smirks, the most knowing of all from Singleton.

"Laws will always seem unjust to those who want to break them," Drake said. "By your argument, even murder might be justified."

"Who's talking about murder?" cried Travell. "I'm talking about man's inalienable rights – that means no one can take them away – to the game that roams wild and free. Since it belongs to no man, by what right does anyone stop us taking it?"

"It seems that no one does stop you," Drake said drily.

The remark was aimed at the whole company, who showed their appreciation with raucous cheers, foot-stomping and tankard-drumming.

"No, no, Drake, I'm talking about the principle of the thing," Travell said.

"Oh, it's principles, is it? If the game was free and wild, maybe I'd grant you your principles. But it isn't. It's fed and bred by His Lordship, and therefore he owns it."

"And how does he feed and breed it? By stealing the land from under people's noses. By shutting off the wood that has been open to the people of Barcombe as long as anyone can remember. Those are our paths under the trees, and we've walked them to gather food and fuel for generations. And now are the poorest families to starve in summer in the sight of plenty, and die of cold in winter while firewood lies rotting on the ground?"

There were loud cries of agreement. Travell was in full liberty-spouting flow when a small boy arrived with the message that his dinner was ready and Mrs Travell said he was to come now. The alehouse revolutionary drained his glass and hurried out after his pupil.

The rest made room for Dan and Singleton. Politics was forgotten in the more important matter of the fight. They relived the match blow-by-blow: the hits on Ben's *smeller*, the damage to his *sparklers*, the *pegs on the lug,* and hits to the *bread-basket*. It was a source of great pride to them that one of their own – they had adopted Dan as a Barcombe man for the purpose – had stood up to Bold Ben when Stonyton's champions fell.

Drake had as much part in the talk as if his sympathy for Lord Oldfield's rights had never been uttered. They respected him, and it was not hard to see why. He disapproved of their thieving ways and was not afraid to say so, but he would not sell them to the hangman for it, not even with Lord Oldfield's reward dangling before him. A pity, thought Dan. In Drake's line of work, out and about in the fields at all hours, there was probably not much he missed.

The door latch rattled and a young man came in.

"Evening, Abe," they chorused.

Abe Wicklow brought a whiff of the farmyard in with him. He was a good-looking lad, and he knew it. He had dandified his work boots, breeches and jacket with a spotted scarf, striped waistcoat, and a band of ribbon around his flat, round hat. A key and a seal hung from a watch chain beneath the waistcoat. When he sat down, he flicked back his jacket to show them off. He was dressed like a man who had been courting, which turned out to be the case.

He took a long draught of beer, licked his lips, and announced with a grin that exposed teeth as big as old Joe's, "I've just been up at the Hall to see Sal. She tells me they called in another doctor last night. He came all the way from London with that lawyer fellow."

"Did he bring Josh Castle back to life?" guffawed a squat, dark, hairy man who reeked of sweat, onions and muck. That was Pip Higgs, who worked with Drake on the common, where it was his job to impound stray or confiscated animals.

"No, he's still as dead as dead," Abe shot back solemnly.

"Bloody good thing too," said gangly, squint-eyed Jem Cox, who had a habit of blowing his nose into his fingers and wiping them on his breeches. "Hope his broken bones rot in hell."

"Here's to Bloodie Bones, I say," cried Singleton.

They all raised their glasses. Dan dutifully swallowed some beer. So far he had been careful to answer more questions than he asked, but he thought a bit of curiosity would not look out of place now.

"Who's Josh Castle?" he asked.

"Lord Oldfield's gamekeeper, found dead in the wood on Thursday with his head broke," Singleton said.

"And Bloodie Bones done for him!" Abe crowed.

"What's Bloodie Bones?"

Answers came from every side.

"He's someone you don't want to mess with, he is."

"You'll hear him of a night, his bones rattling behind you."

"If you cheats or robs the poor, he'll crush you bone by bone, like he done the old Lord."

"So this Bloodie Bones is a ghost, a buggybow who rides out to punish wrongdoers? Like Jack Straw."

Pip Higgs looked impressed. "You've heard of Jack, have you?"

"He's been known to appear at London riots," Dan answered. "That is, a man dressed as him, in a straw mask."

"Bloodie Bones is no man in a straw mask. I see'd him."

They all turned and gazed at the speaker who sat on the edge of the group, casting forlorn glances at his empty glass. He had unkempt hair, a straggly beard, and grimy weather-beaten skin, and was bundled in a much larger man's cast-off coat.

"Garn! You've never seen anything, Girtin," said a farm labourer in a smock, whose mouth was in a permanent miserable down-turn. Dan had forgotten his name.

"Or seen it double!" quipped Abe. Everyone laughed.

"But what did you see?" Dan asked.

Girtin tapped his glass on the table. Dan took the hint and ordered him a refill.

Though the others had teased the old man, they all leaned forward to listen. Everyone likes a ghost story, Dan thought. He did not have much time for tales as a rule, but last Halloween he had been at home and they had all sat around the fire: his wife Caroline, her sister Eleanor and their mother. Mrs Harper had a fund of old tales from her Yorkshire childhood. Her daughters knew them all, but Eleanor still shivered at the delightfully dreadful monsters and demons that stalked the pitch-black, storm-lashed moors.

All that talk of spirits had made Caroline thirsty. Dan took no notice; he knew better than to suggest moderation and provoke a diatribe on spoiling her fun. He had been enjoying himself too much in any case, watching Eleanor's eyes widen and her hands fly to her mouth, joining in her rueful laughter against herself. Caroline morosely emptied her bottle. The merriment had been at its loudest when she threw her cup into the fire. It smashed against the brickwork.

"If I was dead, do you think I'd come back to haunt you, Dan? What do you think, Nell? Would I come back and find you still making eyes at my husband? You can have him. Oh, no, I forgot – you can't, can you? Ask Dan. He knows all about the law. Tell her, Dan. You can't marry your wife's sister, so it's no good wishing I was dead." Her voice grew thick, tears and snot bubbled down her flushed cheeks. "I wish I was dead. I know that's what you'd all like."

Eleanor was white-faced. She could not look at Dan; he dared not look at her. All the pleasure they'd had in one another's company was poisoned. She and Mrs Harper got Caroline to bed, Mrs Harper trying to smooth it all over: Caro didn't know what she was saying; she didn't mean it; it would all be forgotten in the morning…Dan sat by the hearth all night, while the flames died and the ashes cooled.

Why hadn't he seen the signs earlier? Why during their courtship had he found Caroline's sudden rages, her bouts of unreason, so alluring? Because afterwards she would smile, and cajole, and caress; because she was beautiful; because all the men loved her, and not one of them had the sense to appreciate her sister's quiet and tender beauty.

Bitter for a man to dwell on his mistakes! Dan shook off the memory and attended to Girtin.

"I was passing through the graveyard one night when I heard a terrible groaning and footsteps behind me. Like this." Girtin clattered an empty tankard on the table. "I tell you, the hair stood up on my head. My flesh crept. My heart was going like this." He pounded the table with his fingertips. "I didn't want to turn round, but I knew I had to. And when I did, there he was." He lowered his voice and they all leaned in closer. "As big as a house, and the dark blood streaming down him. I could see his heart inside his ribs, black and rotten. His eyes glowed like coals. His nails were a foot long. He clutched at me with his bony fingers, and when he opened his mouth, his breath was the stench of the charnel house. 'Girtin,' he said, with what a voice! My bowels turned to water at the sound of it. But it seemed to break a sort of spell. I turned and ran for my life. I didn't stop until I was out of that graveyard and well away. When I looked back, I saw him sitting on a gravestone eating an owl, whole and raw, the gore spurting from his mouth."

It was a very satisfying tale, as the sigh that went up testified, and earned the man his drinks for the night.

"He'll be sitting on Castle's grave before long," Singleton said, when Buller had pulled more ales all round.

Abe was the only one who had been impatient during Girtin's story, and he wrested the attention back to himself. "Now the doctors have finished with him, he's as good as lying in state up at the Hall."

"Lying in state? Like one of them?"

"'Sright. Just like one of them. They say when Lord Adam saw the body brought into the gamekeeper's cottage, he was so beside himself he smashed the place to bits."

"What did this Castle do to make himself so unpopular?" Dan asked.

"Do?" said Buller, who was standing behind them, wiping his

hands on his apron. "He was Lord Oldfield's head gamekeeper and a bastard into the bargain, ready to do any dirty work."

"And there'll soon be another one stepping up into his place," Singleton said.

They all nodded gloomily.

"I'm not so sure." Abe, that fount of knowledge, again. "Caleb Witt may want Josh's place right enough, but that doesn't mean he'll get it. It's rumoured in the servants' hall that His Lordship is going to bring in a man from outside."

The spectre of the unknown keeper cast a morose mood over them. They devoted the next few minutes to thoughtful drinking.

Drake, who had no cause to be troubled by keepers, said, "That's me done. I'm off. Goodnight, lads."

His departure distracted the rest from their misery and the talk moved on to other matters. While Dan pretended to listen, and even threw in the odd remark, he mulled over what he had learned. It was not much, but the snippet about Caleb Witt was interesting. Witt had discovered the body, and it was often the case that the man who found the corpse was the one who had put it there. And he had a motive: he wanted Josh's job.

They said their goodnights and left Buller to lock up. As Dan settled down for the night in the forge, he heard Singleton shoot the bolts on the cottage door. Dan did not blame the blacksmith for his caution; he was still a stranger to them.

The next day was Sunday. "Pah!" grunted Singleton when his wife said she was off to church. Too used to his contempt to be affected by it, she calmly finished getting ready and left the men to eat up their bread and bacon.

When Singleton had reached the teeth-picking stage, Dan announced his intention of exploring the heath.

"I've nothing else to do," Singleton said. "I'll come with you."

This was a nuisance as Dan had been planning to take

a look at Castle's cottage, but he had no choice but to accept the offer. They left the village by the Stonyton Road, walking along the side of the church. The bells were silent and no sound issued forth: the parson must have started his sermon.

After the last few straggling houses, the ground rose gently. On the right was open country, with the road to Bath running through it. On the left, beyond the heath, the dark mass of Barcombe Wood spread to the top of a shallow valley and down the other side. How much further it went Dan could not tell. On the side nearest Oldfield Hall the trees stopped at the edge of the park, where they had been felled to create an arc-shaped border around the rear lawn beyond the ornamental garden. There was a large, dark oval in the middle of the green, and what looked like cottages dotted around it. That seemed odd so close to the Hall.

"Not cottages," Singleton explained. "His Lordship's improvements. That was the fish pond. Now it's going to be a lake. They'll be bringing water down from the Seven Springs at the head of the valley. It's to have a bridge over it and an island in the middle with a castle on it, and what they call a temple on the far bank. He's getting married soon, and he and his wife have a craze for such things. Lady Helen Burgh. She's a dainty young lady, no denying it, but like all her kind. Maybe she'll improve Lord Oldfield's temper. Maybe she'll make him worse."

They came to a spur of the wood which had encroached onto the heath, and turned left to follow the line of the wooden palings around the trees. The ground was smooth and level closer to the fence and would have been easier to walk on, but when Dan moved towards it, Singleton pulled him back.

"They keep a particular eye on this part of the wood. Don't go too close, else they'll accuse you of going in."

"There's no one about."

"Looks like it," he agreed. "But the keepers are in there somewhere. Remember that, my lad. It's transportation now for a man to walk in a forest his dad and granddad knew as well as their own gardens."

Further on they reached a patch of recently abandoned cultivated land at the edge of the wood. The soil was trampled and the plants broken or gone to seed, and weeds and nettles had sprung up in the midden. In the centre of the plot was a rectangle where a dwelling house once stood, the abandoned hearth with its ring of blackened stone a forlorn sight. Beams and bits of reed from the thatch still lay about, but the site had been stripped of anything of any use to other builders.

"Has there been a fire here?" asked Dan.

"No. This was Bob Budd's house. Lord Adam threw him off the land. Wants to clear the area so it's nice and tidy for his hunting friends. Bob had a family too. Didn't mean nothing to His Lordship, though. Betty, Budd's eldest, came to fetch Travell, and he fetched me, and we went to Drake to ask if he knew what was going on. Budd only had one cow and was poor enough to be allowed to graze the beast on the heath, but Drake had heard no complaints about him. He said perhaps Budd had tried to loose his pig into the forest without taking notice of the new rules. New rules!"

Singleton spat in the direction of the fence and continued his story.

When Singleton, Drake and Travell reached Budd's place, Lord Oldfield's steward, Mudge, and his men were emptying the cottage while Castle stood looking on, his gun over his arm. Budd was loading whatever he could onto his cow. The little ones were bawling, Betty was trying to keep them quiet, and their mother was screaming at him to stand his ground, but he just went on tying up the bundles.

Travell demanded to know what was going on, and Mudge said they were evicting a trespasser.

"On what grounds?" asked Travell.

"On the grounds he shouldn't be here," Mudge said. "We've got an eviction notice."

"Signed by Lord Oldfield, the man doing the evicting," Travell retorted.

"If there's a complaint against Budd, surely it can be dealt with the way we do on the heath, with a fine," Drake said.

"And you'd all put the money in," Mudge said. "Anyway, it isn't commons business. The forest belongs to His Lordship and he doesn't want squatters on it no more."

"Budd's father and grandfather lived here before him," Travell said. "They have rights in the parish."

"Not unless they pay rent, which being squatters they don't," Mudge answered.

The woman, her hopes raised by Travell's defence, came up to Mudge and said, "You can't throw us off. It's not a hut, it's a proper house, it has a chimney. That means we can stay."

"I don't know where you got that from, and it makes no difference," the steward answered. "The house shouldn't be here, and neither should you."

"Your father came from out the parish, but no one thought of throwing him out," Travell said.

"My father was no squatter," Mudge snapped. "He had a proper settlement here through marrying my mother, and kept himself by business too, not scavenging on another man's land. Now get out of my way, before I make you."

Singleton stepped in front of the door, his fists clenched at his side. Drake moved up beside him. Travell followed and ducked behind them. The steward's men looked uncertainly at Mudge, who waved his riding whip: *Get on with it.* There was some pushing and shoving, Travell hopping about without doing much, and it would have come to blows, but Budd said, "Leave it, lads. We're going."

His woman latched onto his arm, cursing and yammering at him to stick up for himself. He bloodied her nose and she let go. She prowled up and down, still cursing him.

"You don't need to go," Singleton said.

Mudge grinned. "But you want to, don't you, Budd? We offered him a choice and he took it, ain't that right, Mr Castle?"

Castle pointed at the heap of gear at his feet: purse nets, wire snares, and an old gun that looked as if it had been used in Cromwell's war. "This is illegal," he said. "Budd's had plenty of warnings. It's transportation now, if he stays in the parish. But if he leaves, he can go free."

Singleton and Drake looked at Travell. He nodded. Transportation: that was the law.

Drake asked Budd where he was going.

"Kingswood. Forest is all I know."

"At least wait a day or two and we'll get up a collection," Travell said.

"I don't want money."

Budd called the children and their mother over to him, told them to carry what they could. They had to leave their bits of furniture. He cracked his whip over the cow's head and they moved off, his mongrel dog trotting behind.

Mudge jerked his head at the dog. "Mr Castle." He would have shot the animal himself if Drake and the others had not been there, but after all the talk of legality, he did not dare. He did not have the right: that was the gamekeeper's.

Castle shook his head. "It's enough."

Singleton finished his story and fell silent. He stared into the wood. "It was enough," he said softly, "to throw a man out of his home for wanting to feed his family a bit of rabbit every now and again. Budd was the only one who looked back. Not at the cottage. Into the wood. He knew every tree, every track, every warren in that wood, Dan. He knew where to gather mushrooms in autumn, where the reeds to thatch his roof grow, where to collect hazelnuts and herbs, where to send his children to gather blackberries and rosehips, cranberries and sloes, where to harvest acorns for his pig, where to collect furze, bracken and fallen wood for his fire. He knew where the deer hid and the pheasants roosted, where wrens sang and adders basked, which paths were quagmires in winter."

He looked at Dan. "You don't know what I'm talking about, do you?…They knocked the house down the next day. Wattle and daub. Caved in easily under hammer and axe. Two or three families who had also set themselves up close by didn't wait to be told to move. They had nothing but rough hovels, no sense of belonging to the parish, wanting only somewhere wild and quiet where they can be left alone. They could have moved to the heath, which still has its wild spots. But they preferred to put plenty of distance between themselves and Lord Oldfield."

"A sad story," Dan said, thinking that Kingswood was not all that far away. Budd could easily have come back one night to wreak his revenge, but why on Castle and not Mudge? Perhaps the gamekeeper, out and about in the forest at all hours of the day and night, was an easier target. But then he was armed, and Mudge too must spend a lot of time riding about the estate on his own. No doubt the steward was also armed. Dan would be if he was in his place.

Perhaps Budd resented the gamekeeper's part in the affair more than the steward's. It was the gamekeeper who had the power to search his place, knowing full well he would find only a few old nets that could not have done much to deplete Lord Oldfield's game, but which could be turned against Budd. Or perhaps Budd meant to come back for Mudge.

While Dan was thinking all that through, a most peculiar figure stepped out of the wood.

Chapter Five

He was a wiry little man, swamped by a long coat tied at the waist with cord. The ragged cuffs of a jacket that had once been green but was now faded almost white poked out from his coat sleeves. His hobnailed boots were much repaired, and he wore thick gaiters over coarse woollen stockings. He was a dark, secretive-looking man, his age hard to guess. Dan put him somewhere in the middle years.

"'Day. Who's your friend?"

"Good day to you, Tom Taylor," Singleton answered. "This is Dan Fielding, who pulverised Bold Ben Jones yesterday."

"Don't look up to it."

"He might not look it, but he's the real go."

"Will you walk up with me?" the gypsy asked.

The blacksmith winked. "That I will."

Something more than a walk on the heath had been agreed on, but Dan fell into line without giving any hint he had noticed. Taylor's step was brisk and light. His eyes flickered from side to side, sometimes glancing skywards, sometimes raking the dense bracken as if he was following something moving through it, though Dan could not see anything. Suddenly he stamped his foot, stooped, and picked up a tiny brown scrap.

"Field mouse," he said, tossing the mangled creature aside.

Dan had no idea why Tom had destroyed it. Perhaps it was a reflexive action with him to catch and kill whatever he could.

They climbed towards the top of the heath through the browning fronds, which were criss-crossed with narrow paths. Sheep grazed on the green pasture on the lower slopes. The outline of a long, low mound appeared above them.

"Barcombe Barrow," said Singleton. "They say there were kings buried in it once, with gold crowns and jewels."

"If it's true, I never found none," said Taylor.

The barrow was covered in smooth grass, though the end of the ancient structure was hidden by an impenetrable wall of briar. Underneath this the roof had caved in, exposing two or three stone-lined chambers. Great stone slabs lay in the grip of the thorns, their surfaces softened and stained by lichen and moss. Some had faded lines and whorls carved into them. Led by the smell of woodsmoke and stewing meat, they walked around the barrow, scattering the hens pecking in the short grass.

Here a dirt path led through a short, roofless tunnel to a doorway covered with an old blanket. Between the tunnel walls a fire burned inside a circle of stones. A woman sat beside it, tending a cooking pot slung from a crook. She was fairer of skin than her husband, and wore a ragged skirt and jacket and an apron of sacking. Two boys with dirty hands and faces sat near her, carving spoons to hawk around the neighbouring villages. The younger one was wearing the elder's cast-off breeches, untidily patched and too big for him. A little girl crouched beside the fire, throwing herbs and onions into the pot. They all wore heavy boots like Tom's, but without stockings.

"Dad!" the little girl squealed, abandoning her work and running to hug her father's knees. Tom clouted her out of the way, though not roughly, and not before he had managed to hide his smile. He glanced about him then opened his coat and from a deep, stained pocket drew out a rabbit with its head crushed, the fur sticky with blood.

"Nice and fresh. Still warm." He grinned. "Found him dead on the road."

Dan thought this very unlikely, but being a mere townsman pretended to believe it.

"Two?"

"Two," Singleton agreed, taking out his purse and counting

out some shillings. When he produced a canvas bag from his pocket and stuffed the coneys into it, Dan knew he had walked this way on purpose to buy Sunday supper.

"I wouldn't like to live in a cold, damp barrow," Dan remarked on the walk home.

"You'd be surprised how snug it is inside."

"They look very settled there."

"They've been there for years. They used to camp here with their tribe every summer, then one year Tom and the woman stayed. I don't know the whole of it, but it seemed her family didn't approve of him for her husband. He goes off with them some years, but she never does."

"He goes off when things look hot for him?"

Singleton laughed. "Maybe. The keepers are always sniffing around, but they never find anything on him, nor ever will. He doesn't keep a dog and he hasn't a gun or any nets. They say he sings the hares and coneys to sleep, catches them that way."

Dan shot a glance at the blacksmith, but he was straight-faced.

Back at the cottage, Mrs Singleton snatched the rabbits off him to prepare them for the pot. Dan did not have to pretend to enjoy the stew, illegal though it was.

On Monday morning, a hearse draped in black and drawn by horses wearing black plumes drove slowly along the High Street. Lord Oldfield's carriage followed. The men of Barcombe vanished, slipping into houses, shop or inn rather than take off their hats to Castle's coffin. The women continued with their errands, willing to pay a curtsey for the spectacle of the fine equipage. Singleton had gone to deliver a horse he had shoed to one of the farmers, and as Dan did not object to baring his head, he was free to join Mrs Singleton at the yard gate and watch the liveried men carry the casket into the churchyard.

Lord Oldfield alighted from his carriage and Dr Russell got out after him. The rector, Mr Poole, waited by the lychgate. He was a freckle-faced, ginger-haired individual with colourless, anxious eyes. He bobbed and bowed to the aristocratic mourner.

A young lady accompanied by an older, corpulent woman stood in front of one of the headstones. Lord Oldfield nodded politely as he passed, but Dr Russell stopped to speak to the young mourner, bending over her with a concerned expression, murmuring a few kind words while she struggled to put on a brave face. Her chaperone gazed vacantly about, her mind apparently on less solemn matters.

"Who are the ladies?" Dan asked.

"Miss Louisa Ruscombe and her aunt, Mrs Hale," Mrs Singleton answered. "Poor young lady! She lives in Yew Tree House, about half a mile up the road, next to Mr and Mrs West. The Wests used to be in the theatre."

"Why do you say 'Poor young lady'?"

"Her brother Frederick died in February, leaving her all alone. She thought she'd have to give up her home and go to one of her father's relatives, until Aunt Joanna turned up on her doorstep. Miss Louisa had no idea she had an aunt on her mother's side. Very lucky for Mrs Hale it was too, finding her out just then, for she'd not long been left a widow with nothing of her own."

Miss Ruscombe and Mrs Hale moved off, the niece adapting her walk to her aunt's waddle. The doctor watched them go. Dan could not blame him for his interest. The girl was a beauty in the fragile style, though her delicate features were blemished by tears.

Russell rejoined the party at the graveside and Mr Poole began the service. Mrs Singleton remembered that *he'd* be back for his dinner soon, and Dan returned to his tasks.

The afternoon passed quietly, if a forge can be called quiet. They did not go to the Fox and Badger, but Mrs Singleton fetched a jug of beer for her husband. Dan drank water. When they had finished work, he said he was going to the village shop to spend some of his prize money on new shirts. As he had hoped, Singleton was more interested in emptying the jug and did not offer to go with him. Dan's plan was to get through his errand quickly, then go on to the keeper's cottage.

Travell was in the middle of sorting a delivery from his suppliers in Bath, so Dan had time to look about him. It was a typical village shop, crammed with a hotchpotch of goods: soaps, tea, umbrellas, teapots, knives, boots, cloth, seeds, bacon and much else. The only paper Travell stocked was a cheap ream sold by the page, and some pocketbook tablets. The paper on the Bloodie Bones dummy had not come from here.

The door opened with a 'ting' of the bell and an old couple came in. The woman was small and fat with an enormous bosom, above which was a quivering, timid face. She had thick lips, pasty skin and dull, dark eyes. Her husband wore a smock and corduroy breeches coated with flour. He shuffled in and stood sag-kneed beside her, twisting his battered hat in his hands.

"Are you the man from London?" she asked.

"Yes, I'm Dan Fielding."

"Have you seen our girl?"

"Your girl?" Dan glanced at the husband, but there was no help to be had from his grimaces and twitches.

"Sukie. Have you seen her?"

"Should I know her?"

"She's in London. Have you seen her?"

"Now, now, Mrs Tolley," Travell said, coming to Dan's aid. "London is a big place. How would Dan know your girl?"

She switched her uncomprehending gaze to him, and with a peculiar wet, sucking motion of her lips repeated, "She's in London."

"We don't know that," the shopkeeper said kindly. "And even if she was, Dan couldn't have met her."

She did not seem to grasp this but turned back to Dan and said, "If you see her, will you tell her we asked? Will you tell her to come home?"

Dan glanced at Travell for guidance. He nodded.

"Of course I will, Mistress. If I see her."

"He says he'll tell her," Mr Tolley shouted into her face. "Come away, Mother."

He plucked at her arm and she allowed him to guide her out of the shop.

"What was she talking about?"

Travell shook his head. "A sad business. They had a daughter, Sukie. God alone knows how they managed to raise her. She was dropped on her head so many times as a babe she turned out as addled as her parents. You've never known a pair less able to look after themselves. The number of times we've had to haul him out of a ditch he's tumbled into or run into the house to beat out a fire she's started with her cooking. Tolley works for the miller. Shifting sacks is about all he's fit for, and he's none too bright at that."

"And their girl has gone to London?"

"No one knows if she's even alive. It's nine or ten years since she disappeared and there's been no word. There was no clue as to why she went either. Her parents doted on her and she had no reason to run away. Then a month ago, Lord Oldfield drained the old pool. He's turning it into a lake."

"With a bridge over it and a temple."

"The workmen found a baby's bones. They'd been wrapped in a cloak once, but all that was left was the buttons. They were so large that was how we knew it was Sukie's. She couldn't manage anything else, never learned to tie a ribbon or do up a pin. She'd always been a plump girl, so it's no wonder no one guessed she was expecting, least of all her mother. Whether the infant was born alive no one knows, but we were supposed to think she'd had the baby, buried it, and run away rather than risk being hanged for child murder."

"Supposed to think?"

"Sukie conceal a birth and run away? She hadn't the gumption."

"So someone told her what to do. The father?"

"Shut her up for good, more like."

"You don't think she was murdered?" Dan whistled. "And no one has any idea who he was?"

"Ah, as to that. Well."

"Well?"

Travell glanced about him as if there might be eavesdroppers in the empty store. "Look at the evidence. The bones were found on Lord Oldfield's land. And it was summer when Sukie disappeared, and Lord Adam was home from school. And Abe's old dad remembers seeing the three of them, Lord Adam, Castle and Sukie, talking in the woods. In France they call it dwots de senna."

"Droits de seigneur?"

"Yes. The aristos think they can take the village girls whenever they like."

"And you think Lord Oldfield...?"

"Maybe both of them. Him and Castle were thick as thieves, did everything together, if you get my meaning. So perhaps they didn't know which of them got her with child, but it was Castle who cleared up the mess. It was him who brought the bones down to the church, though Poole refused to put them in the graveyard because they were unbaptised. That's the kindness of the church for you! Castle dug the hole himself on the other side of the wall and stood over it while the rector said a prayer. It's said the keeper's face was hard as nails as he watched them tiny bones put in the ground. And who knows if that's the only grave he dug?"

"But Mr and Mrs Tolley think their daughter is still alive."

"They can't face the thought that the girl might be dead. That's the trouble with starved minds, Dan. They cling on to irrational beliefs. I keep trying to tell them it's what we're up against in this world that matters, but superstition gets the better of them." He shook his head. "There are some silly tales told. They say the discovery was engineered by Bloodie Bones himself to take place just before His Lordship's marriage."

Dan could not imagine any tale sillier than the one he had

just heard, but he reacted as if he thought it likely that a young, handsome lord who could afford to bed the finest ladies in the land would take a tumble in the woods with an unattractive village girl, then get his boyhood friend to commit infanticide and murder to cover up for him.

"Now me," Travell continued, "I abandoned superstition a long time ago. It's the power and corruption of the aristocracy that's at stake here."

If Citizen Travell believed that every member of the aristocracy lived by the code of the Hell-Fire Club, who was Dan to stop him? The point was not what he thought, but what the people of Barcombe believed – and what Travell said made it clear that they were prepared to believe the greatest evil of Lord Oldfield and Josh Castle.

Old wounds had been reopened with the discovery of the baby's bones. Even if the Tolleys' daughter was still alive, she was lost to them as surely as if she had been murdered all those years ago. Were they singly or together capable of taking their revenge on Josh Castle?

Dan did not think so. But perhaps someone might take revenge on their behalf. Someone like Travell, who saw himself as the champion of the oppressed.

Chapter Six

Dan bought two ready-made shirts, a scarf and some stockings, and left with the parcel under his arm. He waved at a group of boys kicking a ball around on the green. They were too shy to respond and gazed after him in awestruck silence. Barcombe had never had a fighting hero in its midst before.

Dan continued to the lane leading to Oldfield Hall, walking slowly so he did not miss the entrance to Drovers' Way. It was nothing but a grassy trail now, but Mrs Singleton had told him that it had once been an important thoroughfare used by men driving cattle to the markets of Bath and Bristol. One of Lord Oldfield's hated new fences ran parallel with the road on the far side of a ditch, its line broken by a gate that Dan had not noticed in the dark. He jumped over the trench, hid his parcel by the gatepost, climbed over, and dropped down into the wood.

The change in the atmosphere was immediate. There was a stillness and silence under the trees which the twittering of the birds could not disturb. Their chatter seemed cheerful at first, but as Dan went further down the track it began to sound shrill and hostile. All around him twigs snapped and leaves rustled. Sometimes he twisted round, expecting to catch a glimpse of something behind him, and often, in the spinning of a leaf or vibration of a branch, he was sure that some creature had just darted into cover. He felt that there were eyes upon him: secretive, unwelcoming, inhuman. He would have felt more at home in the alleys around Chick Lane.

Yet the forest was also man's kingdom. This was his road, and the forest bore signs of his activity. Old or diseased trees had been cut down, others planted, copses cleared. This was Castle's world, and if it told Dan anything about the keeper, it was that he must have had steady nerves.

The keeper's cottage lay in a clearing on the other side of a stream. The only bridge was a tree, left in the state in which it had fallen with its surface unlevelled, though its branches had been cut for firewood years ago. It would be a difficult crossing in wet or icy conditions, but today was dry and the stream was not running high. Even if Dan tumbled he risked nothing worse than wet feet. And tumble he almost did when halfway across a crow launched itself from a tree with a loud croak and flapped low over his head.

The cottage was an old, stout building, thatched and gabled, and surrounded by outhouses. There was a chicken coop, and a row of kennels where Castle had kept dogs he was training or nursing, both empty. He had decorated the outside of the largest shed with rows of corpses: rats, moles, jays, magpies, squirrels and others too decayed to recognise. Taking these as his starting point, Dan followed Lord Oldfield's memorised directions into the wood until he came to the clearing where Josh Castle had been bludgeoned to death while he was cutting down the Bloodie Bones effigy. It was easy to recognise because the ground was so churned up.

The trees closed behind him, but he could still glimpse the cottage. Josh would have been able to see the lights at his own window if he looked back. In every other direction there was nothing but forest. Perhaps the keeper had been able to read its shapes and sounds, but Dan could not, even in daylight. Not a very bright daylight either, and growing dimmer. He shuffled about the mossy ground for a while, though there was little hope of finding any trace of the killer after five days. During that time it had been trampled by Lord Oldfield's men, and then the coroner's thirteen-man jury who, as was the custom, had been brought to view the murder scene.

Dan went back to the shed with the gibbet. Inside were neat stacks of spades, billhooks, rolls of twine, nets, and a couple of sprung animal traps that he took care not to touch. There was a large copper for preparing animal feed. Another outhouse contained straw-lined hutches which had held ferrets used for chasing rabbits out of their warrens.

After prowling about outside, he went to the house, where there was nothing more gruesome than a horseshoe nailed over the door. The latch was stiff, but the door opened easily once he had worked it loose. He stepped down onto the brick floor. The furniture was simple, but clean and not uncomfortable: a table and bench, a wooden chair with cushions on it in front of the hearth, rugs on the floor. Though the hearth had been cold many days, the smell of smoke mingled with the scent of the dried herbs hanging from the oak rafters. There were hooks in the beam where Castle's favourite gun had been kept ready to hand, but all his weapons had been removed.

The room was tidy, and Dan was beginning to doubt Abe's claim that Lord Oldfield had smashed up the place until he noticed pieces of broken earthenware heaped on one of the shelves. He lifted the lid of a feed bucket and found it full of broken glass bottles. Their contents had oozed out to make a slimy mess at the bottom, with a predominant aroma of aniseed. The lamp on the mantelpiece had no glass shade. Presumably that too had been shattered.

Near the window was a small bookcase. Besides the usual sort of books such as a family Bible and a well-used edition of Archer's *Every Man His Own Doctor,* there was a *Tom Jones* which looked well-read, as did a *Works of Shakespeare*. There was also a copy of Lord Chesterfield's *Letters to His Son* with several passages underlined: *'Your manner of speaking is full as important as the matter…loud laughter is the characteristic of folly and ill-manners…an awkward fellow eats with his knife to the great danger of his mouth; picks his teeth with his fork, puts his fingers in his nose, or blows it and looks afterwards in his hand-kerchief.'* Castle must have had a self-improving turn of mind.

In the sideboard, Dan found neatly organised copies of the *Sporting Magazine*, probably passed on by Lord Oldfield after he had read them. There were bundles of receipts for feed, gunpowder and other items connected with Castle's work. The only documents in the keeper's handwriting were a book of accounts, and a game book recording dates of shoots and number of kills.

Dan poked about in the pantry among animal feed bins, a meat safe, cheese dish and milk jug, all empty. There was a bath tub propped against the end wall with a dish of soap nearby. Like the newspapers, the soap came from the Hall and was quality, scented stuff. Washing under a pump or in the stream had not been good enough for Castle.

He opened the door at the foot of the stairs and went up the steep, dark steps. There were three rooms under the eaves. Two of them were small, and the lingering smell in one of these suggested that it had recently been used to store apples and vegetables. A beer crate held empty bottles.

In the other store room were boxes of old clothes, walking sticks, balls of string, dismantled guns and other bits and pieces. Castle's bedroom was at the front of the cottage, overlooking the stream. Like the downstairs quarters, it was tidy and simply furnished. There were curtains on the windows, rugs on the floor, and a clean coverlet and sheets on the bed.

Most of the clothes in the press were of workaday corduroy, coarse linen and durable leather, and were well-worn. There were also half a dozen fine cotton shirts and three sets of Sunday-best breeches and jackets, with hat, scarf, and a smart pair of shoes to wear with them. These fancy items were all new and hardly used. Even if Castle had been a regular churchgoer, they were more than Dan would have expected him to own or have occasion to wear. A gamekeeper-dandy was not a breed he had come across before.

Lord Oldfield must have given Josh the clothes. The hand-me-downs theory also explained the items on top of the chest of drawers: a mirror, shaving set and silver-backed hairbrush. What Dan could not account for was the posy, carefully dried and placed in a small blue jug. It was hard to imagine a gamekeeper taking the trouble to pick and preserve wildflowers with no medicinal value, but there they were.

Dan had found nothing of any relevance, though he had learned a little about Castle: the gamekeeper had not drunk anything stronger than beer, he had been clean and tidy in his habits, fastidious and even vain about his appearance, and had spent his evenings teaching himself how to behave in polite society, though why a gamekeeper needed to know was a puzzle.

The light was fading fast and the cottage, with its small windows, was already dark. Dan left everything as he had found it, made his way back along Drover's Way, and retrieved his purchases. He was glad to leave the cottage and wood behind him.

Whatever Singleton and Dunnage had planned for Thursday might have something to do with Dan's investigation, or it might not. Whatever it was, they had been furtive about it, and he kept his eyes and ears open. All day Tuesday people came and went at the forge, but the talk was never about more than the job in hand or snippets of local gossip. Singleton did not go to the Fox and Badger in the evening, so there was no chance of picking up anything there either. The next day was the same, and Dan was no closer to making a discovery. If all else failed, he would have to take the risk of following Singleton on the following evening. Then, after supper on Wednesday, Singleton announced a trip to the Fox and Badger.

There were already a few of the regulars in the bar. Girtin was on the scrounge as usual. Dan bought him a drink on the principle that it is always wise to win the trust of a skulking fellow – you never know what he might see. Abe and a few of his young friends were making a racket over a game of dominoes, shouting in each other's faces and clacking the pieces on the table.

A tall, grizzled man in heavy, travel-stained garments sat quietly in one corner, smoking a pipe. Buller placed gin and hot water in front of him and left him stirring sugar into his glass. When they'd had their tankards filled, Singleton led Dan towards the stranger, who carried on mixing his drink as they sat down.

"Warneford, this is Dan Fielding, the man who beat Bold Ben."

Warneford put down his spoon. "He doesn't look – "

"I know, I don't look up to it."

The man blew on the steaming liquid and took a pull at it. "I hear you're pretty handy with your fists, though."

"Handy enough."

"Is that how you make your living?"

"Not unless I have to."

"Pity. I know a man who wants to arrange something with one of the Bristol boys at Kingswood Fair at the end of the month. You'd make a bit of money."

"Good fighters in Bristol," Dan said. "But no thanks."

He had never wanted to go professional, though Noah once had hopes in that direction. He did not want to make his fortune, if fortune he was to make, fighting for a purse. Not that there were not huge sums to be made, but Dan knew of few boxers who had managed to hold on to their money. Few, too, who had not died young with their insides punched to pulp; or wrecked their constitutions by trying to live fast with their aristocratic patrons; or fought beyond the powers of their dwindling strength and ended their careers in humiliating defeat.

"How about you?" Dan asked.

"Animal doctor. Travelling. Ever been in prison?"

"Never been caught."

"At what?"

Singleton had cited honesty as a desirable quality when he took Dan on, but Dan knew that with most men honesty was a shifting notion. It depended on how it related to their own convenience. A tasty rabbit stew, for instance, was a great convenience. He had no fear that Singleton would dismiss him after his confession, which would be true so far as it went – and Dan always found that a little bit of truth went a long way when it came to making his cover more convincing.

"Shops and pockets."

Warneford laughed. "So that's your game?"

"Not now. Seen too many hanged or transported."

"What if you could make money with your fists outside the ring?"

"What do you mean?"

"I can use men like you."

"To do what?"

"Take a risk. Keep your mouth shut. Step up to the mark if it becomes necessary."

"I can do all that."

Warneford leaned forward. "Then join the others tomorrow night in Barcombe Wood. I've orders for game from a number of poulterers in Bristol. Guaranteed sales, and a good share of the profit for you."

Even though the sale of game was as illegal as the taking of it, pheasant, rabbit, and partridge hung in many a shop window.

"I know nothing about hunting."

"You don't need to. Just be prepared to put up a fight if the keepers get in the way."

"Who else is going? Do I know them?"

"Are you in?" countered Warneford.

"I need to know who I'd be trusting."

"Me," said Singleton. "And I'll vouch for the others."

"How many keepers?"

"Three," Singleton said. "Caleb Witt, George Potter, Dick Ford."

Dan took a drink and pretended to think about it. "Very well."

Nothing was said about the night's arrangements during work next day, and Dan thought it wiser not to ask. After supper, Singleton made his usual announcement, and he and Dan went next door to the Fox. Mrs Singleton must have known about her husband's nocturnal activities, but she also knew better than to let on that she did. The world was full of wives pretending ignorance about where the money came from. Sometimes it was safer for the women that way, sometimes not. Since a wife could not testify against her husband it made no difference to Dan's work.

They had their regular drink and chat with the people who came and went. Warneford had left the village, wisely putting himself miles from Barcombe on the night of a raid. Yet still no mention was made of it. At ten Singleton gathered up their tankards and carried them to the bar, where he had a low conversation with Buller. When they were done, he beckoned to Dan, who rose and followed him out.

"Where are we going?" Dan asked.

"Dunnage's."

That made two poachers Dan knew about. Singleton did not want to talk though, so Dan did not ask who else would be there. Acting nosy with gossips like Mrs Singleton and the shopkeeper Travell was one thing, but Singleton was not the man to quiz.

They set off down Back Lane. Where it turned a corner to run parallel to the High Street, they carried straight on along a stony path between tangled, sharp-thorned hedges. They followed this covered track for about a mile before emerging into open country and a blast of cold wind. They crossed three fields to the top of a low rise. A shallow valley dipped below them with a farmhouse standing snug at the bottom of it.

Singleton knocked and they were admitted to a large, flagged kitchen with a low-raftered ceiling. The room smelt of smoked ham and punch. It was clean but bare, not a homely place. The rest of the house was dark and silent. There was no one else living there, no wife or maidservant to help Dunnage with his housekeeping. Two black and white sheepdogs dozed beside the fire.

"Well, here he is," Singleton said, stamping the mud off his boots.

So Dan was expected. They must have agreed on his admission beforehand, possibly with one dissenter. Abe, who was slouching against a wall trying to look tough, uttered a contemptuous, "Yeah?"

Travell stood near the fire and gave a friendly nod. He was not all talk then, thought Dan, though he did not look the most stout-hearted of the crew, judging from his nervous gulps at his drink.

A young lad leaned against the table, gnawing at his fingernails. When he was introduced as Walter Halling he gave a preoccupied smile, then went back to his brooding.

While Dunnage doled out cakes and wine, Abe sidled up to Walter.

"We're a player short for the skittles on Saturday. We've never been beat yet, and don't want to be, not by the Paulton lot. You've got to make up the team."

"Can't," Walter mumbled.

"What do you mean, *can't?*"

"I'm working. Uncle's had a big order for boots from the mine."

"On a Saturday afternoon? Tell the old bugger what to do with his job and come to Paulton with us."

"No," Walter said, and whatever else he might have said was lost when Dunnage called the company to order.

The farmer raised his glass. "Here's success to our venture!"

When they had drunk the toast, which made Walter choke, Dunnage put down his glass and took up a Bible from the dresser at the side of the room. He laid it in the middle of the table and they shuffled in a circle around it. Each man placed his hands on the book, Dan following their lead.

Dunnage fixed his eyes on the sooty ceiling and chanted, "Gathered here by moonlight, we swear – "

Abe pouted. "Do we have to go through this rigmarole every time?"

A spasm of irritation passed through the clasped hands.

"You know the rules," Dunnage said.

"I'll swear a thousand oaths," Walter cried.

"Just get on with it, blast you," growled Singleton.

"All right, all right! No need to huff it," Abe grumbled. "I only wondered."

Dunnage began again. "Gathered here by moonlight, we swear..."

They muttered the words after him. "That we are here as brothers. That we will defend and protect one another as brothers. That he who betrays or deserts his brothers will pay in blood. His blood we will drain from his body. His skin we will flay from his back. His flesh we will feed to the crows. His bones we will burn and his soul we will curse to Hell and Damnation. Amen."

Dunnage held out the book and they kissed it in turn. Then he produced a piece of white chalk and drew a star on their hats so that they would know one another in the dark. Next came some pieces of charcoal with which they blacked their faces. Finally, the farmer rolled back a muddy rug and lifted up some floorboards to reveal a number of guns, which he handed round.

Dunnage thrust a gun at Dan, who hesitated. "Warneford mentioned fists, not guns."

"You'll need it," Dunnage said. "The keepers shoot to kill."

"They what?"

"You've sworn now – " Abe began.

"And I won't go back on my word," Dan snapped back, wishing for the chance to exercise his fists on the young coxcomb.

"It's true though, Dan," Singleton said. "But if we run into the keepers, they'll think twice about starting anything if they see we are armed."

In Dan's experience, the more guns there were, the more likely was a confrontation, but he kept that thought to himself and said, "Is that how that gamekeeper – Castle? – got killed? You had a run-in?"

Abe laughed. "Bloodie Bones killed him."

"And three cheers for Bloodie Bones!" Walter added fervently.

Dunnage silenced the youngsters with a look. "I've no idea who else was in the wood the night Castle got done, but we were nowhere near him. Take the gun."

Dan shrugged and did as he was told. If they did nothing else in the woods that night, they had already committed a capital offence. Under the Black Act, anyone who went armed and disguised into the forests could be hanged, even if he had not fired a shot or taken so much as a rabbit. Another instance of a law that was so harsh it defeated its own purpose, for many juries were unwilling to convict under such a bloodthirsty act.

They refilled and drained their glasses. Dan had managed to keep his full from the first round, and Walter only drank half of his. They muffled their faces. Dunnage and Abe each shouldered a bundle. The dogs leapt to their feet as if they had never known what sleep was, quivering and keen to be out. Dunnage banked the fire and extinguished the candles. They set off, but not by moonlight as in the oath. It was a dark night, friendlier to thieves of any stamp, in city or country. The wind rose and clouds ran across the sky, bringing the promise of rain. They travelled in single file, keeping in the shadows, dodging from tree to tree, crouching low alongside walls and hedges.

So it was done, Dan thought. He had identified the poachers, and all that remained for him to do was arrange the arrests. Everyone would be pleased: Sir William, Lord Oldfield, even Garvey would have to admit the thing had been carried off efficiently. It would be smiles and handshakes all round, and then he could go back to London, and Eleanor – except that when Dunnage denied they'd had anything to do with Castle's murder it had sounded like the truth. It would have been easier and safer to say they were not in the forest at all the night Castle died. Hard to be sure, though. Dunnage might be a skilful liar. Or perhaps he thought it was true. One of the gang could have slipped away and killed Castle without the others knowing, or sneaked back into the woods after they had finished.

They had reached the ruins of Budd's cottage. There was a man with a grievance. Then there were the Tolleys, unlikely though they seemed. And Caleb Witt, who wanted what Castle had had: the job, the cottage, the pay.

Dan would not be going home just yet. He hitched his collar higher. Too late. The rain had already dripped from the leaves and down his neck.

They stopped to listen and, hearing nothing but the steady whisper of light rainfall, nocturnal animals, rustling leaves and creaking trees, hopped over the fence into the wood. Abe, who knew where there was a covey of partridges, took the lead. They stayed close to the fence, the dogs circling ahead. Dan thought they would move like the Red Indians in the American forests, but no one took any particular care to avoid treading on twigs or blundering into trees, though if they spoke they did keep their voices low.

They stopped on the edge of a field. Dunnage hissed a command and the dogs lay down, taut and ready to spring.

"Wide or narrow net?" Dunnage whispered to Abe.

"Narrow. I know the exact spot they are roosting."

Dunnage pulled a net from his pack. "Walter, you take the rear."

"What do I do?" Walter asked.

Abe sneered. "Don't you know that?"

"Everyone's got to learn," Dunnage said. "Walter will do it... You just have to make sure the net doesn't catch on anything."

Dan waited with Travell and Singleton while the other three crept out onto the grass. Abe and Dunnage pulled the net after them, keeping it three or four feet above ground. Walter walked behind, twitching it now and again if it looked like snagging anywhere. One minute there was nothing but grass, the next there was a whirr and scuttle and the ground was alive with brown feathers. They let go of the net over the startled birds. All that remained was to wring their necks and drop them into their bags, which was quickly done. This was a part of the business Dan did not much like. There was nothing sporting in it, for the panicked fowl were helpless.

"A good haul," Travell said. "Should fetch fifteen shillings a brace."

Walter's teeth flashed in a white grin. "And give His Lordship a nice shock when he finds his covey gone."

The rain was falling harder when they set off for home, the pattering covering any noise they made. The conditions were ideal for creeping about the woods – and not only for them. They had been walking for about twenty minutes when a beam of light shot across their path. It was extinguished immediately, but not before the lantern-bearer had seen them. There was the unmistakable sound of flintlocks being cocked.

"Drop your guns!"

Chapter Seven

The voice came from a short, bulky silhouette which Dan guessed was Caleb Witt's. He was flanked by the underkeepers, Dick Ford and George Potter. Their white cravats gleamed faintly in the dark, the marks distinguishing them from the raiders' chalked stars.

The first thing Dan did was throw his gun aside. Dunnage flicked his hand at his dogs, and the well-trained animals flung themselves at the keepers. One raced between Ford's legs and knocked him flying. His gun fell out of his hand without going off, and Singleton jumped in on top of him.

The other dog fastened its jaws around Potter's arm. It was lucky for the keeper that he wore a thick coat. His gun fired harmlessly into the sky, the dog's fangs gleaming in the flash. He shook the animal off, but it came snarling back. Abe dropped the sacks of poultry, and he and Dunnage closed in on Potter as he struggled to kick the dog away. Travell snatched up the haul and retreated to the edge of the clearing.

That left Witt for Dan and Walter, but it was not Witt Dan went for. It was Walter, who had his gun pointed at Witt's chest. Dan lunged at him and knocked the weapon out of his grasp. It went off, and for a few seconds Dan was blind and deaf. When he could see again Walter's enraged face loomed in front of him, and Witt was charging towards them. Dan shoved the boy out of the way, ducked, and met the big man with a head butt. He hit Witt square in the chest, feeling rather than hearing the 'oof' as the air rushed from the keeper's lungs. They crashed to the ground. Dan straddled Witt and did the only thing possible. He knocked him out cold.

He looked round to see how the others were doing. Dunnage and Abe were running, leaving Potter on his hands and knees with blood streaming from his nose. Ford lay motionless on his back while Singleton pounded him with fist and boot. Dan got up and dragged Singleton off, the blacksmith aiming a last, needless kick at the unconscious man. Dan picked up Walter's gun, grabbed his own, and hustled the lad out of the clearing. Travell was already well away.

They stopped to draw breath at a lonely spot on the heath. They stood doubled up, panting, listening for the sounds of pursuit. Either no one had heard the shots, or those who had were not the sort to trouble themselves about it.

Abe wiped the sweat from his face. "That was a good do!"

Then they were all laughing, back-slapping, boasting about the battle in the wood. Not to seem odd man out, Dan crowed about knocking out Witt. He flung back his head and guffawed, but he still saw Walter coming. He sidestepped the youth, twisted him round, and pinned his arms to his sides.

"What's all this?" Dunnage demanded.

Walter struggled in Dan's grip. "I had a clear shot at Witt and he stopped me. Whose side is he on?"

"I'm on ours, you bloody young fool," Dan said. "Or do you want us all to swing for murder?"

"We'd hang anyway," Walter retorted.

"You shoot a man at point-blank range when there's no need for it and it's a certainty." Dan let him go.

"Bastards deserve it." Walter went for Dan again, but Dunnage hauled him back.

"That's enough," the farmer said.

"Hold on," Abe said. "Walt has a point. Why should he care what happens to a gamekeeper? And who is he anyway? No one in Barcombe had met him until a few days ago."

Travell twitched nervously. "That's right, isn't it? No one had met him."

Dunnage looked at Singleton. It was Singleton who had introduced Dan to Warneford and got him into the gang, but it was Dunnage's lead the others would follow. If Singleton could not reassure the farmer, Dan was in trouble. Singleton was the key to getting out of this in one piece.

He rounded on the blacksmith. "What is this? You told me these men were all right, and the next thing I know they're accusing me of Christ knows what. If you think I'm going to put my head in a noose because of some stupid boy, you can think again. Damn the lot of you. I'm off."

He thrust the gun into Singleton's startled grasp, spun on his heel, and strode away. One step, two, three...how many guns on his back? No one moved. No one called him back.

"Dan!" Singleton's voice.

He must not give in too easily. He raised his hand in a dismissive gesture and kept going.

"No, wait!" Singleton cried. Dan stopped and turned. "Dan's right. Walter had no right to put the rest of us in danger. We're not here to settle scores." It sounded odd coming from the man who had just given Ford such a pounding.

Dunnage nodded. "They were outnumbered. There was no need to fire and make a bad case worse."

Dan walked back and said huffily, "That's what I said."

"There's no need to take stupid risks," said Travell who, true to his own advice, had kept clear of the fight.

"All right," said Dunnage, "let's get a move on. We got a good haul and that's what we came for. And no one's going to hang, not if you remember what we agreed."

"But – "

"Stow it, Walter," Singleton said.

Abe jabbed his finger at Dan. "I say we can't trust him."

"He's taken the oath, hasn't he?" Dunnage said. "So let's have no more of it." He gave his orders. "Walter, you cut off home. You're sure your mother doesn't know you're out?"

"Course," the youth muttered sullenly.

Abe, seeing that Walter had given up the attack on Dan, vented his anger with a contemptuous "Your mother!"

Walter shot a furious glance at him, but before another

quarrel could get going, Dunnage told him, "Dust off your hat and wipe that stuff off your face. Now go…Dan and Singleton, you were leaving the Fox and Badger when Jem Cox discovered his horse had thrown a shoe. You did a temporary fix so he could get home. Buller heard you at work, and Jem will be back in the morning when the forge is up and running to have a permanent shoe fitted. Travell…"

"I went to Bath on business and spent the night at a friend's house. He'll back me up."

"And me and Abe were over at Farmer Hippisley's wetting his grandson's head. Singleton?"

Singleton stepped up, and Abe and Travell handed him the sacks in what was obviously their usual routine, except that this time the blacksmith had Dan to share the load. Abe and Dunnage collected up the guns and the group separated.

"Friendly lot," Dan said, still acting the aggrieved part.

"Just careful," Singleton answered. "No harm meant." After a moment, he added, "No one has ever broken the oath, but if he did…it's not just words."

Dan stopped dead and flung out his arms, palms open. Singleton skidded to a halt. They stood facing one another.

"Say what you mean, Singleton. If you want me out, I'm out. It's no skin off my nose whether I stay in Barcombe or not."

An owl hooted. Something flitted in the dark above their heads. Singleton shifted the load on his back and started walking again. "You coming?"

When they had gone a few paces, Dan said conversationally, to show all was forgiven, "Where are we taking the birds?"

"Fox and Badger."

"What happens to them then?"

"Sam Bryer, the Bristol carrier, delivers them to Warneford tomorrow."

"Does he know what he's carrying?"

"Maybe he does, maybe he doesn't. We never speak of it in so many words."

They were close to the church now, and continued in

silence until they reached the forge gate. Singleton took the sacks from Dan and told him to go in. Dan climbed over the gate and paused, one hand resting on the top bar. He heard a soft rap on an un-shuttered window. It opened immediately; Buller was waiting up. If he and Singleton spoke it was in whispers, and Dan did not hear their voices. After a moment the window closed with a soft snick. Dan sprinted across the yard and got into the forge before Singleton appeared.

Dan was tired when he lay down, but he could not sleep. He was still tense from the confrontation. He wondered what Walter was doing with the gang. Abe belonged there, but not a lad like Walter: steady at his trade, not used to drinking, filling his spare time with something other than the Fox and Badger. Yet he had been the only one desperate enough to point a gun, and while the others were not men of peace, they had baulked at murder – which lent more credibility to Dunnage's claim that Castle's death was nothing to do with their poaching activities.

"*We're not here to settle scores,*" Singleton had said. Did Walter have a score to settle with the keepers, and if so, had Josh Castle died for it?

Whatever was eating at Walter, Dan needed to find out what it was and if it was enough to drive him to murder.

Dan was filling the bucket at the pump in the morning when he saw Sam Bryer loading his wagon outside the Fox and Badger. Sam was a whistling, open-faced young man with blue eyes and curling golden hair. A girl sat next to the driver's seat, fiddling with her hair ribbons. When he had loaded the baskets, crates and boxes – a score of Lord Oldfield's birds among them – he climbed up beside her and put his hand around her waist. She wriggled up close to him.

"Cottom's girl," said Mrs Singleton, stopping halfway across the yard with a basket of washing in her arms. "Her father's the rat-catcher, when he's sober. Who can blame her for going with Sam, with such a wastrel for a father and no mother or sisters to care for her? She was sweet on Abe once, but he's always up at the Hall now, sniffing around Sal."

Before long, Dan had the girl's life history. Her future he could guess. He hoped for her sake Sam was the marrying kind.

Singleton appeared in the forge doorway. "Stop your maundering, woman. And where's that water?"

She sniffed and went into the house. Dan hurried back with the pail. He had been promoted to striker, which meant that while Singleton cut a heavy bar with a hammer, he pounded it with a sledge. The strength in his shoulders made him good at the task.

Jem Cox turned up to have his horse shod, replacing a perfectly good shoe with a new one. Dan did not see any money exchange hands, though no doubt Cox and others like him got some reward for providing the poachers' alibis – probably something with fur or feathers. Perhaps keeping the silence itself was its own reward. Lord Oldfield had said every countryman was a poacher if he got the chance. Why would he peach on his own kind?

And as Dan discovered at the Fox and Badger that evening, the bolder the poacher, the more esteemed he was. Sam Ayres and Drake stayed away. Whether this was deliberate or not, Dan did not know. He had only seen Ayres there on the day of the fight, and Drake did not come in every night. But he did not imagine either man wished to be in the Fox and Badger the night after a poaching raid.

Dunnage was not there either. He preferred to drink at home in the gloom of his kitchen. Nor was Walter. But Dan, Singleton, Abe and Travell were treated as if they had performed some marvellous feat fighting six against three (counting the shopkeeper, which Dan did since he'd had a gun), and leaving one man so badly beaten he might be lame for the rest of his life. The man's suffering did not soften the people of Barcombe. As they saw it, it might easily be one of them lying injured, and there would be no comfortable bed, no physician, no pension from Lord Oldfield for their families.

In between pouring jugs of ale, tapping barrels, and slamming tankards on tables, Buller reported that he had seen Dr Russell earlier in the day and learned that Dick Ford had two broken ribs and a smashed kneecap, and there was no way of knowing what damage had been done to his insides.

"That's proud Ford – now peg-leg Ford!" yelled some wag, to gusts of laughter.

Travell called it striking a blow for English liberties. Everyone cheered and Jem Cox started to sing. Though an ugly, dirty man, he had a surprisingly fine voice and he did not forget a word.

When I was bound apprentice
In famous Somersetshire
I served my master truly
For nearly seven year,
Till I took up to poaching
As you shall quickly hear
For 'twas my delight of a shiny night
In the season of the year.

They all took up the chorus, and had belted out several more verses when the door opened and in stepped Caleb Witt.

Dan had seen the same thing in a score of London taverns. He would walk into a room, and for a couple of heartbeats there would be dead silence. Then it would break with a noise that almost blew him back into the street, everyone talking and laughing, the smokers puffing on their pipes, the drinkers quaffing their ale, the whores wriggling in men's laps. They all knew who he was, though they all pretended not to. And either none of them had heard of the man he was after or his crimes, or they could all swear he was somewhere else at the time.

By the time Witt had fastened the door, the villagers were engrossed in their cards and dominoes, their beer and baccy, their chat about dogs and horses. There was even a smattering of "Good evening, Caleb" as Witt pushed his way to the bar and placed one large, red fist on the counter. Dan doubted the gamekeeper had missed the momentary pause, or that he was fooled by the innocent bustle.

"And how," asked Buller, pouring out Witt's beer, "is poor Ford? That's a bad business, a very bad business."

Witt did not answer until he had slaked his first thirst with a long pull at his drink. "He's well enough."

He turned and surveyed the company.

"I'll join you, Singleton."

He strode over, dragged a stool from under the next table, and straddled his thick legs over it. He was younger than Dan had realised, only in his late twenties. His face was ruddy, the skin coarse and crinkled around the eyes. He had a large, bulbous nose, a wide mouth, and pale eyes set beneath a bony brow.

"Damp night," he remarked.

They all agreed on this. He looked at Dan. "I don't think I know you."

"Dan Fielding," said Singleton. "My new forge assistant."

"Ah, the boxing cove." Witt rubbed his jaw where Dan's knuckles had left a purple stain.

"Nought but a milling cove," said Dan.

Witt nodded slowly and switched his attention to the shopkeeper. "Well, Travell, how's business? Prospering?"

"Times are hard, Mr Witt, for us poor tradesmen," Travell answered, his voice a nervous whine. "Two bad harvests in a row. Money's tight."

"Yes, I dare say the best goods are those that cost you nothing to get but bring a high profit when you sell 'em," Witt replied. "Makes you wonder how poor labouring folk manage to put their dinners on the table, eh, Abe?"

"I'm lucky I'm in regular employment," the lad answered, smart but not too jaunty. Witt was a tough man. It would not do to annoy him.

"I hear he's a good master, Farmer Dunnage. Good dog trainer too." Witt drained his glass. "Well then, I'd best be off. Me and Potter will be at the west warren all night."

Leaving them to digest the information that the west warren was precisely where the keepers would not be that night, he rose, wrapped his many-collared coat about him, and made for the door. It was an old game, Dan realised, this bantering between keeper and poacher, where much more was said than was spoken. But it was a grim game when the stakes were so high on both sides. There was no more singing, and the gathering broke up soon after.

On Saturday afternoon, Singleton and Dan had planned to drive to Stonyton to fetch some coal, but an urgent job came in – one of the farmers needed some tines on his plough replaced – so the blacksmith had to heat up his forge and stay behind.

"Do you think you can manage the cart without overturning yourself?" he asked Dan, fastening the horse into the traces.

Dan was getting used to the big, gentle workhorses, and as long as he was not expected to ride one he could manage a horse well enough. He did not let on that he was glad he was going on his own. There was someone he wanted to talk to: Walter Halling.

Stonyton was a large village strung along the Stony River valley between the Old and New Pits. The pits were connected above ground by the High Street, and below by tunnels. A black canal, crowded with vessels carrying coals to Bath and beyond, flowed sluggishly along an embankment behind the street.

The dwellings around the New Pit, known as Upper Stonyton, were modern terraced cottages, purpose-built for the miners and mean in size, material and workmanship. The older properties in Lower Stonyton were no better. They were run down and uncared for by landlord or tenant, most of whom were content to live surrounded by their rubbish heaps and middens. Half-naked, barefoot children hung around squalid homes where pale, dirty housewives had admitted defeat in the battle with the coal dust.

What chiefly struck the senses, though, was the noise. Steam rose in roaring clouds from the winding engine above the offices and stables of the original working, to which Dan was heading. Chains rattled and squealed as the bulging coal baskets were winched up to the surface, where the ore was tipped thunderously into trucks, trundled across a short track to the quay, and loaded into barges. Bogies clanked down the rails from the New Pit to add their loads to the cargoes. Saws whined in the carpentry workshops where they made the pit props. The men had to shout to be heard above the din, and shout they did, every other word a curse or blasphemy.

Dan had arrived at shift-change. A group of girls hung around the gates, exchanging obscenities with the loaders. The men who had finished below were walking and crawling back to the lift shaft, a journey of several miles for some of them. They would be thirsty after hours in the hot tunnels. The girls stood a chance of getting a drink as well as earning a few pennies for favours granted in alleyway or field.

Dan turned into the yard, ignoring their shrill invitations. Coal dust glittered on the ground, and the ruts and potholes were filled with black sludge. The pit manager poked his head out of the office and directed Dan to the coal shed. The horse stood patiently while the pre-ordered sacks were loaded. Dan watched the men drift in for the next shift. They clustered around the lift shaft, where the overseer handed out candles.

The cage trundled up from the pit. The men in it were so dirty they looked as if they had brought the darkness to the surface with them. They carried mattocks and the satchels they had taken their food and drink down in. Most were stripped to their shirtsleeves, many to their drawers.

They handed their unused bits of candle to their foreman, exchanged greetings with their replacements, gathered up the girls, and set off down the road to the rough alehouse Dan had passed on the way. He climbed back into the cart and asked the coalmen for directions to the shoemaker's.

Chapter Eight

The shoemaker's at the end of the High Street was a poky place with bare, dusty floorboards. Dan had to stoop to avoid hitting the boots and shoes hanging by their laces from the rafters. Walter was just rising from the workbench behind the counter, which was set beneath a window to take advantage of the light. He held a new pair of miner's boots with reinforced toecaps.

Dan did not expect him to be pleased to see him, and was not offended by his "Oh, it's you. What do you want?"

"I need my shoes repaired. The soles are worn."

Walter glanced at the open door to the workroom at the back of the shop. There was someone moving about in there; someone who could hear every word and would know if he turned a customer away.

"I'll just be a minute," he said, and carried the boots next door. "This pair's done, Uncle."

The unseen uncle must have taken the boots and inspected them, for a moment later he said, "Good work. Why don't you see what's wanted in the shop and then get off home?"

"We've still ten pairs to do."

"They can wait until Monday."

"I don't mind stopping."

"No, lad, you've done enough today."

Walter came back to Dan and said grudgingly, "Let's have a look, then."

Dan took off his shoes and handed them over. They were big, heavy things with nails around the soles and stiff uppers.

Walter grunted. "The heels need replacing too."

In spite of his dislike of Dan, he was a craftsman. The work soon absorbed him, and the job he did was neat and strong.

"This is your uncle's place?" Dan asked as Walter cut and hammered.

"Yes."

"How long have you been apprenticed?"

"Five years."

"Will you stay here when your time is up?"

"No. I'm going to set up my own shop in Barcombe." Walter brightened. "It's going to be in the house to start with, but once I get going I'll be able to afford something better for me and Mother." Then he remembered whom he was talking to and lapsed into sulky silence.

"I wish you luck with it."

"These're done." He banged the boots on the counter. "A shilling and sixpence."

He dropped Dan's payment in a box and took off his apron. "I can give you a lift if you like. I've got the cart."

"I'd rather walk."

"Look, Walter, I'm sorry about what happened. Can't we talk about it?"

He shot a nervous look into the workshop. "I'm off now, Uncle."

"Have you left the bench tidy?" Uncle Thomas called back. "Then see you Monday."

Dan held the door open. "Well?"

Walter glowered then looked away. "All right."

"Is it just you and your mother?" Dan asked when the noise and smoke of the village were behind them.

"Yes."

"And she doesn't know what you're getting up to at nights?"

"No."

"She wouldn't like it?"

Walter did not answer. Dan had hit a soft spot. He let the silence grow between them for a few moments to give the blow a chance to sink in. Then he said, "The reason I stopped you the other night is because there's a big difference between killing a man and taking a deer."

"I don't see it. Either could get us hanged."

"Yes, but in the first case there's never a chance the court would show mercy. In the other there is. You're young. Juries don't like hanging boys for a first stealing offence."

"You know a lot about it."

"When I was younger than you I fell in with a bad lot and took to thieving. But I had no parent looking out for me. In the end, I was lucky, I got out in time. If I hadn't I'd be dead by now, at the rope's end or from gaol fever. Is that what you want, Walter? To swing at the end of a rope or die in a stinking hulk? Is it what your mother wants for you?"

"What's it to you?"

"It makes me angry to see someone like you throw it all away. You've got a home, an apprenticeship, you've got plans. You are decently dressed and you get enough to eat. Boys like you don't know you're born."

"And you had it really tough. Too bad."

"I don't want your sympathy. I just want you to stop and think about what you're risking, because when it's gone, it's gone."

"It's my life."

"Well, I've said my piece."

"Thanks very much."

Walter folded his arms across his chest, pursed his lips, and glared at the horse's ears.

"Why do you think the keepers deserve it?" Dan said after a while.

The youth started. "What?"

"The other night you said they deserved to be shot. Is that just because they are keepers, or what?"

"It's because they are bastards."

"They're just doing their job. What else do you expect from them? That they'll welcome you into the woods with open arms? Say, 'Go on, take the deer, we don't mind'?"

"The woods have always been ours. Now they won't even let us walk through them."

"It's unfair, but you can't truly think the keepers are going to do anything other than obey their master."

"It's because of Jack," Walter mumbled.

"Who's Jack?"

Before the woods were fenced, Walter said, he used to walk through them on his way home from the shop. He always had Jack with him. His face lit up when he described the mongrel terrier with his lopsided run, stout drum belly and short, sturdy legs. He had found him as a pup, wandering in the lanes about Barcombe where he'd been abandoned by his owner.

On this particular day it was hot. The woods looked cool and shady. Walter paused in the middle of the road by one of the new *Keep Out* signs. Jack flopped down beside him, his pink tongue hanging from the corner of his mouth.

Walter knew that there were things called Game Laws under which the old Lord had allowed them to take rabbit and the occasional bird, had sometimes even ignored the loss of the odd deer. Now, under the same laws, young Lord Adam wouldn't let anyone take anything. It didn't make much sense to Walter. Surely, though, Lord Oldfield didn't mean to stop them going on the paths. The tracks through the woods were ancient; the people of Barcombe had always used them to go about their daily business. Since he wasn't here to hunt, there could be no harm in entering the wood. He jumped across the ditch and ducked under the fence. Jack bounded after him.

He had been walking for a few minutes when he ran into Lord Adam Oldfield and Josh Castle. The gamekeeper had his gun over his arm as usual, though they had not been hunting for Lord Oldfield was unarmed. Walter raised his hand to his cap and tipped it respectfully.

His Lordship's father would have nodded gruffly and passed on, but Lord Adam stopped and demanded, "Can't you read?"

Walter had forgotten about the sign and the question confused him.

"Answer His Lordship," Castle snapped.

"Yes, I can read," Walter answered, and added helpfully, "Mr Travell taught me."

"I don't care who bloody taught you," said Lord Oldfield. "What the hell do you think you're doing in here?"

Walter looked nervously at Castle. "I'm on my way home."

"It's His Lordship is talking to you, not me," the gamekeeper said.

Walter's bowels seemed suddenly full of icy water. "I – I am on my way home, Your Lordship. I always come this way."

"Not any more, you don't," Lord Oldfield snapped. "The signs say 'Keep out' and that's what you'll do from now on."

"But – "

"But?" repeated Castle.

"Everyone uses the path. It's a shortcut."

"There are no shortcuts," Castle said. "Don't let me or His Lordship catch you in here again."

"No, sir – thank you, sir – I won't do it again, sir. Come on, Jack."

Jack, who had been happily sniffing at trees, trotted to his heel.

"Will you look at that smart little fellow?" Lord Oldfield said. "Your dog, is it?"

Walter felt his knees go limp with relief. He'd had his warning and now His Lordship was smiling, showing there was really no harm done. "It's Jack, sir. He comes with me, sir, to work."

"I'll bet he does. Enjoys himself too, no doubt?"

"Oh, yes, sir. He likes a run around."

"After rabbits?"

Walter laughed. Things were going much better now they were chatting about dogs like any young men might. "No, he's not a hunting dog, sir. He couldn't catch a rabbit if it was in a pot."

Castle guffawed.

"Josh, what's the penalty for keeping a dog if you don't have a licence to hunt?"

An odd question coming from a magistrate. Even Castle looked puzzled.

"Five pound or three months," the keeper said.

"Well then, what's your name, I fine you five pounds." Lord Oldfield held out his hand. "Come on, pay up."

"I haven't got five pound," Walter stammered. To his dismay, tears sprang into his eyes.

"That's a pity. Don't cry. I'll let you off. We'll have to carry out the rest of the sentence though."

Walter blinked. "Sentence?"

Lord Oldfield stared gravely at the little dog's eager, upturned face. "I hereby find you – Jack, did you say? – find you, Jack, guilty of the charge as proved and sentence you to be hanged by the neck until dead."

"Hanged?" Walter shrieked.

Castle laughed. The boy crashed onto his knees and swept the dog into his arms. "You won't have him, no you won't!"

"Won't have him?" repeated Lord Adam Oldfield. "Look'ee, Josh, at our merry little man! Won't have him, he declares."

Castle, still chuckling, jerked his head at the boy. "Get out of it."

Comprehension dawned. It was a joke. A cruel one, but a joke nevertheless. Hugging the terrier, Walter scrambled to his feet.

"Wait a minute." Lord Adam grabbed Walter's arm. "Aren't you forgetting something, Josh?"

"My Lord?"

"The sentence." Lord Adam wrenched Jack out of Walter's arms, dandled him by the scruff of the neck. "I have some twine in my pocket."

"But this is no hunting dog," said Castle. "He's not even fit as a ratter."

"I said, the sentence, Josh."

The two men stared at one another. Then Castle lowered his eyes, took the twine, stepped aside from the path, and threw it over a low branch. Walter, petrified by disbelief, watched as the gamekeeper tested the knots, took the dog from Lord Adam, looped a noose around his neck, balanced him in the air, his legs flailing, and dropped him.

Walter sprang forward, but Lord Oldfield held him back. The branch dipped, the rope creaked, the noose tightened. Jack's pink tongue lolled sideways out of his mouth.

"Like I told you, bastards," Walter said.

"After that you joined the gang?"

"Yes."

"I'm truly sorry, Walter. But you can get another dog. You can't get another life."

"I don't want another dog. I want Jack. And I'd do anything to get back at them."

"And if Lord Oldfield heard you talking like this, how would he know it wasn't you who killed Josh Castle?"

"So that's it. You're going to pin it on me for the reward, are you?"

"Could it be pinned on you? Were you out with the gang that night?"

"Of course I was. Was a good haul too."

"Did you kill Castle?"

"No. But I would have done if I'd had the chance. And smashed his bones."

Before Dan could make any answer to this, they were interrupted by an explosion.

Chapter Nine

Walter was already out of the cart and running up the hill towards the barrow. Dan pulled up and followed him into the smoke. On the other side of the choking tendrils, Mrs Taylor sat on the ground rocking her little girl on her lap.

"Ai-ai-ai!" the woman wailed.

"*Dya, dya – Mother!*" the child screamed.

The metal cooking pot lay several feet away and the hearth stones were scattered in all directions. One side of the girl's face was scalded and peppered with bits of kindling, and clumps of her hair had been burned off. Mrs Taylor's hands were scorched red from beating out the flames. Dan could staunch bleeding, bandage wounds, even make a temporary splint for a broken limb if he had to, but he knew nothing about treating burns.

"We must take her to Mother," Walter said.

"I don't think we should move her. Can you fetch your mother? Take the cart."

"Quicker if I run. It's just there, on the edge of the forest." He sprang away.

Most of the fire had been doused by the contents of the pot. Dan stamped out the last flames as Tom came tearing into the encampment, his big coat flapping. He dropped to his knees beside his wife, gathered his daughter into his arms, half-sang, half-chanted her name: "Kiomi, Kiomi". The girl's screams faded to sobs and whimpers. Over her head, the woman told her husband her tale, speaking in what Dan supposed was Egyptian, her rapid speech punctuated by Tom's curses.

The Hallings arrived, the boy carrying his mother's bag of remedies. Dan had an idea of a village healing woman as a dirty old crone. Anna Halling was a neat young woman in white cap, striped neckerchief and checked cotton gown with a clean blue apron over it. She had a trim figure, and the concern that shone from her blue eyes made a naturally pleasant face more pleasant still.

Tom's boys stood nearby, shocked and singed but otherwise unhurt. Mrs Halling sent them off to fetch water. They were glad to have something to do and raced down the hill with the pail. Tom stood up and Mrs Halling took his place. She gave the girl a drink from a bottle, which after a short delay sent her into a muttering sleep.

"It's valerian," Walter said in answer to Dan's enquiring glance.

"What did your wife say?" Dan asked Tom.

"She set Kiomi to stirring the pot while she threw some more wood on the fire. It just went up."

"But why? This was more than damp kindling."

Tom did not answer. His attention was fixed on Mrs Halling's deft fingers as she washed his daughter's wound and picked out charred splinters.

Dan turned away and raked through the gravy-soaked ashes. The fire had been carefully laid from branches and twigs, but among the natural kindling were some wooden stakes. He picked up the remains of one of these. A tube a few inches long had been hollowed into one end, the opening distorted and cracked by some internal pressure. He poked his finger inside. It came out covered with black dust. He sniffed. Gunpowder.

"Taylor, do you know what this is?"

Tom took the stake, examined it, and beckoned to the boys.

"Where did you get this?"

The younger lad started to cry. The elder turned pale and mumbled something in his own language. Taylor's hand shot out and the stake cracked across his son's face, leaving a red and black streak.

"I've told you a hundred times to take only snap wood, furze and bracken."

The boy sobbed out excuses. Taylor struck him again. When he raised the stick a third time, Dan caught his arm. He had seen enough children beaten in his lifetime.

"Thrashing them won't do any good. They know they've done wrong. But what did they do?"

Taylor jerked his head. The boys scuttled to the other side of the barrow, from where their sad, white faces peeped out at their father.

"They took this from a pile of rails left ready to repair a gap in the fence around the wood. It's an old keepers' trick. They fill one or two stakes with powder, plug the hole, and leave them for someone to gather for firewood. I've heard of it. Never known it done around here."

"A nasty trick," Dan said, and meant it. If Lord Adam Oldfield had been standing in front of him at that moment, no consideration of rank would have stopped him from punching his noble face.

"Will the child lose her sight?" he asked.

"I don't know," Mrs Halling answered. "We should ask Dr Russell to look at her."

"No *gadso* doctors," Taylor said.

"But Dr Russell has more skill in such matters than I," she said.

Taylor stuck stubbornly to his refusal, so in the end she promised to look in on Kiomi herself in the morning. She put away her salves and stood up. Walter picked up her bag. Dan walked down to the road with them.

Walter's face was grim, his fists clenching and unclenching. "Those bloody bastards!"

"That's enough, Walter," Mrs Halling snapped.

"I'm sorry, Mother. But it's true."

"That's no reason for you to start swearing."

Dan wondered what she would say if she knew that swearing was the least of the mischief her boy got up to. They said their goodbyes, and he watched them until they disappeared around a spur of woodland. He had indeed said his piece to Walter and had not meant to say any more, but that was before he met Anna Halling. A kind woman, ever ready to help others, she had brought her son up well – the way she rebuked him for cursing was evidence of that. It must have been a hard struggle without a husband, and a unique effort among the mothers of Barcombe – Abe's mother had not taken much care over her son's morals. Not that Dan thought the Barcombe women particularly vicious; it was just that poaching was a way of life around here.

He had seen enough to know that there were vicious mothers; mothers who pimped their own daughters; mothers who hired out their babies to beggars; mothers who kept their children hungry and in rags while they spent what little money they had on gin. His only memory of his own mother was of himself standing in a filthy cot, gripping the bars with his thin fingers, peering out through the holes in the tattered sack hung over the alcove where he slept, looking at her shadowy form straddling a man. He did not know where the room had been, nor how he knew the woman was his mother, nor when he had learned that if he did not keep quiet when she brought a man back, pain and terror would follow. So he watched and waited for the man to finish and pay, for her to pull down her skirt, stumble out to the shop, return with a bottle, and drink herself to death.

It was one of the things he had not told Caroline, even when he asked her to marry him eight years ago and made a confession of his background. He had been honest about never knowing his father and losing his mother, and having to live on the streets, but the details he did not share. He'd had to tell her something, though he had been afraid she would refuse him, but she had called him her 'wild boy', seen it all as a great, glorious game, violent and glamorous at the same time. Like his boxing.

Perhaps she had expected life with him to be more exciting. She had never taken him seriously when he said he did not want to be a pugilist. His boxing would make them rich and famous; she would have servants and a carriage, and a husband other women envied. Instead, as she never tired of complaining, he left her alone for hours on end while he went about his work, and he kept that a big secret, and while he was out having fun – for she didn't suppose he spent all his time tracking thieves – what was she supposed to do?

He would not talk about his work. He wanted to protect her from the depths to which people can sink, but somehow she had managed to sink there all the same. She did what his mother had done. She drank.

"Look who I've brought!" Abe cried, dragging Walter into the Fox and Badger that evening.

"Can't stop," Walter muttered. "Said I wouldn't be long."

"Go on with you," Abe said. "You're here now. Two of your best ales, Mistress Buller!"

The landlord's plain, fat daughter raised her eyebrows at this unusual extravagance, turned away from the barrel of ordinary, and drew two of Buller's special brew. Abe thrust a tankard into Walter's hands. He sipped cautiously. Abe nudged his elbow. "Get it down you...That's a bad business up at the barrow, ain't it?"

"It's tyranny, that's what it is," Travell said. "It's the yoke of the Hanoverian kings. I tell you it wasn't always like this. We were a free nation once. Men were at liberty to roam the forests, hunt what and where they liked, even to vote for the Parliament men. All men, not just the rich."

"In Paradise before Adam and Eve, was that?" Drake asked.

"Not so long ago as that," Travell answered earnestly. "Under a great ruler called Alfred, Englishmen elected their king, voted, and had yearly Parliaments. Then King William of France invaded and made the forests his own, stole our land to give it to his nobles, and bled us dry with his taxes."

Dan could see how Travell got his reputation as a wise and learned man. His audience had never heard so much history. It came straight from the radicals in the London Corresponding Society. From their centre in London, they sent pamphlets and speakers to their friends in the regions, spreading the word of the coming revolution.

"We have rights over Barcombe Wood," Travell continued, "as inviolable as our rights over Barcombe Heath."

"*In*-what?" asked Abe.

"No one can take them off us."

"Oh. I thought that was in-ailey something. Hey, Walt, it's your turn to buy."

"It's a bit strong – " Walter began, but Abe cut him off by calling out to Mistress Buller, "Two more of the same when you've got a moment."

Travell went on, "We have deeds and field awards written down which prove our right to the heath. There must be something proving the same for the wood."

"How do you work that out?" asked Drake.

"Because that's what they did, the lords of the manor. They wrote things down. All we have to do is find the parchment."

Abe turned out his pockets. "Not here."

The others took up the joke, looking under the table, picking up their glasses, groping under their chairs.

"You can laugh, my friends," the shopkeeper said, "but if we found that deed we'd be able to make Lord Oldfield give us back the wood."

"And where do you think it is?" Drake asked.

"In the parish chest in the church."

Drake rolled his eyes. "What makes you think Mr Poole will let any of us go rooting through the parish papers? Or that we could make head nor tail of 'em if we did?"

Walter cried, "We must make him!"

Abe laughingly patted his protégé on the back. "That's right, Walt! We'll make him."

"And how will you do that?" Drake demanded.

"Never you mind," Walter said. "We'll do it, that's all."

Drake shook his head and drained his mug, unimpressed by beer-bravado. Dan did not pay much attention to the lads' wild talk either.

"It's a constitutional matter and needs handling by someone who understands such things," Travell said. "I shall give the matter more thought."

He leaned back and furrowed his brow as if he was there and then solving the complex legal problem. Dan had a vision of Garvey: wigged, robed, pitiless. He put Travell's chances of standing up to the sharp London lawyer at nil.

"How is Kiomi?" asked Buller, who had just come up from the cellar where he had been clattering about among the barrels.

"Mother says she thinks she will recover, though whether she'll lose her sight she can't yet tell," Walter said.

"We should get up a collection."

"Taylor wouldn't thank you for money," Singleton said. "He's no use for it."

"Then we could send food and blankets," Buller's daughter suggested. "I've got a bit of ham left over from dinner. I'll send that."

This went down well and the men began to pledge their womenfolk to making up food parcels. Girtin looked hopeful at all this talk of charity, so Dan asked Buller to fill his glass. Shortly after, it being closing time, Singleton and Dan left. Abe was buying another round for himself and Walter.

Dan turned over in his straw for the hundredth time. The country was a noisy place at night. There was a never-ending chorus of hooting, barking, snuffling and whining. Things rustled, skittered, bumped in the darkness. A man could not sleep for the racket. The streets around Covent Garden with its brawlers and prostitutes were more peaceful. At least there he knew what animals were outside.

After a while he fell asleep, only to be woken a short time later by the sound of breaking glass. He sat up in the dark. It came from the direction of the rectory. He listened for the sound of running footsteps, but heard none.

He pulled on his clothes, cautiously opened the forge door, and crept out into the yard. No light appeared in Singleton's window. Either he was a heavy sleeper or, as seemed more likely, he took no interest in protecting the rector and his church from night-time marauders. If Mrs Singleton was trying to persuade him to turn out, she was not going to succeed.

Dan climbed over the gate and slipped across the road. He jumped onto the wall in front of the churchyard and hauled himself onto the high garden wall to look over into the rectory grounds. A moving light appeared through a jagged hole in one of the downstairs windows. Dan scrambled up to the parapet and lowered himself into a flowerbed on the other side.

He crept up to the window and peeped over the sill. The rector and his wife were inside in their nightgowns, her long, dark hair twisted in a plait falling to her waist. Poole put his lamp on the desk and fussed over the scattered books and papers.

"Villains! Robbers! Where is that wretched constable when you need him? What do we pay our rates for?"

"The mess can easily be cleared up," Mrs Poole soothed, "and there is not much damage."

"Not much damage? Look at the scratch!"

She stooped and examined the desktop. "We can repair it."

He snatched up the lamp and shone it about the room, pounced, and scooped something from the floor. He thrust a large stone under his wife's nose.

"If I had been in here, this could have killed me!"

"You were not likely to be here in the middle of the night," she said mildly.

"That's not the point, Laura. What's this? There's a note."

He put the lamp back on the desk and unfurled the paper wrapped around the stone.

"This is an outrage! They dare to speak of oppressions – which they can't spell – under the fairest government, the mildest king, a constitution the envy of every nation, a system of justice – "

"What does it say?"

He flung the note at her.

"Oppressions! Oppressions! Does our Government spy on its own subjects? Do we have a Bastille? Do we – " He broke off. "You've decided to show your face, have you?"

This was addressed to the shawled and curl-papered maidservant who stood wringing her hands in the doorway.

"Oh, oh, oh, it's the French!" she wailed. "We are to be murdered in our beds!"

"Don't be ridiculous, Martha," snapped the rector.

"Oh, sir, they'll cut our throats! They'll burn the house down with us in our beds. They'll – "

"Now, Martha," Mrs Poole said, laying the note on the desk, "they will do no such thing. It is nothing more than an annoying prank."

"It's a great deal more than that," Poole corrected her. "It is an act of subversion and must be reported at once. Martha, run for the constable."

This gave rise to more trembling and weeping. The girl could not be persuaded that the streets of Barcombe were not lined with Frenchmen.

"Pah! I'll go myself," Poole said at last. He ushered the women out of the room and hurried off to dress. After a few moments, the bolts on the front door shot back and he emerged from the house carrying a stout stick. He strode down the path, unlocked the garden door, and set off to Ayres's house, which was at the other end of the village.

Dan had about ten minutes before Poole came back with the constable. He took off his jacket, wrapped it around his hand, and reached through the hole in the window. The sash lock was easily undone. He slid the window up and clambered inside.

Poole had left the lamp burning on the hall table. Dan tiptoed across the room and paused at the doorway. The women had gone upstairs and all was quiet. He darted out, grabbed the lamp, and carried it back into the study.

The paper lay on the desk where Mrs Poole had left it. It was a page torn from a ballad, *The Merry Broomfield: Or, the West Country Wager*, blank on one side. Dan glanced at the print. '*I will lay you an hundred Pounds / A hundred Pounds, aye, and ten, / That a maid if you go to the merry Broomfield / That a maid you return not again.*' Lucky Poole had not noticed that, or he might have been driven to apoplexy.

Dan turned the page over to read the writing on the back: '*Parsons and tyrants friends take note. We have born your oppreshuns long enough. We will have our parish rights or else Bloodie Bones will drink your blood. BB His Mark.*'

The paper matched neither the note left near Castle's body, nor the earlier note sent to Lord Oldfield. The writing too was different. It was childish and clumsy. Lines ran diagonally across the sheet, and the last few words were squeezed into the corner because the first were too big.

The ballad had probably been bought from a peddler or at a fair, impossible to trace. The sheet was creased and dirty as if it had lain in a pocket for a long time. Abe's pocket at a guess: it was the sort of bawdy a young man like him would enjoy. As an apprentice, Walter would be able to read and write, though not necessarily all that well. This was their way of making the parson help the parishioners restore their rights to Barcombe Wood.

As Dan laid the paper back on the desk, it struck him that, of the three notes, one was odd man out. The note sent to Lord Oldfield threatened '*blood and fier*'. The rector's note warned him that Bloodie Bones meant to drink his blood. But the scarecrow note had been short and made no specific threats: "*Tirants Bwar Bloodie Bones.*"

There was something else. The first note to Lord Oldfield and this one to the rector were written on grubby scraps of old paper, recycled from their original uses – a tavern bill, a ballad, the sort of paper people who did not do much writing were likely to use. Farm labourers and shoemakers had no reason to lay out money on stocks of writing paper. By contrast, the *Tirant* note from the scarecrow was written on a clean, fresh sheet of paper of better quality: heavy, cream coloured and deckle edged. Bought paper, not re-used. Whoever wrote the *Tirant* note was someone who did sufficient writing to make the cost of his materials worthwhile. If that was the case, he must get plenty of practice at writing and spelling.

Had the *Tirant* note been written by an educated man pretending to be semi-literate? Someone like Travell, for example, the self-taught taproom lawyer who had set himself up as a school teacher? Although Travell did not seem a likely murderer, he was a man with a cause that might make him capable of striking a blow for justice on behalf of people like the Tolleys.

Was Caleb Witt likely to be a skilled writer? Gamekeepers kept game books; Dan had seen one in Josh Castle's cottage. The penmanship had looked competent enough, but then Josh was a special case, a boy befriended by a lord who might have been given more schooling than other village lads because of it. Could Witt's fists wield a pen as well as he?

Singleton used chalk and slate. Dan doubted Abe would have to pretend to be illiterate. Dunnage spent more time in the fields than the study. He could not see any of them being accomplished writers. Perhaps the handwriting was not disguised after all. It was possible that someone had found or stolen the paper. It was puzzling, though.

Footsteps overhead reminded him that he ought to leave the rectory. He returned the lamp to the hall table. He had just got outside and pulled the window down when he heard voices in the road. Ayres's high-pitched tremor: "How many of them were there, do you think, Reverend?"

The rector and constable passed inside. The light reappeared in the study and danced over to the broken window, where the constable carefully – and uselessly – examined the broken glass. Dan could not get out the way he had come in without being seen. He crept behind the house to the top of the garden and climbed over the garden wall into the graveyard. He was threading his way between the tombs when a figure rose up before him. Girtin's tale of Bloodie Bones sitting on a gravestone with the blood of a live owl spurting from his jaws flashed into Dan's mind, then he saw that it was Girtin himself.

"I wonder what Dan Fielding is doing sneaking about the rectory in the dead of night?"

"I heard the window smash and came to see what was happening. Did you see who threw the stone?"

"Maybe I did. Maybe I didn't."

"Did you see anyone running away?"

"I seen you running away."

"No one else?"

"Who else might there be?"

"You were in the Fox tonight. I think it was that young fool Walter. I wanted to make sure he'd got away."

"Why?"

"Because I've taken a liking to the boy."

Girtin smirked. "To the boy, is it?"

Dan grinned. "Well…You won't tell anyone I was here? I don't want this pinned on me."

"Tell on such a generous man as yourself, Mr Fielding?"

"I will be a generous man, but you must keep this between ourselves. Is that a deal?"

"Deal."

Dan had had to depend on flimsier safeguards than the discretion of a drunk before now. He said goodnight and crept back to his bed.

Chapter Ten

On Sunday, when Dan brought in the water from the pump, the blacksmith was shovelling down his breakfast while Mrs Singleton packed cakes and bread into a basket. They were going to a nearby village called Peasedown to spend the day with his older brother. This brother was also a blacksmith, as was their father, though the old man had retired from the active part of the business. Dan had heard the history of the clan from Mrs Singleton, who was looking forward to a day swapping recipes with her sister-in-law and playing with her nieces and nephews.

"He's a strange one, that Girtin," Dan remarked, as if he had just seen him flitting among the graves. "What's his story?"

"Girtin?" said Mrs Singleton. "He used to be tenant at Tenner's Farm. The Doggets have it now. He had two sons, fine, big lads. I remember as how all the girls used to run after them."

"Run after them!" Singleton muttered.

"They met a West Country fish merchant at Bridgwater Fair – must have been ten years gone now – and he told them that if they signed on with him they could make a fortune in just one summer, fishing in Newfoundland. They don't have much summer there, they say it starts in May – "

"June," said her spouse.

" – May and is over by October. Cod."

"What do you mean, *cod*?"

"Cod. That's what they fished."

"And what difference does that make?"

"Well, it was cod. Anyway, the boys thought if they could be rich men in so short a time, they'd take him up on it. And they did make a good sum, but in a fortnight they'd spent it all, as young men will, with nothing left for their passage home. The eldest got food and lodging for the winter with a merchant by promising to spend the next summer fishing for him. But he never saw the summer. He died of frostbite hunting in the woods. When he was found he'd been half ate up by wolves."

"Don't be daft. There are no wolves in Newfoundland."

Dan thought there were, but did not want to start an argument with Singleton by saying so.

"His brother," she went on, "went to America."

"Which was against the law. Tell him that!"

"But on the way – "

"How is the man to get a grip on things if you only tell him the half of it?...There's a law against fishermen from Newfoundland going to fish in America. But the lad never got there. He died of sickness on the ship."

Mrs Singleton, as she so often did, continued as if her husband had not spoken. "His mother never got over her grief. She died a year later. Girtin tried to manage on his own, but he turned to drink."

"He'd turned to drink long afore that."

"And before long he was behind with the rent and the place was falling to rack and ruin. In the end, Lord Oldfield – the old Lord – turned him out."

"Phew! They're a hard lot, the Oldfields," Dan said.

"Not the old Lord," Singleton answered before his wife could. "He gave Girtin plenty of chances and he didn't hound him to the debtors' prison, as I have no doubt our present Lord would do. But in the end good land was going to waste. Girtin knows who's to blame for his plight."

"Does he always sleep in the churchyard?"

"Not always," Mrs Singleton said. "In a barn or the fields sometimes."

Singleton grunted. "Rector Poole would rather he went over to the poorhouse at Stonyton, but Girtin will never wear the pauper's badge. People give him clothes and food. He gets by…Have you done with your gossiping, woman? We'd better go if we're to be there before midnight."

Dan helped them carry their things to the cart, opened the yard gate, and waved them along the road. That was an interesting detail, he thought as he closed the gate – Girtin's boys going off to America about the same time Sukie Tolley disappeared.

He stripped and washed in the wash house, liberally dousing himself in the warm water Mrs Singleton had provided in honour of the Sabbath. She had also given him soap and a mirror for shaving. When he had finished he put on one of his new shirts and set off for the heath. At the common he turned in the direction Walter had pointed out yesterday and, after a bit of crossing back and forth, found a grassy track. A curl of smoke above the trees told him there was a cottage at the end of it.

It stood in a lonely clearing close to a section of Lord Oldfield's fence, surrounded by a well-tended vegetable and herb garden. The door was ajar. Dan knocked and, when there was no answer, pushed it open and called, "Anyone at home?"

A few pieces of wooden furniture stood on a clean, flagged floor. Various bits of household paraphernalia hung from hooks on the walls: a warming pan, cooking pots, spoons. Earthenware mugs and plates stood on plain wooden shelves, and dishcloths hung on a line slung across the chimney breast over a small fire of crackling wood. A cupboard held a few pieces of pewter and china. The room was fragrant with the drying leaves hanging in bags and bunches from the rafters.

It was the kind of house a working man could look forward to coming home to: quiet and well-ordered. Not like his own. Once he had gone through the door to find Caroline trying to set the kitchen on fire, staggering about the room with the hem of her skirts ablaze. She had fought and screamed obscenities at him as he beat out the flames, too drunk to see her danger. Another time it had been his collection of boxing mugs smashed, including his treasured *Humphreys v Mendoza 1788*. One evening he caught her chattering like a child to a leering stranger, whom Dan sent away with a split lip.

Then came getting her into bed, and in the morning sickness, suffering and remorse. Except the remorse got less and less, and turned to hatred of him – the Puritan who would not let her have a bit of fun; who took all the sunshine out of life; who had only married her to make her miserable.

Things had improved since he had taken the house in Russell Street and her mother and Eleanor had come to live with them. Some things. These days it was her mother and sister who put Caroline to bed. She was more manageable with them. When she was not drunk, she spent hours sitting in front of the fire, letting them do all the work of the house around her.

The sound of a light tread interrupted his memories. Mrs Halling appeared, a bowl in her hands. She had been feeding the hens he had heard squawking behind the house.

Her hand flew up to tuck in some strands of loose hair. "Good day, Mr Fielding."

"I hope you don't mind me dropping by. I came to ask after Kiomi."

"Won't you come in? Can I offer you something? I have some beer."

"I'd prefer water."

She put the bowl away and poured him a cup from a stone jar. "She is in a great deal of pain. I've given her mother an ointment to apply to the burns, which may help. I wish I could persuade Tom Taylor to let Dr Russell look at her eyes."

"I suppose he cannot pay for it."

"Dr Russell runs a weekly charity clinic. And, given the feeling in the village about the incident, I think it very likely that a subscription could be raised for any special treatment she needed. A cartload of food, blankets and clothing was sent up to the barrow after church."

They sat down at opposite sides of the table.

"Is Walter here?" Dan asked.

"No. He's gone out with Abe and some other friends."

Dan hoped they were up to nothing worse than a Sabbath game of football or skittles. "Good. I wanted to talk to you about him."

"I hope he is in no trouble."

"Well, that's the thing. I think he is, or likely to be. He's sore angry against Lord Oldfield because of what happened to his dog, and he's behaving foolishly because of it."

"If you'd seen him the day he brought Jack home, you'd be angry too."

"Though I haven't been in Barcombe long, I'm already discovering how high-handed Lord Oldfield can be. But the power's all on His Lordship's side, and Walter will only bring ruin on himself if he carries on as he is."

"Why, what has he done?"

"I'm sure it was Walter and Abe who broke the rector's window last night."

"And I'm sure you are wrong."

"Maybe. But there's more than window breaking. Do you know where Walter was the night Ford was injured?"

"He was here, in bed."

"He wasn't. He was in the woods helping himself to Lord Oldfield's birds."

"You are not accusing my boy of having anything to do with that?"

"It's not my accusations you need to worry about. He was in the wood the night Josh Castle was killed too."

She sprang to her feet. "You go too far, Mr Fielding!"

"He has already told me, Mrs Halling."

"Why would he tell you?"

Dan hesitated. He did not want to tell her that the reason he knew Walter was in the gang was because he was in it too. In his line of work he often had to allow good people to think ill of him. Usually he accepted it as part of the job, but he did not want Anna Halling to think ill of him. He could not tell her why he was out poaching either. He had been in the business long enough to know it was never safe to reveal his cover.

"I work at the forge. I see things. I see a lad getting himself into trouble. I've been in trouble myself. So I talked to him."

"He talked to you and not to me?"

"I suppose there are some things boys can't talk to their mothers about."

That hurt. She sank back into her seat.

"He wouldn't…he has always kept away from those people."

"He thinks he's getting his revenge on Lord Oldfield by joining them. You had no idea?"

"No, though I thought there was something. He's been so jumpy lately. And Abe has been hanging around him, which he wouldn't do if Walter's father was still alive. Davy worked on the estate, you see. Estate and village don't mix."

"Was he a keeper?"

"No, a woodsman…but Walter never told you he killed Josh? You can't think he did that? He knew that Josh didn't like killing the dog, that he had no choice. Cousins or no, Lord Adam was still the master. Walter knew that."

"Cousins? Who?"

"Lord Adam and Josh."

"They were cousins? How?"

"All I know is that Josh's father, John Castle, was born on the wrong side of the blanket."

No wonder Lord Oldfield had taken Josh's death so hard. They were not just friends, but family – only one lived in a mansion and the other in a cottage in the woods.

"Josh was a good man. He used to bring me and Walter a bit of rabbit or fish sometimes. He didn't deserve what happened to him – and it was not my son who killed him."

"I don't think so either, but it doesn't matter what I think. They're looking for someone to blame, and if Walter isn't careful he'll find it landing on him. He hates Lord Oldfield, and he's reckless and loud-mouthed. You must stop him, Mrs Halling, before he gets in any deeper."

Dan stood and picked up his hat. "I hope I haven't spoken out of turn."

"I'm not sure yet." She got up to show him out.

He paused in the doorway. "What happened to his father?"

"An accident, the day after Lord Adam's eighteenth birthday. He wanted a play, so they had one of the barns turned into a theatre. Mr West brought some theatre people from London to help, and Lord Adam and his friends acted all the parts. The whole village went to watch, and there was drinking and dancing after. The next day, Davy went to help take the stage and seating down. One of the scaffolds collapsed on top of him. Lord Oldfield felt so bad about it he said we could stay on in the cottage for my lifetime."

Dan wondered if there was any doubt that the present Lord Oldfield would honour the agreement, but he did not mention it in case it touched on a source of anxiety. He imagined, though, that being dependent on His Lordship's whim made Walter's feelings all the more bitter – and the boy and his mother all the more vulnerable.

He said "Goodbye" and hurried back to the forge. If Mrs Halling did not know the full story of John Castle's birth, he knew who would. Disappointingly, the Singletons did not get back until late and he had to go to bed with his questions unanswered.

Truth to tell, they were not all about Lord Oldfield and Castle. Mrs Halling was the first villager he had met with a good word to say for the head keeper, who had brought rabbits and fish to the little cottage in the wood. 'Josh' she had called him, and she knew he had not liked killing the dog. How did she know how he felt? Had he confided in her? Why would he, unless they were close?

A pretty young widow – a handsome young man – and a jealous, resentful son? Had he only succeeded in finding another motive for Walter to be rid of Castle? Yet Walter – not a boy of great discretion – had not given any hint of an affair between Josh and his mother. She had not given the impression of a woman bereft of her lover either.

Perhaps he should ask Mrs Singleton about it.

Or perhaps not.

It was none of his business who Anna Halling fell for.

Mrs Singleton was busy assembling the ingredients for the morning's baking when Dan brought in the pail. Given the chance, she would waste the little time he had with a detailed account of her nephews' and nieces' exploits. He pitched in before she could start.

"I went to see how Tom Taylor's girl is yesterday."

He relayed Mrs Halling's bulletin while she clucked sympathetically, lamented Tom Taylor's stubbornness in refusing Dr Russell's attendance, and sang the doctor's praises. "Though he's only been in the village four year."

"I heard a funny thing too while I was out," Dan added. "Daft, more like. That Josh Castle was cousin to Lord Oldfield. As if!"

"But it's true," she said, the gossip-light gleaming in her eye.

"Go on! A lord and a gamekeeper?"

"That shows how much you know of the world."

He wondered how the worldly knowledge of a country housewife and a Bow Street officer would compare, but only grinned sheepishly at her.

"Josh's father, John Castle, was the son of Lord Adam's great uncle, Francis."

"Born out of wedlock?"

"That's right," she confirmed happily. There was nothing like a bit of scandal among the upper classes to bring a smile to the face of the lower orders, no matter how stale it was.

"Fell in love with an actress, did he?"

"A Spanish girl." She made this sound worse than being an actress.

"How did he come across one of those around here?"

"It was in America, where he'd gone to be a soldier after

a falling-out with his father, a hard, mean man he was. He brought her back with him. Elena, she was called, and she was already expecting. Pass me that flour dredger, Dan."

Dan handed her the tin shaker. "He brought her back but didn't marry her?"

"Well, it was a sad thing. They thought they were, you see. Hold that oven door open for me, will you? No, use a cloth."

Though he was used to the blazing furnace in the forge, he meekly accepted the cloth she passed to him and wrapped it around his hand. She slid a tray of loaves into the oven and banged the door shut. When he turned round she was already taking another measure of dough out of the bowl to pound on the floury tabletop.

"It turned out that it wasn't a proper marriage, but Francis died of a fever he'd caught in America before they could make it right. It's said his father was sorry for the way he'd treated his younger son, so he gave her a cottage on the estate and something to live on. When John was old enough he was apprenticed to the gamekeeper. In time he became head gamekeeper himself, and Josh followed in his footsteps."

"Did you know Elena?"

"I remember seeing her when I was a girl, but no one knew her to speak to. She was too grand for the likes of us, as my mother used to say. She always dressed in black and wore a veil like those Spanish ladies do. She must have been a beauty when she was young. But she kept herself to herself. Kept her son close too. It was a wonder he managed to find himself a wife, and no one envied Sarah Jordan when she went to live under her thumb, which wasn't for long, poor soul. She died when Josh was born. John wouldn't look at another woman, or more likely his mother wouldn't let him, and she brought the boy up herself. Didn't do him any favours, either, letting him spend all his time with young Lord Adam."

"Thought he was a cut above too, did he?"

"He did that all right, did Josh Castle. Him and Lord Adam were always together, trailing all over the estate after Josh's dad, hunting and shooting, and never mind if they trampled someone's corn or frighted someone's animals to death. Even when Lord Adam went to school and university and then travelled about a bit, as gentlemen do, they kept friends."

"Castle. Why was he called that?"

"It was her name. His grandmother's. Called herself Mrs Castle because her name was castle in foreign. Castilliam? Castillar?"

"Castillo?"

"Something like that. Do you know the lingo, Dan?"

"What lingo?" Singleton stood in the doorway. "What are you clacking on about now, woman? How many times have I told you not to keep him from his work with your bloody twaddle? And you, Dan, what are you doing standing there like a great gabey, listening to her?"

Dan winked at Mrs Singleton and scurried off to the forge. The delay had put Singleton in a foul mood and he hardly said ten words all morning. Dan did not mind. It gave him time to think about what he had learned.

Josh's Spanish descent explained his exotic looks, and the story of his aristocratic background must have added a great measure of romance to the man too. His history might also explain his passion for self-improvement. Perhaps he thought there was a rightful place for him somewhere other than a gamekeeper's cottage in a wood. A woman, such as a widow with a boy in need of a father, might easily have found him attractive, especially if he had expectations, or thought he had.

Lord Oldfield had not mentioned that he and Castle were cousins. Natural enough, perhaps; no one likes to talk scandal of his own family. Besides, what relevance could ancient family history have on the case?

Every relevance, if Josh had taken it into his head to make some sort of claim upon the Oldfields. Only what claim could the son of an illegitimate child press? And could it have been so compelling that only murder would rid Lord Adam of it?

The fact that it had been Lord Oldfield who had called in Bow Street did not in itself prove he was innocent. Many a killer had tried to deflect attention away from himself by crying "Murder" first and loudest. Still, it was a risky thing to do for a crime that could so easily have been hushed up in Barcombe. The poachers were there to be blamed, and there was no need to have Dan in to fix it on them.

If His Lordship was playing a double game, it was not a very clever one. He did not strike Dan as a stupid man – but he had kept something back.

Chapter Eleven

Tuesday was a mild, hazy September day. The air was full of mellow scents: damp leaves, straw, woodsmoke, horses. It was still warm when Dan and Singleton finished work. They stood in the yard cooling off, Singleton taking his last pull from the beer jug, Dan drinking water. When he had finished, Singleton washed while Dan tidied up the forge. Then Dan sluiced himself and followed Singleton indoors for a hearty meal. He went to his straw and blankets drowsy with hard work and a good supper.

It felt like only minutes later that he was woken by the clanging of the church bells. He pulled on his clothes and scrambled into the yard. Singleton was already out of the house, a knife thrust into his belt, a hammer clutched in his hand.

"What is it?" cried Dan.

"Alarm," Singleton said. "The Frogs." He waited for Dan to come up to him and handed him the knife. "Here, take this."

There were already a number of men standing around the church door, and more running along the street, their wives calling after them. Doors slammed, dogs barked, lights flickered. Dan looked up at the church clock, a pale circle in the starlight. It was two in the morning.

He and Singleton joined the others. Some had axes, billhooks, knives and cudgels. Drake had a blunderbuss. The farm labourer with the miserable face, Creswick, was armed with a swingel – a long stick with a shorter stick of hard holly wood attached by a loop of leather – a weapon poachers and keepers often used against one another in pitched battles.

They were ready to defend their homes, waiting only to learn where the French were to be met. Even Travell, with his radical ideas, did not go so far as welcoming the invader.

Ayres emerged from the bell tower where he had been with the rector, who was still working the bell rope. A tense, expectant silence fell.

"There's a fire at Oldfield Home Farm!" the constable announced.

There was a stir of surprise, but otherwise no one moved or spoke. Dan could hear the distant, shrill clanging of the fire bell at the farm above the church bells.

"What are you waiting for?" Ayres cried.

Singleton spat into the churchyard. "We'd better go, or forfeit house and livelihood when the Lord marks our absence, damn him."

So, with no very good grace, they left their weapons in the porch and trotted after Ayres. They saw the arc of red light over the barn long before they reached it, and by the time they clustered in the farmyard the blaze was well underway. Flames fuelled by bales of hay roared out through the gaps in the barn roof, trailing sparks that threatened to set other buildings alight. The men had got all the animals out and driven the terrified beasts to a safe distance.

Mrs Mudge and the female servants ran in and out of the house carrying armfuls of belongings. Lord Oldfield, in his shirtsleeves, directed the stable boys and gardeners who had hauled the fire engine down from the Hall to the pond. It would take a while to get the pumps going. Mudge formed the villagers into a line to pass buckets of water along.

Only Dan, Drake and Ayres worked with any sense of urgency, and Dan had to be careful not to be caught out. He was not the only man concealing his feelings. Many of the villagers were hard pressed to hide their grins. They passed the buckets slowly and managed to slop away most of the contents before they reached the top of the chain. But once the engine got going, the fire's time was up, though it was not

112

completely out until dawn broke.

Lord Oldfield ordered beer to be served and there was a sudden surge of energy from the firefighters. Under cover of the hubbub caused by the arrival of the casks, Dan pretended he had a casual interest in the charred ruins and strolled off to look at them. He circled the smouldering heap, searching for any sign of what might have started the fire. The flames had burned from the inside out, but that did not mean the fire was accidental. It would have been easy for someone to sneak up to the rear wall, prise loose a board, and throw burning coals or wood into the hay.

His foot kicked something hard. An irregular yellow globe rolled into the long grass beneath the paddock fence. He picked it up. When he saw what he held, he almost dropped it again. It was a human skull with two streaks of red paint running from the eye sockets and the initials *BB* daubed on its shiny head.

The skull looked old. Dan thought of the graves of the dead kings in the barrow and wondered if the fire was Tom Taylor's return to Lord Oldfield for the injuries to his daughter. Could the Romany write? The letters were not well formed. Anyone could have daubed them.

He heard footsteps behind him, and a harsh, "Here, you, what do you think you're doing?"

Dan turned and saw the steward, Mudge.

"Just looking," he said, putting on a sullen face.

"What's that you've got there?"

Dan handed the skull over. Mudge examined it, whistled and swore. "Right, you're coming to explain this to Lord Oldfield."

"I found it," Dan said.

"You can tell that to His Lordship." Mudge grabbed Dan's arm and pushed him back towards the farmhouse.

Lord Oldfield was talking to one of the herdsmen. He was as filthy as the workmen, his fine shirt stained with smoke and sweat, his breeches soaked and muddy. Even so, it was obvious that he was the authority here, the man with the power: a power Dan knew he had already abused, and that most cruelly, when he hanged Walter's dog and set traps for Tom Taylor's unsuspecting children. And when he enclosed Barcombe Wood? That was what the villagers, who had been forced to turn out tonight and offer him their services, thought. Travell would call it feudalism, though that was supposed to have been done away with in England.

Dan kept his head down, secretly scrutinising Lord Oldfield. Was he a murderer? There was no way of telling what crimes someone had committed just by looking at them, though Dan had heard of men who thought it was possible to detect criminals by the shape of the head. One thing was certain: Lord Oldfield had not set fire to his own barn.

His Lordship glanced at Dan and looked away again before any sign of recognition could escape him. He flicked his hand in dismissal and the herdsman hurried away.

"What's all this?" he demanded.

"Caught him with this." Mudge held out the relic.

"I found it," Dan repeated.

Lord Oldfield turned the skull over. "Bloodie Bones. Of course. You have no idea how it got there?"

"Whoever started the fire must have put it there, M'lud," Dan answered.

"Don't be smart," Mudge growled.

"That's enough, Mudge," His Lordship said. "You're the fellow who out-boxed the blacksmith, aren't you?"

"I am, M'lud."

"Wish I'd been there to see it. Tell me next time you're planning to fight."

"I'm not planning to fight again, begging your pardon, M'lud." It was enough that he was risking his life at His Lordship's request; he was damned if he was going to fight for his entertainment as well.

"Pity. Well, what am I to do about this? Did you put it there?"

"No, M'lud, as God is my witness," Dan answered.

"Well, Mudge, there you are," Lord Oldfield said. "Get rid of it."

The steward protested, but was interrupted by Rector Poole who came running up, mud-splattered, red-faced, almost sobbing with the effort. He must have run all the way from the church, and left his dignity there too.

"Lord Oldfield! I must speak to you."

"Can't it wait?"

"No, My Lord. I hardly know how to put it into words. I have never in all my days seen anything so wicked. So diabolical – so foul – such depths of evil – "

"What is it, Mr Poole?"

"When I went into the church to sound the alarm last night, I found the door unlocked. I was in too much haste to give it much thought at the time, given the urgency of the situation, though I do remember thinking that I'd locked it at the end of the day as usual, especially after what happened at the rectory the other night...those dreadful threats...Ayres of course has got nowhere with finding the culprits."

Lord Oldfield clicked his tongue. The breaking of the parson's window was old news. Poole recollected the matter in hand, and continued, "It was only after everyone had gone that it struck me as odd, so I examined the door. The lock was covered in scratches and the wood around it was scored and splintered. Someone had picked it, and rather clumsily."

"I hardly think this is the time to report the theft of a pair of candlesticks."

"The candlesticks were untouched, My Lord, as was the rest of the silver plate. What had been tampered with was – was – your family chapel. The contents of one of the sarcophagi were scattered all over the floor."

"The devil! Not my father?"

"No. You will remember that when we interred your father, we had to move some of the older coffins. The lid of Lord Mandeville Oldfield's was broken in the process, leaving it easy to open. I gathered up the – the remains – but the – "

"The skull was missing," Lord Oldfield said. "Here it is."

Poole reverently took charge of the skull and wrapped his black silk scarf around it. "I shall see that Lord Mandeville is properly reinterred. There must be a service, of course."

"I suppose so. Yes, Mother will insist on it. Private. Family only."

"But surely you should insist everyone in the village attends. It will be an ideal opportunity to preach to them about their crimes. Or would you prefer it if I admonished them on a Sabbath?"

Lord Oldfield shrugged. "Mother will decide about that. Come in for breakfast. You can discuss it with her."

If Poole had been invited to take a seat among the saints in heaven, he could not have looked more pleased. His Lordship, who was more interested in hot coffee and rolls than stoking the rector's ambition, moved off.

"Mudge!" he snapped.

The steward grabbed Dan's arm and hissed, "I'm watching you, Fielding. Now clear off."

He shoved Dan away, caught up with Lord Oldfield, and was immediately drawn into a discussion about the arrangements for settling the livestock and rebuilding the barn. Poole trotted after, and it was hard to say who had the wider grin: the rector or Lord Mandeville Oldfield.

"I hear you've been having exciting times."

Warneford tamped down the tobacco in his pipe and reached for a spill from the mantelpiece. He stood by the fire in the Fox and Badger, one foot on the dog iron. It was Wednesday evening and could hardly have been wetter or more miserable. "Shame for Lord Oldfield it wasn't like this last night," Singleton had laughed.

Apart from Girtin, who sat dozing in a corner, a strong odour of dirty, damp wool steaming off his coat, they were the only customers in the bar. Buller sat on a stool by the fire, a glass of brandy in his hand. His daughter had taken advantage of the lull in trade and had the night off.

Singleton chuckled. "Oh, yes. Bloodie Bones has been busy."

"You and your Bloodie Bones. Bloody nonsense."

"It's more than that."

"It's a way of bringing the law down hard, that's what it is. And that's bad for business. I tell you what, Singleton, you ought to tell your lads to lay off it." He took a deep puff at the pipe. "Who lit up the barn anyway? Was it one of your lot?"

"No, and I don't know who did it," said Singleton. "But it was well done whoever it was."

Girtin opened his eyes and made a great fuss and fidget about resettling himself.

"Something to tell us, Girtin?" Buller asked.

"Not me. I don't look when there's people sneaking around the churchyard of a night. Isn't that right, Mr Fielding?"

"Eh?" said Warneford.

The old drunk was on the verge of giving Dan away, and from the inane grin on his face he did not even realise it. Dan kept his hand steady on the table while he sized up his situation: *The door is ten steps to my right. There's a window behind me. Singleton on my left: dangerous. Warneford's hand has moved to his pocket: he's armed. Buller's no problem. Act innocent.*

He let his jaw drop open. "What's he talking about?"

"Just what I'd like to know," Warneford said.

Singleton guffawed. "Is it Dan you saw in the churchyard last night? Must have been in two places at once then. He was up at the fire with me. You was there, Buller."

"That's right. Looks like what you saw was your bird-eating bugaboo, Girtin."

Girtin shook his fuddled head, looking uncertainly from Buller to Singleton. "I saw the fire. I saw him breaking into the church."

"Me breaking into the church?" Dan said. "Sounds like the liquor talking."

117

Girtin's perplexity lifted. "A drop of rum on a damp night would be very welcome."

Dan laughed. "Go on, Buller. Get him a rum." The drunker Girtin got, the less sense he would make.

"Hang on," Singleton said. "It was you found the skull, wasn't it?"

"Yes," Dan said, "and I didn't take it up with me if that's what you're getting at. The church lock was broken before the bells started, remember?"

"You could have sneaked out earlier and got it."

"And got up to the farm, started the fire, and back down again before the alarm sounded? And why would I? I've got no grudge against your Lord Oldfield. If it comes to it, why couldn't you have broken into the church and got the skull yourself, Singleton?"

"If you couldn't do it, I couldn't do it," the blacksmith said.

"Well then," said Dan.

"Hold on!" Warneford said. "I'll have this out. What did you see, Girtin?"

Girtin grinned. "It warn't Bloodie Bones. But his letters was BB."

"Rot you, you bastard, I'll get it out of you!" Warneford shouted, raising his hand above Girtin's head.

In one swift movement Dan was out of his seat, his fingers tight around Warneford's wrist.

"Leave him be. He's drunk, that's all."

Warneford swung around, his fist clenched.

"Stop it!" Singleton leapt to his feet and stepped between the two men, holding them apart with his strong arms. "BB? Don't you get it? It was Bob Budd you saw, wasn't it, Girtin?"

Girtin nodded. "That's right. What about that drop of rum?"

Singleton chuckled. "Bob Budd. Good on him. You happy now, Warneford? It had nothing to do with us."

Buller mopped up the spilled beer and glass. Warneford straightened his coat and offered Dan his hand.

"No hard feelings."

"None here," Dan answered, and they shook on it.

"But you move fast!" Warneford said as they sat down again. "Took me right off guard. Buller, bring us a bowl of rum punch."

"Punch is all right," Girtin said.

The landlord went to the bar and busied himself with spirit, lemon and hot water. No one said anything while they waited for the drink. Dan weighed up what had just happened, and found it was more to his advantage than anything. If Girtin did talk about seeing him at the rectory the night the window was broken, it would just be put down to drunken rambling.

The question now was: would a man capable of arson also be capable of murder? Dan had already wondered about Budd. He had a motive for murdering the gamekeeper who had played such a large part in getting him thrown out of his home. It was not beyond thought that Budd had managed to get the paper for the note on the scarecrow from somewhere. Filched it perhaps, from pocket or house. Dan would have to find a way to get over to Kingswood and meet this Bob Budd.

The drink arrived, and in the business of mixing sugar and water, cordial relations were resumed. Warneford had come to the village with a purpose, which he now disclosed.

"I have orders for rabbit," he said. "Hare if you can get them."

Singleton looked doubtful. "When do you want them?"

"Can you go out tomorrow?"

The blacksmith shook his head. "We had a set-to with the keepers last time. We should give it a rest for a while."

Warneford smiled. "I understand. There's a big difference between a lord who turns a blind eye, and an enclosing lord. It's another game now. A professionals' game. Well, no matter. If you don't want to do it…"

Singleton was quick to pick up the emphasis on *you*.

"You'd bring in strangers?"

"Well, it's more than just the odd coney for the pot, isn't it?

119

You don't relish your night sport quite so much now it means the hulks or seven years' transportation if you're caught. Hanging even. I don't blame you." Warneford looked regretful. "But I have my business to think of."

"Oh, no. We're not having outsiders in our woods."

Warneford spread his fingers. "What else am I to do?"

Dan knew that Singleton was going to give in and saw an opportunity to make himself look good. "Wait a bit, Singleton," he said. "This could work to our advantage. If they won't be expecting us to be out so soon, they'll be off guard."

Warneford grinned. "A shrewd observation. You could go far, Fielding."

Dan swallowed this compliment to his criminal tendencies.

"That's true, I suppose," Singleton said. "And they are a man down…it has to be tomorrow night?"

Warneford nodded. "Got to keep my customers satisfied."

Dan was washing in the yard early in the morning when he saw Warneford emerge on horseback from the Fox and Badger's stables and set off at a slow amble towards Bath. It was wise of him to make himself scarce before the poaching raid. He did not know that, for tonight at least, he and his gang would be safe – provided Dan could get a message to Lord Oldfield in time.

He went into the forge to light the fire. Under Singleton's tuition, he had become skilled at the task. The main thing was to clear out the clinker from the previous day's work. It was like black glass when it was cold, but turned to sludge when hot. Then he needed the right amount of coke over the kindling to get it going, just a breath of air through the blast pipe, and if he got all that right he would have a good blaze.

When it was drawing, he made sure there was plenty of coal in the bin and the water trough was full. Things were going nicely when Mrs Singleton appeared at the cottage door and called him in to breakfast.

In the forge afterwards, Singleton unhooked an old

harness from the wall. "I want you to go to Dunnage's and tell him about tonight. Take this with you, making out it's his and we've just repaired it. Make sure no one's listening, unless it's Abe. I'll go down to Travell's by and by – he'll get a message to Walter."

Dan, who had thought it would be late afternoon before he could get away from the forge, was glad to obey. He grabbed his coat and set off up the road alongside the Fox and Badger with the harness slung over his shoulder. The sky had cleared, but the fields were muddy from last night's rain. He found Dunnage in one of his barns, looking at some bags of seed with one of his labourers: a short, bow-legged man with a wrinkled face.

"I've brought your harness back."

The farmer nodded as if he had been expecting it. Dan waited while he finished giving the man his instructions and sent him away.

"What is it?" Dunnage asked, tying up one of the sacks.

"Warneford was in the Fox last night. He wants us to go out again tonight."

"And Singleton said yes?"

Dan described the conversation with Warneford.

Dunnage grunted. "A persuasive man, Warneford. What about Travell and Walter?"

"Don't know yet. Singleton is getting a message to them."

"Doesn't look like we have much choice. I'll see you later."

Dan turned to go.

"Better leave me the harness, then."

Dan did not go back the way he had come. Instead he struck off across the sodden fields and down to a lane that came out on the Bath Road. Spaced at generous intervals along it stood three large houses built of the local stone. At the last of them, the house belonging to Louisa Ruscombe, the track dwindled and ended in a high hedge. He pushed his way through a gap, passed the Wests' place, and hurried down to the doctor's, which was nearest the road.

121

Russell was driving out of his gate, but drew up when he saw Dan.

"Ah, Foster!"

"Fielding," Dan corrected, with a warning glance into the garden. The gardener was crossing the grass on his way to the glass house built against the wall in a sunny spot at the top of the lawn. A few moments later he could be seen moving behind the panes of glass, picking nectarines.

Dr Russell laughed. "Yes, of course. What can I do for you?"

"I have to get a message to Lord Oldfield. I thought you could deliver it under pretext of visiting his mother."

"You are ready to make an arrest?"

"No, not yet. The poachers are going out again tonight, and I need Lord Oldfield to keep his men out of the woods."

The doctor clucked his tongue. "His Lordship won't like that."

"I don't much like it myself, but I want to avoid a repeat of what happened to Ford."

"Yes, he is badly smashed up."

"I know. I was there."

"You were there? You already know who is in the gang?"

"I found that out easily enough."

"Then what are you waiting for? They are dangerous men, and no one will be safe until they are behind bars."

"And they will be, but so far all I've got against them is the poaching and the attack on Ford. I don't know who killed Castle."

"You mean which of them did it?"

"I'm not sure any of them did. It turns out Castle had other enemies in the village."

"Poachers and thieves. Of course they were his enemies."

"True, but was it poachers and thieves who killed him? Can you take the message?"

"His Lordship must wonder if he'll have to let them burn all his property before you get a result. Still, I suppose you know your own business. Can I at least tell him who the poachers are? He will want to know."

Dan did know his business. If Lord Oldfield had their names, he might not resist the temptation of taking action against them, especially if he intended them as scapegoats for his own crime. Dan would be exposed as a Bow Street man before he had finished his investigation.

"I'll tell him when I'm ready to make a full report."

The doctor frowned. "I'll go up to the Hall now. Good day, Fos – Fielding."

"There is one other thing. Have you heard what happened to the little girl at the barrow?"

"The gypsy child? They've not brought her to me. Some of them look on a doctor as something akin to the hangman, I think."

"Mrs Halling is looking after her."

He tutted. "These village women do a great deal of harm with their eye of newt and tail of toad."

"There's nothing of the hocus-pocus about her cures. And she'd like you to look at the girl. It's the father who refuses."

"Would she? That's rare. But there's not a lot I can do if they won't bring the child in."

"Couldn't you call on them?"

"I don't make house calls to non-paying patients. The free clinic is on Mondays."

"Taylor won't come. What if you happened to be going past the barrow one day? Would you drop by? I'll see that your fees are paid."

"No, I won't take your money…I do go that way sometimes. Lady Oldfield has recommended me to Squire Douglas in Stonyton. But if Taylor refuses to admit me, I shan't stand arguing with him. Will that satisfy you?"

"Yes," Dan said, touching his hat for the benefit of the gardener as the doctor's gig rattled away.

Chapter Twelve

"Walter's not coming," said Travell. He drew a bottle of brandy from a deep pocket in his coat and put it on Dunnage's kitchen table. "Says he's had enough."

"I always thought he was chicken," Abe said.

"Leave the boy be," Travell retorted. "Gi'us some of that brandy, Dunnage."

Dunnage reached for some greasy glasses from the dresser and poured out the spirit.

"We don't want anyone whose heart isn't in it," the farmer said. "Funny though. He seemed eager enough last time. Well, it's his choice."

"What if he starts blabbing?" Abe grumbled.

"Wouldn't that incriminate himself?" asked Dan. As soon as he'd said it, he knew it was a mistake. Incriminate was too technical; the sort of word he used around lawyers.

"Hark at him!" cried Abe. "Incriminate!"

"It means – " Travell began, but Abe cut him off.

"I know what it means. I just want to know if Walter can be trusted."

"We can trust him," Singleton said. "He's not got such a big mouth as you."

Everyone laughed except Abe, who glowered and lapsed into resentful silence. Travell held out his glass for a refill. Dan avoided the bottle by taking a sip of his brandy when it came his way. Travell helped himself to another while Dunnage fetched the Bible. When the oath had been taken, Dunnage and Abe handed out some sacks and sheets of heavy cloth.

"What's this for?" Dan asked.

"For catching rabbits," Singleton explained. "You put the cloth over the warren and let the dogs start digging."

"Then pick the coneys off as they come out," Dan guessed. "Won't they make a noise?"

"No. Rabbits don't squeal when caught. But trap a hare and you'll hear him fields away."

Dunnage distributed the guns.

"No," said Dan. "Not after what happened last time."

Abe took his weapon with a derisive glance in Dan's direction. The shopkeeper took one too. Dan, reckoning Travell was on his fourth glass, decided to keep out of his way if he started waving the gun about.

The farmer whistled up the dogs and they set off to Barcombe Wood. They skirted the edge of it until they came to the west warren, a hummock just outside the trees. The meadow was a moonlit sea of dun-coloured bodies, until the rabbits got wind of them and dived into what they thought was safety. The dogs dug with bloodthirsty eagerness, and before long the rabbits were squirming under the men's blows.

As Dan did his share in doling out skull-shattering thumps, he kept an eye on the woods. Dr Russell had been right to say Lord Oldfield would not like his message. It would not surprise Dan if he ignored it. Dan was just beginning to hope his fears were ungrounded when he thought he saw a light between the trees. It was gone before he was sure, but a moment later it flickered again.

"What is it?" whispered Singleton.

"I thought I saw something."

"I can't see anything."

"It isn't there now, but I'm sure I saw someone moving about."

"If it was keepers they'd be on us by now," Dunnage said.

They could hear nothing but the occasional feeble twitch from beneath the blood-stained cloth. The light flashed out again, further away.

Dan handed his cudgel to Dunnage. "I'm going to take a look."

"Abe, you go with him," Dunnage ordered. "The rest of us will start bagging up what we've got."

Dan did not want to be stuck with Abe, but could not refuse. They crept towards the fence. Dan paused to signal to Abe, but he was already climbing over. Dan lost sight of him almost at once.

Dan jumped down into the wood and set off towards the spot where he had last seen the light. He stumbled over roots, slipped on dead leaves, was snagged, slapped and torn at by branch and briar. Every now and again the light flashed in front of him. Sometimes the beam shot out to his left, sometimes the right. He veered about after it.

When a good fifteen minutes had passed without any sign of his quarry, he gave up the chase. By then he had completely lost his bearings. He had no idea how to get back to the west warren, how far he was from the edge of the wood, or where he would come out when he eventually found it. He risked calling softly to Abe, but there was no answer. One tree or copse looked much the same as another to Dan, especially in the dark. For want of a better idea, he continued in the direction he had been heading.

After he had been walking for a while, the ground dipped down and became soggy underfoot. He heard gurgling water, and before long came upon a thin, shallow stream weaving its way over a stony bed. He decided to follow its course. It would at least mean he was not going around in circles.

The trees thinned out, and ahead of him he saw a dark open space with a rectangle of yellow light lying upon it. He stopped at the edge of the wood. He was looking at a lawn around a mansion. There was a large, shallow hollow in the middle of it, its edges churned by footprints and the passage of the carts and barrows that stood about it. Nearby lay piles of bricks and heaps of scaffolding. The skeleton of a crane rose above a peculiarly-shaped building; Dan supposed it was the temple Singleton had spoken of. To his right, set close to the border of the wood, was a small castle with pointed arches and towers.

He had been following the course of the spring that started in the top of the valley, and which Lord Oldfield planned to harness for his improvement works. The bowl was the half-built lake, and the mansion was Oldfield Hall. A dank, weedy miasma from the drained pool filled the air. This was where Sukie's baby had been found. A nasty grave for an infant.

The upper windows were dark; the light came from the little green room where Lord Oldfield had first received Dan. His Lordship must have been unable to sleep, knowing that the men he accused of Josh Castle's murder were at large in his wood while he had to let them roam.

Dan turned left, intending to dodge through the trees and so come out onto the lane into the village. He stopped. There was someone else standing under the boughs and looking in at Lord Oldfield's window: a man muffled in a dark coat, with a scarf and hood over his face. As Dan caught sight of him he began to run across the lawn, using the building works as cover.

He stopped behind a cart, swung a gun to his shoulder, and fired into the drawing room. The sound of the shot and breaking glass boomed and echoed from wall to wood. From the house came a shouted oath, and Lord Oldfield appeared at the shattered window. Dan plunged into the trees after the fleeing gunman, but lost him after a few yards. There was no point in losing himself in the woods again, so he abandoned the pursuit.

Lights were coming on all over the Hall. Dan went back to the spot where the man had been standing. The long grass around the trees was trampled, but it was too dark to make out any footprints. He crouched down and groped around on the off-chance of finding something. A twig snapped behind him. There was a searing pain on the back of his head and he toppled forward.

*

Dan opened his eyes, the world tilted several degrees, and he immediately shut them again. Not for long. Someone was slapping his face and whispering, "Wake up, you bugger."

He opened his eyes again and, when the nausea had passed, recognised Abe's blacked-up face.

"We have to get out of here. Stand up, blast you."

Dan struggled into a sitting position and discovered the pain was not all in his head. Abe had dragged him into the forest, as the bruises on his back testified.

"Give me your hand," he said.

Abe hauled him up.

"Did you fire that shot?"

Abe laughed. "Must 'a been Bloodie Bones."

"Give me your gun."

"Why?"

"Give it me."

Abe knew that, shaken and in pain as he was, Dan could still give him a good pounding. He shrugged and handed the weapon over. It was cold. Dan returned it.

"Did you see who did?"

"Nah."

"Because I owe whoever it was. So if you know, you'd better tell me, Abe."

"I didn't see him. I just found you lying there."

By now the grounds around the Hall were full of shouting servants, their lanterns zigzagging across the lawn. Dan felt another wave of sickness and gritted his teeth.

"Let's go."

He was impressed by how surely Abe found his way, but well and truly sick of the forest by the time they hopped over a fence into a field. After they had crossed three or four more, Abe stopped on a low rise. To their left was a long, dark stretch of open land – Barcombe Heath. After a bit of effort to focus, Dan saw the silhouette of the church spire a little below and in front of him. They had taken a circuitous route to get there, away from Lord Oldfield's search parties.

"You can make your way back from here."

"What about you?"

Abe gestured in the direction of Dunnage's farm. "I'm going that way."

"Do you live with Dunnage?"

"In one of his cottages, near Tanner's Field."

"Do you think the others are all right?"

"Yeah. They'll be well out of it by now." Without another word he was gone.

Dan crept down to the church and scrambled over the low stone wall into the graveyard. Threading between the gravestones, he wondered why the gunman had come back to attack him. The man was well covered up, it was dark – he had no reason to think Dan could identify him. Even if Dan did, why would that worry him? What Barcombe poacher would turn in a fellow recruit in the army of Bloodie Bones?

Unless the gunman was Walter, and Dan had been too optimistic about the effect of his talk with Mrs Halling. What if he had stayed away from Dunnage's not for his mother's sake, but so he could make this attempt on Lord Oldfield's life? If it *had* been an attempt to kill him. The gunman could not have known His Lordship was sitting up late, and even if he had, his aim had been hurried and he'd had only one chance at it. It seemed more likely that the shot was intended to alarm and annoy.

Still, Dan would have to check up on the youth in the morning.

He climbed over the gate into the forge yard. The back door of the cottage opened and the blacksmith appeared, candle in hand. His voice hissed into the darkness.

"Dan!"

Dan tiptoed into the kitchen and whispered, "Did the others get away?"

"Yes. All well. But what about you and Abe?"

Dan told him what had happened.

Singleton laughed. "Hope that put the wind up His Lordship."

"I should think it did. But I don't know why I had to get a bashing."

"He probably thought you were one of Lord Oldfield's men."

"Well, I'd like to repay the compliment, so if you find out who it was, let me know, eh?"

"If it means seeing you in action with your fists again."

"It will, I promise you."

Dan felt shivery and was glad to get into the warmth of the forge. There was a bit of water left in the tank so he washed the blood off his head in it. As far as he could tell, the cut was not very big or deep, but it did hurt. He lay down on his straw, hitched the blankets over himself, and shut his eyes.

His headache had not gone by morning and it was not helped by the heat and hammering in the forge. A forge was a good place to gather and gossip, and there was plenty to gossip about: Lord Oldfield's warren raided in the night and a shot fired at His Lordship. There were people in and out all day to tell Singleton and Dan what the two men already knew. They grinned, winked and nudged the blacksmith, well pleased with the secret that was no secret.

Singleton enjoyed his notoriety, but Dan kept his head down and went about his business, listening. While everyone knew who had robbed Lord Oldfield of his game, no one had a clue who had fired the gun at him. It looked as if the gunman was not going to step up to bask alongside Singleton in well-deserved glory.

Mrs Singleton kept out of the way and served their meals in silence. She noticed the cut on Dan's head, but did not offer to tend it for fear of touching too closely on her husband's nocturnal activities, nor did Singleton suggest that she should. He was well able to bear another man's discomfort without offering to relieve it.

By mid-afternoon they had done all the jobs needed for collection that day. Singleton decided anything else could wait; he was going to the Fox to talk to Buller. Dan refused the invitation to join him and said he was going for a walk to clear his head.

He washed off the day's grime, put on a clean shirt, dusted down his breeches, and set off for Anna Halling's cottage. He had not made himself welcome last time. He did not suppose this visit would be any better.

Anna opened the door with floury hands and a face flushed with heat. To his surprise, she smiled and invited him in. The table was covered with cutters, mixing bowls and jars, and the smell of the first batch of scones rising in the tiny oven by the hearth filled the room. He sat down and helped himself to a currant from a twist of paper. She slapped his hand away.

"Don't pick! They're all I've got. Mr Travell let me have them in return for a jar of rosehip jelly...You've come at the right time. I'm making a treat for Walter's supper, and no one deserves to share in it more than you."

"Why, what have I done?"

"You spoke out of turn."

"You talked to the boy then?"

"I wasn't going to. I didn't think my son could be so stupid. But what you said stuck in my mind: '*There are some things boys can't talk to their mothers about*'. I couldn't sleep for worrying. So I asked him."

She paused, busying herself with adding milk to the mix. Dan guessed there had been a painful scene: a son's denials, a mother's recriminations, tears on both sides.

"He promised me that he will not go out again."

"And last night? He stayed in all night?"

"Yes." She removed a tray from the oven and put the next batch in. "He had nothing to do with what happened up at the Hall, and this time you will believe me."

She gave him a look there was no arguing with and wiped

her hands on a cloth. "How did you get that cut?"

"I walked into a chain hanging down from the rafters in the forge."

"Let me take a look."

What with the fragrant heat, the singing of the fire, her soft breath close to his ear, and the light touch of her fingers on his scalp, he almost fell asleep. He watched drowsily as she went over to a shelf and selected an earthenware jar. She lifted the lid, releasing a whiff of honey and lavender. The salve, gently applied, was warm and soothing.

"I'll put some in a cup for you. Put it on three times a day. It will help the healing. And don't waste it. I don't know when I'll be able to make some more with the wood being closed off now."

"The loss of Barcombe Wood is serious for you?"

"Many of the herbs I need grow there."

"Nowhere else?"

"I might be able to get some on the heath and in the lanes, but not in the same quantities. I should be collecting and drying mushrooms for the winter now. Then there's fuel. I'll have to use more furze off the heath, and it burns much more fiercely than wood. There's the rushes too. I don't know how we'll manage for light, though heaven knows we don't stay up much after dark..." she stopped. "There, I'm grumbling at you. Try one of these, Mr Fielding. I'll pour you some ale."

"My name's Dan. And I'd prefer water."

"Then I'll get some ale for Walter. He'll be in in a minute."

She went out to the scullery. Dan shut his eyes. There were moments like this in the kitchen at home, when Eleanor was baking and Caroline was not there to spoil things. If he let himself, he could imagine that it was Eleanor pottering about in the scullery, Eleanor who would bring him his water, Eleanor who would blush when he put his hand over hers and smiled up at her as he took it.

The front door latch rattled and in burst Walter. "Mother, I'm – what are you doing here?"

"I've come to see you."

"Checking up on me?"

"Yes."

Walter glared, then noticed the baking things. A boyish gleam lit up his face. His mother came back into the room with a tray of drinks.

"I thought I heard you. I've made you some scones."

"So why is he eating them all?"

"Mr Fielding has had one. And I don't think that is any way to talk to a visitor."

"Didn't ask him here, did I?"

He dropped into a chair by the fire and unlaced his boots. Dan said, "They're delicious."

"Have another," she said.

"Don't mind if I do."

Walter gave in. His hand shot forward and he took one of the scones. After tasting it he could not hurt his mother's feelings by having nothing good to say about it. So, against his will, he found himself siding with Dan in praise of her cooking.

"Have you seen Abe today?" she asked.

Walter flushed. "Yeah." He turned to Dan. "He told me he'd seen you last night. Told me how you cut your head."

Dan caught and held the boy's gaze. "He came by the forge just after I did it. I walked into something."

Walter dropped his eyes and muttered, "That's what he said."

"Are you going to Paulton with him tomorrow afternoon?" she asked.

The boy bit his lip. "No."

Dan put down his cup. "I'd better be going. Walk to the end of the lane with me, Walter."

He scowled, but could not refuse in front of a mother who had taught him better manners. While he pulled on his boots, Dan asked after Taylor's girl.

"Kiomi is doing better than I had hoped. But the swelling hasn't gone down and she still can't open her eyes, so I don't know yet if there is any long-term damage."

"I thought I might drop in to see her on Sunday afternoon. Perhaps I will see you there?"

"Perhaps you will, after church."

He took up his hat and pocketed the salve. Walter thrust his hands in his pockets and marched morosely beside him.

"Have you and Abe had a falling-out?"

"None of your business."

"You have, haven't you? Because of last night."

"And whose fault is that? You with your interfering. You've made me a laughing stock."

"Better that than an example hanging in chains on the high road."

"Yeah, yeah. If it's so dangerous, why are you doing it?"

"I've got nothing to lose."

"He said I was a coward. A ninny tied to my mother's apron strings."

Dan felt for the boy's anguish. He knew what it was like, following the crowd because you're young and don't know there's another way to go, and even if you do you don't have the confidence in yourself to take it. He had been lucky; he had had Noah to show him, though at first he had fought him every step of the way. Noah sent him to a day school a couple of streets away, where he had sneered at the neatly dressed boys, the tame boys, the boys he threw sticks and stones at, whose pennies he nicked, whose books he kicked in the mud. He took his canings without flinching and thought he was brave. It had taken him a long time to see the courage there is in picking yourself up off the floor, putting your clothes straight, and carrying on in your own way in spite of the feral creatures snapping at your heels.

"I'll tell you what a coward is. A coward is the man who does what everyone else does because he's afraid of what they'll say. A coward is the man who thinks nothing of hurting someone who loves him just so he can look big in front of his friends."

"Mother would never have known if it hadn't been for you."

"She'd have known all right – the day they came to arrest you."

"What about when they arrest you?"

"Walter, if I'd got a tenth of what you'd got, I'd start caring."

"That again!"

"Yes, that again. You have a home. You have a future. You have a mother who loves you. That should mean more to you than what a jackanapes like Abe thinks."

"I still don't see how you can tell me to do one thing and do another yourself. I don't suppose you're going to tell her you're a poacher?"

"No. Are you?"

"I'm no oath breaker."

Dan laughed. "Meaning I am?"

"You told Mother about me."

"And did you a favour. Anyway, I'm getting bored with it. I don't think I'll stick it much longer." That was as much as Dan dared say, but he hoped that if Anna did hear any rumours about his involvement in the gang, Walter, whom she was sure to ask first, would tell her what he had said.

They came to a halt at the end of the track. Dan glanced back at the house. Anna stood in the doorway, looking after them.

"Your mother's waiting for you."

"All right."

Walter started back to the cottage, stopped and turned back. "Dan."

"What?"

"Have you ever been in prison?"

"I've known people who have. They're dead now." Not a word of a lie in that.

Walter ducked his head and loped back to the cottage. His mother put her arm around him and drew him inside.

Chapter Thirteen

Kiomi's face was swollen and pitted with red wounds, and there was a crusty, yellow discharge gumming up her eyes, but Anna assured Dan that she was healing normally. Kiomi herself was enjoying the attention. She had been given a doll, probably the first she had ever owned, which she was delighted with.

While Anna dressed her injuries, Taylor invited Dan to see inside his odd dwelling. Dan expected something like the seeping cellars of London, where for a penny a night you could share a lousy mattress on a filthy floor with half a dozen other unwashed bodies. Instead it was dry and warm, and the air was not stale. A number of small chambers led off a central passageway that ended in a wall of tumbled brickwork. There were alcoves in the walls where once corpses had been buried in all their finery.

Dan peered into the shifting shadows beyond the faint glow of Tom's rushlight. "Don't you mind sleeping in a tomb?"

"There are no spirits walking here. We had a cleansing ceremony before we moved in."

The alcoves were packed with gifts from the village: bread, milk, a side of bacon, potatoes, apples, a basket of nectarines, and a lifetime's worth of blankets and clothes. There were shoes and stockings too, although Mrs Taylor and her children still went barelegged in their old boots. Dan guessed that many of these items would be discreetly traded away when the donors had lost interest in the family.

They went back to the fire, and Taylor brought out a jug of local cider, dry and strong. To be polite Dan took a couple of mouthfuls, and his host swigged the rest. Mrs Taylor tended the perennial stewpot, which gave out the savoury smell of onions and rabbit. Every now and again Tom threw a log onto the fire and gave it a kick to keep it going. Anna sat beside the little girl, making up stories with the doll. No one said very much and the time passed companionably until Anna got ready to leave. Dan said it was time for him to go too. He picked up her basket and offered her his arm. She hesitated, then took it.

"What do you think, Mr Fielding," she said when they were out of earshot of the barrow, "Dr Russell called on the family yesterday. Tom Taylor would be furious if he found out."

Dan had already guessed where the nectarines had come from. "That's very good of the doctor. What did he say?"

"The child's sight is not damaged, and once the swelling has gone down she should be able to see as well as ever. Isn't that good news? And how kind of the doctor to go out of his way like that. He also said that he was impressed with the speed the wounds were healing and wanted to know what was in the salve. It's only an old recipe of my mother's."

"I'd keep it to yourself. You don't want him patenting it and selling it off as Dr Russell's Balm."

"I don't think he would do that."

"You'd be surprised what people would do."

"I am surprised – that you should take such a dim view of people."

He was a little surprised himself. He could see the doctor's praise of her skill pleased her, so why was he so ungracious about it?

"He must be a very good man," he allowed after a moment.

They had reached the cottage by then. He had no excuse to linger, so bade her good day and loitered back to the forge.

The next morning, a pedlar with an enormous pack on his back trudged along the Bath Road. Dan thought nothing of it; pedlars came and went all the time. Shortly after, a cart laden with parcels of cloth, and the dismantled timber and awning for a stall, rumbled by. When a third merchant's cart appeared with a musician sitting on the back tootling aimlessly on a flute, it was clear that something out of the ordinary was going on.

"What's it all about?" Dan asked.

Singleton peered out of the forge door, recognised the musician, and waved.

"They're here for Drift Day on Wednesday."

"What's Drift Day?"

"The drift on Barcombe Heath. Couple of times a year Drake rounds up our livestock and counts them, makes sure we aren't exceeding our quotas and that none are infected. I've got rights for one horse and five sheep. Dunnage runs them with his flock for me. Gives me a nice bit of extra income. Always a good day, is Drift Day. Most of us go up to the drift, and we always get a bit of a fair set up on the green. Afterwards is the Field Court in the Fox. That's when Drake collects fines, listens to complaints, and reads out any new field orders."

"Who makes the orders?"

"Drake recommends them, the lord of the manor confirms them. Though really Mudge and Drake decide things between them, and Lord Oldfield just says 'Yes' to whatever they put in front of him. That's how the old Lord did things anyway, and Drake says his son is the same, though for different reasons. The father was happy to leave us to ourselves unless he was needed to settle a dispute. The son couldn't care less about our sheep or cattle. Just as well. Don't think we could stomach him interfering in the heath after what he's done in the forest." Singleton grinned. "Oh, and Warneford usually settles up with us on Drift Day."

"He's coming here?"

"Yes. He'll be on the heath to look over any sick animals."

That was good news. Dan had been thinking about how he was going to get over to Kingswood to look for Bob Budd without exciting any curiosity. Something Warneford had said when they first met had given him an idea. The Kingswood

Fair was the following Saturday, and Warneford knew a man who was putting on a fight. It should not be too late for Dan to challenge one of the supporting bouts, and it would be in keeping with the character he had presented to the villagers. With any luck he could get the match over quickly and concentrate on tracking down the arsonist.

The traders set up camp on the green, and those who could afford it crowded into rooms at the Fox and Badger. More arrived on Tuesday. Ayres was busy all day sorting out arguments about pitches and driving mischievous children away. Wednesday came round and Singleton went off to the heath in the morning. Dan stayed at the forge doing a bit of tidying up and cleaning out the furnace.

He had promised to walk Mrs Singleton to the fair. In honour of the occasion he put on clean stockings, one of his new shirts and scarf, gave his jacket a good shake, and wiped the dust off his shoes. Mrs Singleton wore all her finery, the glory of which was an old-fashioned black silk hat, rosetted and ribboned all over. She took his arm. They could have been mother and son strolling along the high street.

The green was crowded with stalls, tents and shies. The smell of meat frying and cakes baking set the mouth watering, and the tunes from fiddle, drum and flute set the feet tapping.

"No wonder you miss the Fence Month festival," he said, "if it was anything like this."

"It was nothing like this," Mrs Singleton said sadly. "Then the stalls went all along the High Street, the gypsies came to play music for us, and there was dancing all night. The mummers' procession to the wood was a wonder! Still," she added, her face lighting up at the sight of the draper's stall, "this isn't bad."

He fidgeted while she sorted through the bolts of printed cotton and lengths of linen, murmuring to herself, "This would make a good shirt for Mr Singleton. I could get an apron out of this piece. This would do for my niece Becky."

He caught sight of a red checked apron moving between the stalls, and all at once his chivalrous feelings towards his companion deserted him. He left her to manage her purchases as she could and caught up with Anna.

"Mr Fielding. Dan. You're not at the drift?"

"Counting sheep isn't really my idea of a good time."

She laughed, and stopped at a stall selling ribbons. After some deliberation she bought a yard.

"It can't be very interesting for you watching a woman buy ribbon," she said as the man wrapped it up.

"It makes a change from ploughs and horseshoes."

As a matter of fact, he liked looking at her as her eyes flickered over the fabrics, her fingers gauged their quality, and her thoughts were absorbed in balancing what she needed with what she could afford.

"I've got some pretty lace, missus," the mercer said, unfolding a piece of white fabric. "Look lovely around a cap, this would. Three shillings the yard."

"It would, but it's too expensive."

"I'll do you a special price. Two shillings and sixpence."

She hesitated, but "No, thank you."

They moved away from the stall. "I've finished for the day," she said.

"Is Walter here?"

"I don't think he's of an age to enjoy marketing with his mother any more. He's gone over to his uncle's in Stonyton. He's got friends there he's been neglecting of late: good, steady lads...Are you going to the Field Court?"

"I thought I would see what it's all about. I gather it starts at five o'clock."

"Yes, and goes on a bit longer than it should for some of the men."

They came to a halt in the middle of the street between the forge and the rectory.

"Well," she said, turning towards the road beside the church, "I'm going this way."

"I think I'll go up to the drift after all. I'll walk with you. I just have to run back for something. Will you wait for me?"

"I can find my way home, Mr Fielding."

He held up his hand. "Five minutes. No, three."

He left her sitting on the wall by the lychgate and sprinted back to the mercer's stall.

"I'll have that bit of lace."

"It's fine Nottingham lace, a very good buy. Four shillings."

"Wait a bit! It was two shillings and sixpence five minutes ago."

"To the lady, yes."

"Reduced from three shillings."

"Give me three and six."

"I'll give you two shillings and sixpence."

"I'll starve!" he grumbled, not very convincingly, and gave in with a wink. "I hope she likes it."

Dan shoved the packet in his pocket and hurried back. She had taken off her straw hat and was twirling it about in her lap. She rose when she saw him and put the hat on. He carried the basket and they sauntered along the lane, chatting of this and that. The trees were beginning to turn golden and were full of little chirrupings and rustlings. After a while they emerged from a strip of woodland onto the edge of the heath. The sound of men shouting and whistling, sheep bleating, and cattle lowing floated across the gorse.

She pointed. "The drift is that way."

"I'll carry the basket down the track for you."

"There's no need."

"It's heavy."

When she had her hand on the door latch he slipped the lace into the basket. His plan was to be well away before she found it, but she was too observant.

"What's this?" she exclaimed, unwrapping the parcel. "That lace!"

"Got to get to the drift," Dan muttered, attempting a retreat.

"Is this what you went back for?"

"You seemed to like it."

"I did like it. But I can't accept it from you."

"Why not?"

"It's a fairing."

"A what?"

"A fairing is a gift from a man to – to – "

"A woman? It's a fairing then."

It had been stupid to give in to the impulse, but good to find out how it felt to make a gift without it being spoiled by the ungraciousness of the recipient. Nothing had ever pleased Caroline: "Didn't they have it in a different colour?" Or, "It's very nice, but I don't suppose I'll ever wear it." Or, "I suppose one of the cheaper ones will have to do." It would be better still to be able to give something to Eleanor without worrying about what Caroline would say if she found out.

He went back to the village and hung around the forge. Mrs Singleton came home. She had made a cake for the holiday and looked on contentedly while he ate. She chatted about the traders: those who were new to Barcombe; those who were old, familiar faces; those who had put their prices up or the quality of their goods down. Singleton would have shut her up, but Dan did not mind. He never knew what he might learn from letting gossips run on.

The church clock struck five. Footsteps clattered outside, and the sounds of men joking and laughing, some singing, came in through the open door. They were on their way down from the heath, ready for a cooling pint in the Fox.

"Thanks for the cake, Mrs S," Dan said, picking up his hat. "See you later."

He stepped out into the shadows lengthening across the yard. As he vaulted the gate, he glanced back towards the door. She was gazing after him, much as Anna Halling had gazed after Walter the other night. He gave a cheery wave. She turned away slowly, as if her knees and hips pained her, and started to clear away the dishes.

*

"There's someone waiting for you," Buller muttered, jerking his head at a closed door off a side passage.

Warneford was sitting in a corner of a small parlour, writing in his pocketbook. A fire burned in the hearth. It had not been going long; the little-used room was cold and smelt musty.

Warneford did not look up from his calculations. Dan sat at the table, put his beer down beside him, and stared into the fire. From the crowded bar came the rapping of coins on the counter, the men's impatient shouts.

"Come on, Buller, you've got a room full of thirsty men here!"

Dan recognised Singleton's voice, and a moment later the door opened and the smith lumbered in. His face was red with more than the sun and wind: he had been taking his turn as the cider jugs circulated up among the gorse.

"Dan! You missed it."

"I fell asleep."

"Never mind. Have a drink."

"I've got one."

Warneford closed his book.

"Good business today?" Singleton asked Warneford as he sat down.

"It would have been better if the stock had needed any attention," Warneford answered.

Singleton grinned. "Animal doctors are like physicians – only happy when there's sickness and disease."

"At least we don't make our patients worse for the sake of a fat fee."

"No, I'll say that for you. But never mind, Warneford. You've other ways of making a living! Ah, here's Dunnage now."

Dunnage joined them, Abe at his heels. A moment later, in sidled Travell. The poachers gathered expectantly around Warneford, who had drawn a purse out of his pocket. He started to open it, then said, "There's one missing."

"Walter's given up the game," said Dunnage.

"Why?"

"I don't know."

"Because his mother asked him," Abe said scornfully.

"What about his share?" asked Warneford.

"What share? Why should he get anything?" Abe demanded.

"It won't take nothing out of your pocket," Dunnage said. "The lad should have his due."

"Is that what you all say?" asked the man with the purse.

Travell cleared his throat. "Abe may have a point. The boy made it clear he didn't want anything more to do with it."

This from the defender of the poor man's rights! Dan did not argue, though. Best that Walter did not take poachers' coin. He said, "I don't think he should have the money."

"Me neither," said Abe.

"Nor me," said Travell.

"The vote's against you, Dunnage."

The farmer shrugged. Losing the argument meant a little more for the rest of them.

"And how do you like the work, Fielding?" Warneford asked when the money had been pocketed.

"Well enough, but I'd like to find a way of making a bit extra."

"Do you have anything in mind?"

"You mentioned Kingswood Fair. Is it too late to do anything?"

Warneford leaned forward eagerly. "You mean you want to go a round?"

"Dan!" Singleton exclaimed. "You never told me you were thinking of it. The Champion of Barcombe – the Barcombe Bruiser! That's it – the Barcombe Bruiser! I'll put my money on you."

"Hold on," Warneford cut in. "You are sure, Fielding? Because if I'm to go to any of the other backers with a challenge, I need to know you will turn up on the day."

"I'll bring him on Saturday morning," Singleton said.

"Better yet, I'll let you take him with you tomorrow. I'll lend him a horse. That way you can keep an eye on our investment."

"That will give me time to do some training," Dan said. "A couple of long walks, swing some weights. In fact, I'll walk to Kingswood tomorrow. What is it, fifteen miles?"

Singleton laughed. "Can't face going a-horseback, eh, Dan?"

"It's true I don't care for riding," Dan admitted, "but it so happens that pedestrianism is the best training there is."

"You can walk all the way on your hands for all I care," Warneford said, "as long as you get there. I take rooms at The Rose and Crown."

"What about the magistrates?" Dan asked.

Warneford laughed. "They know better than to interfere."

So it was all arranged, and now they could hear Drake calling the meeting to order in the other room.

Chapter Fourteen

They joined the rush to get in more ale, then Drake rang a little hand bell, and eventually everyone gathered around the table where the field officer presided. Pip Higgs sat next to him, giving off the pungent scent of the byre. Drake called out the names of those who owed fines, and one by one they brought him their money. Drake entered the amount in his book before passing Pip his share for running the village pound.

It seemed there was no one in the village who did not owe for some transgression on the heath. Dan's mind was beginning to wander when a murmur of astonishment brought it back. The rat-catcher, Davy Cottom, stood in front of the table, counting out his coins.

"Are you going to settle last year's fine as well?" Drake asked as everyone jostled to get a view of Cottom's cash.

The little man grinned, treating them to a view of his rotten teeth. "Outright."

"Don't think that means you can bring your scabbed sheep back to the common."

"You can save your sermons. I won't be grazing sheep on Barcombe Heath any more. I've sold up – house, cattle, everything. I'm off out of here to start a tobacco business in Bath."

"Well, ain't you the swell!" Abe called, preening himself on the laughter of the silly young men who clustered about him.

Cottom agreed with a complacent nod. From hunting vermin to opening his own shop – that was a big step for any man. Dan had seen his house too. Selling it would not have raised enough to buy a shed, let alone set up in business in a fashionable city.

"Who's the buyer?" Travell asked.

"Lord Oldfield."

"What's he want with a tumbledown cottage with an acre of land attached to it?" Travell asked.

"It doesn't even border on the estate," Dunnage pointed out.

"Nor is it in the way of the spring for that bloody lake of his," added Singleton.

"Now then, gentlemen!" from constable Ayres. "Let's have a bit of respect. That's His Lordship you're talking about."

No one wanted to be reported by the constable for speaking out of turn and the fuss died down, though the mystery remained. What could Lord Oldfield want with Cottom's place?

Since no one knew, Drake moved on to the next business. He outlined the tasks to be done on the common over the autumn: ditches drained, pools cleared, thistles pulled up. The men smoked, drank, and nodded their agreement. The meeting wound up and there was a surge of movement towards the bar.

"Hold up!" Singleton roared, banging his tankard on the table. "Warneford here has an announcement to make."

Warneford waved his hand. "You tell them."

Singleton hauled Dan to his feet. "This, gentlemen, is the Barcombe Bruiser, and Warneford is backing him to fight at Kingswood Fair on Saturday!"

"What are the odds?"

"I'll give you four to one on."

"Who's the opposition?"

"The book will open on Saturday," Warneford said, "when I know who he's up against."

Singleton yanked up Dan's arm. "Three cheers for the Bruiser!"

They cheered and applauded, then they drank Dan's

health. Ayres joined in the toast, but as soon as the noise died down, he gulped his beer and slunk out of the tavern.

Girtin sucked noisily at his empty glass. Dan passed him some coins. "Here, get yourself a drink."

"You're a gent, Mr Fielding. What will you have?"

"Nothing. I have a long walk ahead of me tomorrow, so I shan't have any more."

"That's the way!" Singleton cried approvingly. "Keep your form!"

Warneford had already left Barcombe by the time Dan set off in the morning. Singleton drew him a map and explained the route. He was to head to Bath, then swing off towards Bristol, asking his way in villages with odd-sounding names like Combe Hay, Englishcombe, Newton St Loe, and Keynsham, by when he should find himself on the main Bristol road.

Mrs Singleton cooked him a hearty breakfast while a crowd gathered in the yard. They squeezed into the kitchen to watch him eat, a pugilist consuming ham and eggs apparently being a rare spectacle. She made up a parcel of food and lent him a knapsack to put clean linen in. The men clustered around the gate to see him off, and he strode away with their good wishes in his ears.

On the edge of Kingswood Forest, he asked the first man he met, a miner stumbling home with a belly full of beer, if he knew Bob Budd. He belched "No". A farm labourer was no more help. Then Dan saw a woman and two children at the side of the road, gathering blackberries. The woman hesitated before answering that she did not know Budd. Dan suggested the information might be worth a shilling and she remembered where she had heard the name. He produced the coins and she remembered where he lived, and when he handed them over she remembered the directions.

Budd's new dwelling was on the edge of the wood in a setting very much like the one at Barcombe. There the resemblance ended. Even in its ruined state, Dan could tell that his old home had been a snug cottage. This was nothing but a hovel made of bits of wood, sacking and straw.

A girl and two small children sat in the grass outside the hut, washing snail shells in a wooden bucket. They would make a little money selling them at the local market for the bottom of bird cages, along with whatever else they could scavenge from the countryside – berries, nuts, rushes for candles.

The girl stood up and shooed the little ones, under protest, into the hut. She stood in front of the rickety door, arms akimbo, her pinched face taut with hostility.

"Is your dad in?"

She shook her head.

"I'm from Barcombe."

"I don't know you."

"I've not been there long. I'm Dan Fielding. I work at the forge."

"You're the boxer?"

"That's right. Are you Betty? Singleton told me about you."

She stared at him for a moment, then said, "You can wait if you like. Don't know when he'll be back."

"Thanks."

He pulled off the knapsack and sat down. She called the children back to work. He waited in silence broken only by clicking and splashing. The children peered at him, and Betty pointedly ignored him.

Bob Budd appeared half an hour later. He was a man of medium height with sandy hair and eyebrows, pale, watery eyes, and a mouth set in a bitter downturn. He wore leather breeches, a coarse woollen jacket, and a homespun waistcoat made of odd bits of wool found snagged on hedges. He carried a couple of fish, which he tossed at Betty. She sent the children for fresh water, produced a knife from a pocket beneath her filthy skirt, and proceeded to gut the catch.

"Who are you?" he asked roughly.

"Dan Fielding."

"He's the boxer," Betty said.

"I know that."

She glared at her father above the bloodied knife and, determined not to be silenced, added, "He's been waiting for you."

He shot her a look full of hatred and made no reply. She smiled and resumed her gutting.

"What do you want?"

"I think you may owe me something."

"Then you've waited for nothing, because that's what I've got to owe. Nothing."

"It's not goods or money I want. I don't take kindly to being bludgeoned."

"What's your bludgeoning to do with me?"

Dan took off his coat. "It was me you knocked down outside the Hall the night you tried to shoot Lord Oldfield."

"I never tried to shoot him."

"Not so keen on standing up to me face to face, eh?"

"I'll stand up to you where and when you like – " Betty guffawed " – but I've no idea what it's all about. I've never seen you before in my life, man. How do you make out I knocked you down?"

Dan put up his fists. "We're wasting time. Come on."

"I don't know who belted you, but it wasn't me, and I don't know why you should think it was."

"You have good cause to hate Lord Oldfield. I know you burned his barn. No man could blame you if you took a potshot at him through his window as well."

"Now just a minute. I fired his barn, but I never tried to kill him. Wouldn't have missed if I had. But I've got nothing to fire with. Bastards took my gun."

"And I suppose you didn't kill the gamekeeper by sneaking up on him and bashing his brains out, nor try to do the same thing to me?"

"I've danced on Castle's grave, but it wasn't me who put him in it. I'd raise my glass to the man who did."

"That's about all you could do," Betty muttered.

"As for bashing any man's brains out, it's a thing I've never done. If you won't take my word for it, speak to Singleton. He'll vouch for me."

"If it wasn't you, I'd like to know who did do it, so I can pay him back in kind."

"And I'd like to know who the bloody fool was who missed Lord Oldfield."

"You have no idea?"

"I don't."

Dan picked up his coat and shrugged it back on. "No hard feelings, then. The Kingswood road is in that direction?"

"That's right. What makes you think you'll find your man in Kingswood?"

"I'm not looking for him there. I'm fighting in the fair on Saturday."

"Who are you up against?"

"I don't know. Warneford is arranging something. Do you know him?"

"I know Warneford all right. So he's in Kingswood on Saturday?"

"He'll be there tonight. I'm to meet him at The Rose and Crown."

Betty flung a fish's head into the bushes. "I'm taking the childer to the fair."

"You aren't going to any fair," he snapped.

"Got these shells to sell," she retorted. "And don't think you're having it for beer money neither."

He moved towards her, his open hand drawn back. She flung her head back, offering up her face to his blow. His arm fell to his side.

"Bitch. Just like your mother."

"Except I'm still here and she's gone."

She rose, selected some branches from a heap by the hovel, and began to lay a fire.

"Give us your tinder box."

He handed it over. "I'll walk with you, Fielding."

"Glad of the company."

They left the girl striking sparks from the flint.

Budd trudged in silence, his hands bunched into fists in his pockets, his jaw grinding. He began to look about him a little when they reached Kingswood. He knew his way, and Dan was glad to follow him through the ill-lit streets – if such runnels of mire could be called streets.

Kingswood made Stonyton look like paradise. Every other building was a pub or tavern. Snotty children and ragged women hung around the doors. Groups of young miners tumbled out of one bar and staggered a few yards along to another, though what advantage there was to them in the constant change Dan could not see.

Dan and Budd shouldered their way into The Rose and Crown, an old inn on Two Mile Hill. An out-of-date sign on the door advertised last week's inquest of a miner found dead at the bottom of a pit shaft. Inside, the room was crowded but there was a wholesome smell of food, a good fire in the hearth, and the barmaids running up and down with ale and bottles were only as untidy as heat and hurry made them. The company was there for the fair: men with business interests to look after and more on their minds than drinking themselves into a rage or stupor.

Warneford waved from a corner. As usual, he had found himself an obscure spot on the edge of things from where he could see everything and everyone. He called one of the waitresses.

"Well, Dan, you made it. And Bob Budd! I didn't know you two knew each other."

Dan dropped his bag and sat down. "We didn't until an hour ago, and that was only because I was going to give him a beating."

Warneford raised an eyebrow. "I'm glad you didn't. I need you fit and well for Saturday."

"I'm fit enough."

The girl arrived at the table.

"Bring a pint of sack," Warneford ordered.

"Lemonade for me," Dan said. "And I'd like something to eat."

"There's stew and bread," she offered.

"Then I'll have stew and bread. What about you, Budd?"

Budd shook his head.

"Come on. This is on me."

A sudden smile split his face. "All right then. I'll have the same."

"Beer for him and stew for two."

"So, Bob," said Warneford, "how are things going with you?"

"Not so bad," Budd said, and at that moment, eyeing the brimming glass the girl put in front of him, he meant it. He took a long draught and smacked his lips. All thought of the hovel on the edge of the wood, the resentful girl, and the snivelling children dropped from him as the beer went down. He only put down the glass when the food arrived, and this he devoured as if he had not eaten for days – which he probably had not, or at least not enough to keep a grown man satisfied.

Dan signalled to the girl to refill Budd's glass and ate his own meal. Warneford was pouring his third bumper of wine when they pushed the plates away. The food and drink had put heart into Budd. He opened his business with Warneford like a man confident he has something valuable to sell.

"I've been here long enough to find out the warrens and coveys, so if you need anything…"

"I'll take all you can get," Warneford answered. "Get it to Buller by each Friday and he can send it on with Bryer."

A shadow fell across the table, cast by a squat, flashily-dressed man. Though run to fat and well past his prime, his well-formed shoulders and broken nose were evidence of a past spent in the ring. He looked from Budd to Dan, trying to make up his mind who was the challenger. Warneford invited him to pull up a chair, and when he had settled, the two men regarded one another for a moment, Warneford smoking nonchalantly, the newcomer twisting a large gold ring around his thick finger.

"Warneford," he said at last.

"Grey."

"Which is your man?"

Warneford nodded at Dan. Grey flicked a glance at him, calculating with the speed of long practice what he stood to win by Dan's defeat.

"I've got a match for you. A lad from Bristol, about nineteen, new to the ring. Will you take it?"

He was playing down the opposition, trying to lull Dan into a false sense of security.

"We'll take it."

"I'll go back and let his side know. What name does your man go by?"

"Dan Fielding. Budd here's his bottle holder. And yours?"

"Henry Pearce."

"Broughton's Rules?"

"Agreed." They shook hands, and Grey left.

Budd was still blinking in surprise over his unexpected appointment.

Dan grinned. "You don't mind attending me, do you, Budd?"

"Glad to," Budd said. "What does a bottle holder do?"

Chapter Fifteen

By the time Dan, Budd and Warneford got to the fair on Saturday afternoon, the stewards were clearing up after the dog fights and adapting the pit for the boxing. They took down the wooden fence, swilled the gore off the boards, hammered in posts, and attached ropes at the four corners. The ring lay in a natural, shallow amphitheatre, so they did not bother to raise it above ground level.

The crowd, already excited by a morning's drinking, betting and bloodshed, was as rough a one as Dan had ever seen. Kingswood was not a place that attracted the noble amateurs of the Fancy. There were no smart carriages positioned on the high ground around the ring, no huddles of London trainers and backers on the lookout for talent, no weedy quill-pusher to take down a round-by-round account of the battle for the *Sporting Magazine*.

After a night and day in Budd's company, Dan had concluded that the only crimes the man was capable of were sneaking ones such as arson and grave robbery. It turned out he had carried out the latter part of the business while the drink was upon him, and it filled him with disgust now.

Castle's murder had been a sneaking one, the killer unseen and in the dark, and the steeling influence of drink could easily have played a part in it too. Yet while Budd freely admitted to at least one capital offence – arson – he gave no hint that he'd had a hand in a crime of which he thoroughly approved. It was the same with Dunnage and the rest of the gang: consistent denial coupled with outspoken admiration for the killer. Either they were all very good liars – not impossible – or none of them was the man he sought.

Budd was popular with the Barcombe lot, especially when they found out that he had a place ringside. They were all there: Singleton, Travell, Abe, Dunnage, Buller, and the other Fox and Badger regulars. Walter Halling had come too, though whether to cheer for him or shout "Hoorah" for every blow he took, Dan did not know. He was glad to see them. A young fighter like Pearce might be flustered by his opponent's noisy supporters.

The first match came and went. It was mere butchery. Another followed, short and brutal as the first. It ended when the challenger, a saucepan-maker from Bath, left the ring with a broken jaw. If this was the standard Dan had to expect, it should not take him long to finish off his opponent, not with Noah's training behind him.

Warneford and Grey got into the ring to agree on the position of the mark, the square yard chalked in the middle which each man must step up to at the start of a round or within half a minute of a fall, or else forfeit the fight. None of the earlier fighters had bothered with it. It had been straight out of the corner and start swinging punches for them, but Warneford and Grey had agreed Broughton's Rules, and Dan was determined that was what they would have.

He passed the time skipping about to warm up. At least he tried to, but his Barcombe acquaintances kept coming up to slap his back and shake his hand. They beamed proudly at those outside their charmed circle, as if to say, "Here is our hero – what do you have to match him?"

Dan could not help thinking that he did look the part in smart pumps, breeches, and stockings provided by Warneford, with his bottle holder hovering about, dabbing officiously at his back and shoulders with a towel, though he was not sweating yet. Warneford had instructed Budd in the use of the smelling salts, and he had tied the phial on a string around his neck to be ready if needed. His enthusiasm for his duties and his excitement about the coming battle began to affect Dan. As he flexed his muscles, the sense of his own health and strength took hold of him. What with this and the furious betting on him from the Barcombe men, he was thinking very well of his chances by the time his opponent approached the ring.

The minute Dan saw Pearce, he knew that Grey had not just underplayed the opposition. He had lied. This was not some inexperienced youth. He wore a yellow sash around his waist, the favour sported by Bristol pugilists. He was a fighter of some pretensions, and Dan realised how high those pretensions were when he recognised the little man at his side. It was none other than Bob Watson. Dan had heard Watson had become a butcher in Bristol after he left the ring. It seemed he had not entirely given up his interest in the sport.

Among Pearce's entourage were a couple of handsome brothers, the elder about fifteen. The group climbed into the ring, and Dan followed Budd through the ropes on the opposite side to meet them. The brothers gazed at him in frank appraisal. The younger one said something to the elder with a doubtful air.

"No, Tom, he's no match for Hen," he hissed back, the loud whisper reaching Dan's ears as intended.

Pearce came forward and held out his hand. "I'm Hen."

He smiled at Dan as if he expected them to be firm friends, not two men about to batter one another before a baying crowd. Under the cloak of his smile, he weighed up the opposition, as Dan weighed him up. Hen was about five foot ten inches tall, well-muscled, and light on his feet. His apparent warmth might put other fighters off guard, but Dan was more wary.

Usually each side chose their own umpire, and if they did not agree on any point a third would be appointed to settle the matter. There were no suitable candidates among the organisers of the previous fights, so Grey and Warneford agreed to let Bob Watson supervise the match and make all final decisions. Though he was Hen's trainer, he was the only man with the skills, and they could trust him to be fair.

They retired to their corners. Dan rounded on Warneford.

"Who is Pearce, and how does he come to have Watson seconding him?"

"You see his friends?" asked Warneford. "They're the Belcher boys, Jem and Tommy, good little fighters both. Watson is their brother-in-law. Their grandfather," he added casually, "was John Slack."

"*The* John Slack?"

"What's wrong with that?" asked Budd.

"Oh, nothing," Dan answered. "Only that John Slack was the man who beat Jack Broughton in fourteen minutes. Only that Watson is a veteran of the ring – I saw him beat Elisha Crabbe in '88. Only that this new-to-the-ring boy has the backing of what you might call the nobility of boxing. And Warneford knew all along what I was up against."

Warneford chuckled. "But Hen doesn't know what he's up against, and I don't back losers. Come on, Dan, you know you're a match for any man. You know you can win."

He broke off as a buzz of alarm spread through the spectators, who were looking behind them to the top of the field, shifting and muttering, torn between anxiety and resentment. A smart carriage rattled along the track on the rise. Watson grabbed Hen's arm and pushed him through the ropes.

Warneford cursed. "It's the bloody magistrate."

"It *is* a magistrate," Dan agreed, "but I don't think we need to go yet. That's Lord Oldfield's carriage, and unless he's brought a local justice with him, he's no right to stop the match."

"No Kingswood justice would risk interfering with the fair," said Budd. "What's the bastard want?"

Dan watched His Lordship step out of the coach, his pair of hounds tumbling about him.

"I think he wants to see the fight."

"How does he know about it?" Warneford demanded.

"It's not been kept a secret," Dan answered. He thought it probable that, like so much that went on in the village, the information had been carried to Oldfield Hall by Ayres, whom

Dan had seen slipping out of the Fox and Badger after the fight was announced. The constable could not have expected the result to be that Lord Oldfield would turn up to join the spectators.

The crowd fell back to let Lord Oldfield through, eyeing the dogs warily. If it had not been for them, he would not have got down to the ring without at least a splatter or two of mud – and maybe worse – thrown at him. His footman followed nervously with a folding chair.

Nonchalantly, Lord Oldfield leaned on one of the corner posts. "So you are the Barcombe Bruiser, who told me he wasn't planning any fights. Are the odds in your favour?"

Dan was going to fight for His Lordship's entertainment after all! He stifled his irritation. "It's pretty even at the moment, My Lord."

"I had better give you something to fight for then."

His Lordship drew out a leather purse and threw it on the boards. It landed with a satisfying chink. "Fifty guineas for the winner!"

"That's yours, Hen!" Jemmy Belcher cried. Hen grinned and nodded. The prize gave more relish to the match than merely beating a fairground challenger.

Watson darted into the arena and snatched up the purse. The footman placed the chair behind Dan's seconds. Budd glanced uneasily at His Lordship, but Lord Oldfield had no idea he sat within feet of the man who had burned his barn and rifled his ancestor's tomb.

Hen Pearce came back into the ring. Abe, ever the wit, made clucking noises and flapped his arms. Soon the rest of the Barcombe mob were copying him.

Hen had heard it before. He yelled back, "I might be a chicken, but I'm a game one!"

He and Dan shook hands again and went back to their corners to wait for the bell. Dan rolled his shoulders, feeling every breath, every twitch of his muscles, the prickle of each hair on the back of his neck. It was the same before a raid on a den of thieves and murderers or a night-time arrest. Those last few seconds before the action starts, before the world crashes in...

The bell sounded from a million miles away and he moved forward like an automaton, raised his fists, and put his head down. And took a facer before he had gone two steps, and where it had come from, he did not know. Pearce had got in right over his guard. But it woke him up. They spent the rest of the round circling one another, feinting, closing, doing little more than getting each other's measure.

In the next round, Dan went on the attack and put in a blow which Pearce returned. A few more exchanges followed, and Dan's nose started bleeding. In the third he attacked again, driving into Hen with a series of rapid blows. Hen was beginning to look distressed. He swung at Dan and fell with the force of his own punch just as the bell went. Watson dragged him back to his corner.

Round four, and Dan put one in Hen's stomach that left him winded, and there was little doing for the rest of the round. Hen rallied in round five and they swapped several blows. The lad was tiring, while Dan had never felt so full of energy.

Though Watson tried to patch him up, Hen came out in the sixth covered in blood, and Dan got in a tap to the forehead that should have finished him off. Except he was as game as he said he was and he kept coming. The match was nearly over though, everyone could see it. Dan had only to hammer one or two more home, and the fight was his. Guarding with his left, he swung at Hen with his right, slipped on the blood-stained boards, and crashed to his knees.

Dan put his weight on his right hand, tried to raise himself, but the fall had knocked the strength out of him. His breath rasped in and out of his lungs. Watson counted the seconds, beating his arm to emphasise their passing. Dan tried again, but his legs refused to obey him. The crowd yowled, Watson's lips moved, the thirty seconds Dan had to get to his feet and up to the line before he was declared the loser rushed by, and still he could not move.

Hen gave a whoop of triumph and danced in for the winning blow. No matter that it would be a foul: no one in this mob would complain about hitting a man when he was down, and if they did it would not do Dan any good. One easy strike, legal or not, and he was done for. Even if he managed to get to his feet, he would not recover. He had lost the fight.

Hen's sweating face leered above him, the flesh twisted into a swollen smile, his lips and teeth dripping red. His fist feinted in, out, in, out; his feet skipped to the left, to the right, teasing, jeering, showing Dan how easy it was going to be as he danced around to a position where Watson could not see his fists.

The crowd was shouting and howling, and now Dan could hear individual voices; one or two at first, but the cry caught on and spread: *"Kill him!"* Not that the animosity was personal. That was what men came to fights for, and in the excitement the truth often slipped out. Warneford was on his feet, gesticulating and shouting, "Umpire! Umpire!" Bob Budd stood at the corner, screaming and waving his towel, tears running down his face. Lord Oldfield was standing too, one hand gripping the rope. Getting his money's worth.

Dan flung up his left arm to deflect the worst of the blow when it came. He heard the words, "Bloody do it!" He had thought or said them, or someone else had. Hen drew back his fist, his smile gone, replaced by the brutal focus of a man about to annihilate his opponent.

The blow never came. Hen pranced backwards, raised his arms above his head, and jogged around the ring, waving at the yelling crowd. The realisation that Hen hadn't hit him rushed through Dan like new blood, and at last he found the strength to stand. Though his knees sagged and his head wobbled, he was up with five seconds to spare.

The bell rang for the end of the round. Budd and Warneford shot into the ring and dragged Dan back to the corner. Water in his face, brandy on his lips, hartshorn fumes under his nose. Warneford hissed into his face. "He's yours next round. It was only luck, he couldn't have got you down if you hadn't slipped."

Pearce had not hit him, but he had seen him fall, and he came out in round seven with fresh heart in him. For a time they went at it as if they had only just begun. Hen was flagging again when he aimed a most peculiar one – perhaps in error, perhaps deliberate. Dan only knew that if Hen had got that blow in on his throat with any force, he would have been out of the reckoning. As it was, it was easily deflected. Hen was staggering and could hardly see out of his right eye. Dan followed him around the ring, clipped the side of his head and, spewing his guts, he went down. The Barcombe Bruiser had won.

In that instant, the life went out of Dan and he crumpled. Budd and Warneford were back in the ring and propping him up before he hit the boards. Warneford held up his limp and bloodied hands in a victory salute. The crowd bellowed, whistled, cheered. Budd threw a towel around him and wafted the salts under his nose. They hustled him into the corner, where he leaned, gasping, against the post while Budd poured brandy down his gullet. He swallowed some, spat out most, and grabbed the flask off him.

Hen sat on his second's knee, his torso sheened with sweat. Jem Belcher sponged his face and Watson knelt beside him, bandaging his knuckles. Dan hobbled over and held out the flask. Hen winced as he reached for it, flashed a grin that set his split lip bleeding, and took a long swig.

"A noble fight, young master," Dan said.

"And where did you learn to fight?" Watson asked.

"Round and about."

Watson's eyes narrowed. "You've been well trained. Anyone can see that."

"Surprises all round then," Dan said. He winked at Hen, who could not wink back with his closed eye, and returned to his corner.

Budd towelled him down, threw a shirt and jacket over him, and led him out of the ring. They pushed through the crowd, the other two shielding Dan as much as they could.

Walter stood in front of him, staring at his battered face in horrified admiration. He thrust a jar into Dan's swollen fingers. "Mother sent this. She said you probably wouldn't have enough left from before."

"What did she say? I mean, did she say anything? Did she...?" Dan gave up. He was not sure what he was trying to ask. "Thank her for me."

Walter was about to say something, but one of his friends called him. He snapped his mouth shut and hurried off. His place was immediately taken by Singleton, who grabbed Dan's hand and pumped his arm up and down.

"Well done, Dan, well done! Going for the stomach in the fourth was a brilliant stroke – just what I'd have done in your place. And that one-two-one-two in six!"

Dan had not managed to get a word in or retrieve his aching arm when Lord Oldfield's footman stalked up.

"His Lordship's compliments, and will you join him in his carriage?" he said, grinning at Dan before resuming his haughty attitude.

They all knew that Dan had no choice but to accept the invitation, but he had to be careful not to look too keen. It was not difficult: he was far from eager for the interview. It was bad enough that His Lordship had turned up for the fight. Now he was going to want to know how the case was going, and Dan was not ready to make his report.

"I'm all right here," he said.

"Don't be a fool," Warneford said. "Get what you can out of your victory. No one will hold it against you."

"You should go," Budd agreed. "Take the bastard for all he's worth."

This the footman pretended not to hear, though his lips twitched.

"Yes, you should go," Singleton chimed in. "The lads will love it!"

The poacher feted by the lord whose game he had taken.

163

The men of Barcombe would love it, right enough.

"Lead on, then," Dan said to the footman.

They followed him to the carriage, the excited crowd pressing behind them. Dan stopped and shook hands with Budd, Singleton and Warneford.

"I'll sort things out here and see you in Barcombe tomorrow or Monday to settle up," Warneford said.

Budd looked sorry to be losing him, but as soon as Dan turned away, he was surrounded by men who wanted to carry him off to the beer tent and hear all about the Barcombe Bruiser. Dan wondered if his children had witnessed the fight, and if Betty would have any more respect for her father if she had.

But the coachman was holding the carriage door open. Dan stepped inside.

Chapter Sixteen

Dan leaned out of the window, waving as he had seen other boxers do when a rich man took them up: full of hope and pride, thinking the moment of victory would last forever, and they would not be cast aside when some new sensation caught the eye of the Fancy. Eventually the cheering crowd fell behind, preferring the attractions of the beer tent to running along in choking dust.

"You're a mess," said Lord Oldfield. "You'll have a hot bath and then Dr Russell will take a look at you."

Dan thought of the cold pump in the yard and the hot bath at Oldfield Hall, and did not argue.

"Thank you, and for the purse."

"Well earned."

"It was a tough fight. The boy was fast, and the boy was good."

"I thought him a little raw."

"As he is, and not at the peak of his strength yet. I think he has the makings of a champion, given time and experience."

"Do you?" Lord Oldfield said. "But why don't you aim for it? I would back you. I'd like to have a fighter of my own."

A fighter of his own: that was how they thought, these lords. Even the most generous of them thought they could own you. At the best they would dress you like a coxcomb and drag you around like one of their leashed dogs. At the worst they would turn you into a hired thug, a bully boy to protect them while they dabbled in the low life of taverns and stews. Bill Hooper of Bristol had fallen into that trap with that noble hooligan, the Earl of Barrymore, and lost every bit of the respect he had won in the ring.

"Thank you, My Lord, but I have no ambition in that direction."

Lord Oldfield did not like to be refused and said pettishly, "But if you won't box for me, what are you doing fighting in Kingswood?"

"I came to Kingswood on the trail of a murder suspect, and taking on the match was a good way to get here without attracting suspicion. I hadn't expected the opposition to be so handy."

"What suspect? Dr Russell told me over a week ago you knew who was in the gang. You said you needed more time and I gave it to you, with the result that I was shot at and my mother thrown into a fit of nerves from which she has barely recovered. This has gone on long enough, Foster. I want these men stopped."

"And they will be, when I've completed my investigation."

"I don't see what else there is to investigate. You've done what you were engaged to do."

"Yes, I know who the poachers are, but I'm not convinced Castle's killer is amongst them."

"Who else could it be?"

"There are plenty of people who bore a grudge against him. Bob Budd, who he helped evict from Barcombe Wood – he was my bottle holder, by the way. The Tolleys, whose daughter Sukie went missing ten years ago. The dead baby found in your lake is believed to be hers and Castle's, with some even saying he had something to do with the girl's disappearance."

"Nonsense. Josh had no need to go a-whoring."

"My impression is that Sukie was simple, not a whore, and that some man took advantage of her. However, that's not my concern."

"It is not. That is catching Josh's killer. All you have discovered are a few petty grudges, such as are common in rural communities. Can you bring the murder home to any of these people?"

"No, but – "

"Then it is time to draw the matter to a close. I want the poachers arrested."

"What about Caleb Witt? I heard he wanted Castle's job."

"If he did, he isn't going to get it. I'm bringing in a man of Lord Berkeley's."

"But Witt wouldn't have known that."

"Nor does he yet, but he's never been given any reason to think I'd consider him as head keeper."

"All the same, it would be worth checking on his movements that night."

"I expect he was out and about with Potter, doing what I pay him for. If he had not been I would have heard of it. Enough of this, Foster. I will not have these men remain at large to encourage others in the belief that they can break the law with impunity."

"They are certainly guilty of breaking the Game Laws and assaulting Ford, but I cannot prove any of them killed Castle."

"It doesn't matter which of them struck the killing blow. They are all culpable. I insist that you tell me who they are and arrest them immediately."

"I can't do that. Not until I've finished."

"Finished what? You've taken a straightforward matter and turned it into something more than it is. No doubt things are different in the London underworld, but this is the country. It's clear that you are out of your depth here. Sir William should have sent someone who knew what he was doing."

This from the man who had shut the people of Barcombe out of the wood without a thought for the hardship it would cause them. The man who had turned petty poachers into deer stealers, who had caused the near-blinding of a little girl, who had kept back information that might have a bearing on the case, who from the start had steered Dan towards the conclusion most convenient to himself. A conclusion more than convenient – if Lord Oldfield was the murderer.

"I do have one other suspect."

"Who is that?"

Dan had snapped out the words without thinking, too angry to stop himself. He would not back down now, would not let himself be sidetracked by bluff and bluster, whether it come from a lord or a nightsoilman. They could take away his job because he offended the rich and powerful, but not for incompetence – never for that.

"You," he said.

Lord Oldfield started. The dogs, sensing a threat to their master, sprang, growling, to their feet.

"How dare you make such a suggestion!"

"If you would get your dogs' jaws out of my face, I'll tell you…Why didn't you tell me that you and Castle were related?"

"What has that to do with anything?"

"Perhaps Castle thought the Oldfields owed him more than a cottage and a gamekeeper's wage. His father was your great uncle's son, wasn't he?"

"Illegitimate son."

"Wasn't there a marriage?"

"It has nothing to do with you."

"It has everything to do with me."

"I could have your hide for this."

"I've already risked it once today."

"Yes," said Lord Oldfield, "you have…down, Captain, Trusty." The dogs sank back onto their haunches, but still regarded Dan with hostility. Their master gazed at him above their heads, his mouth tight with anger, his fingers drumming on the arm of his seat. If he expected Dan to beg pardon, he was disappointed.

Or perhaps not. No one likes a fighter who refuses to take risks. "If this is what you're like in the ring, God help your opponents," Lord Oldfield said. "But if you think I killed Josh, you are wrong, so very wrong. If Josh had wanted anything, he had only to ask me for it."

"Even half your estate?"

"To which he could have had no possible claim. Yes,

there was a marriage of sorts, but the marriage was invalid. It was performed by Alexander Keith, an excommunicated clergyman of some notoriety who ended up dying in the Fleet Prison. There was at one time a lively trade in illegal marriages in and around the prison; Fleet weddings they called them. It was to put a stop to the career of Keith and others like him that Lord Hardwicke pressed for a change in the marriage laws. My family's case came in for a good deal of unfortunate publicity because of it. So, unless you doubt the probity of Parliament and King, I have them to stand as witness."

Dan could not say he believed absolutely in the probity of parliaments or kings, but if there was no lawful marriage, he could not see how Castle could have had any right to Lord Oldfield's property.

"Then I'm sorry. I had to ask."

"You think you are being conscientious. I suppose I cannot blame you for that, but now let us have an end to this. Give me the poachers' names."

Dan did his best to stall off His Lordship. "It doesn't make sense. If they wanted Castle out of the way while they took the deer, all they had to do was knock him out and tie him up. There's no benefit to them in killing him. You'll only appoint another head keeper, maybe even bring in more men to patrol Barcombe Wood. Why would they risk that?"

"Because they are vicious and stupid."

"I'm not sure they are either of those things. Angry and wily, maybe. And they are not the only people going into the wood at night. I saw the man who shot you and, though I couldn't catch him, I know he was not one of the poachers. He may not be Castle's murderer, but I think we should find out who he is before we arrest anyone."

"Nothing is to be gained by wasting time looking for such ruffians. They will learn to keep the peace soon enough when we've set them an example. Give me the poachers' names. Or must I write to Sir William?"

It was unlikely that Sir William Addington would back

Dan in an argument with a fellow magistrate and a peer of the realm – especially when he had nothing to argue with. Lord Oldfield was right: he could not bring the murder home to anyone else. In addition, there was a strong case against the poachers. They were guilty of theft and a brutal assault on one gamekeeper, and they had been in Barcombe Wood the night Castle was killed.

Still he hesitated. He had lived among them, had seen them sober and drunk, at their work and their thieving; seen how they lived by their own law, which made poaching no crime and disloyalty the worst sin a man could commit. He knew they were men with a grievance, though he knew nothing about the rights and wrongs of that. He knew what their resentment made them capable of: the gamekeeper Ford would have died if he had not dragged Singleton off him. But Castle had not been murdered in the heat of the moment; the attack had been subtle and planned. Whatever else the poachers had done, they had not done that, and if he gave them up now he would never find out who had.

There was one chance, though it was not much of one – if he could get Lord Oldfield to agree.

"Grant me one favour. Let me have your consent to offering his life to whichever of them turns King's Evidence against Castle's killer. If they did it, or if they know who did, that is the surest way to find out."

"No. They are all equally guilty and they will all hang."

"If you don't let me do this, we may never be sure. There will always be the possibility that the real killer has gone free."

"And if I allow you to do this, it will be a certainty that a killer has gone free."

"I only said offer his life, not a pardon. You can still prosecute him for taking your deer. That carries seven years' transportation, which is as likely as not to mean death."

"Damn you, Foster, do you ever give up?"

"No."

Lord Oldfield laughed, a short outburst of irritation and

respect. Probably no one had ever stood up to him before, not even Josh, who had hanged Walter's terrier despite knowing it was wrong.

"To hell with it. I agree."

Before Dan could thank him, the carriage pulled up outside Oldfield Hall. The driver jumped down and handed his whip to a stable boy. The footman lowered the steps and flung open the carriage door. Lord Oldfield and his dogs strode into the house.

Dan stepped from the carriage, straight into the driver, who wanted to shake his hand, the footman, who wanted to clap him on the back, and the stable boy, who wanted to stare. Even the liveried flunky in the hall patted his arm when he thought his master was not looking. None of them minded that he smelt of sweat and blood, but Lord Oldfield had evidently had enough of it while they were cooped up in the carriage. He handed his hat to his footman.

"We will continue our discussion when you've bathed and changed. Be quick."

He summoned the maid, who was waiting in the background, and went into the drawing room, his dogs at his heels. A few seconds later, Dan heard the clink of glass.

Dan followed the girl upstairs and into a small dressing room with a fireplace, narrow bed, wash stand and towel rail. Two boys in the adjoining room were pouring water into a tub.

"You can change behind that screen," the girl said.

He hesitated. She grabbed a towel off the rail and threw it at him. "Use this."

Seeing that she did not mean to leave the room, he went behind the screen, stripped, and wrapped the soft linen around him. He had never used anything like it. All they had in the gymnasium were thin cotton squares.

He padded into the bathroom. The boys had gone, taking their pails with them. A deep tub stood in the middle of a tiled room bigger than Dan's kitchen. Next to it was a marble-topped table on which stood soaps, sponges, and bottles of he did not know what. Another towel, just as large and soft as the one he wore, warmed by the fire.

He no longer cared whether or not the maid peeped. He flung the towel aside, stepped into the water, and soaked his pains away.

When he went back to the dressing room, the girl had gone and so had his clothes. Neatly folded on the bed were clean black breeches and white stockings, a linen shirt, and smart blue jacket. Everything fitted well, and though it was all good quality, it was far from turning him into a fop. He looked about for his shoes. They had gone too, presumably to be cleaned. He sat down on the bed to wait for the girl to bring them back.

Chapter Seventeen

When Dan woke up, it was morning and he was lying under the bed covers. He could not remember undressing, but did have a blurred memory of seeing Dr Russell's face hanging over him while it was still daylight.

He gritted his teeth, rolled out of bed, and hobbled over to the chair where his own clothes, cleaned and ironed, lay next to the new ones. He left the smart breeches and jacket where they were. When he had dressed, he found some water in the jug on the wash stand and splashed his face and hands. Then he examined himself in the mirror over the fireplace. His nose was red and swollen, there was a bruise on his cheekbone, and he had a cut on his lip, but he did not look too monstrous.

A few turns around the room got his limbs moving. After that he opened the door and stepped out onto the landing. A clock chimed prettily somewhere close by: eight. He peered over the stone balustrade. There did not seem to be anyone about, so he decided to make his way to the kitchen and see if he could scrounge a bit of breakfast.

He was at the bottom of the stairs when he heard the swish of a dress on the marble tiles. It came from the alcove beneath the staircase. A woman stood in front of one of the family portraits. Dan would have turned back, but it was too late. She had heard him and was stepping out of the recess. On the canvas behind her, Lord Adam Oldfield's eyes stared out from the puffed, crimson face of a corpulent man in antique clothes, posed beside his hunter with his dogs at his feet. A preview, perhaps, of what Lord Adam would be in years to come. The woman who was so interested in his future must be the one who was going to share it with him: Lady Helen Burgh.

She was beautiful, as all rich young ladies are with their elaborate hair, silken gowns and flawless complexions. Yet there was something in her face beyond the usual insipid attractions of these high-bred females. A certain knowingness: not exactly bold, but not exactly demure either.

Dan stepped aside so she could pass, trying to make himself look like part of the furniture as the servants did. She stopped and looked him up and down.

"You are the pugilist?"

"Yes, madam."

"What's your name?"

"Daniel Fielding."

"Oldfield says you are a Cockney."

"I am from London, but not a Cockney, ma'am."

The distinction did not interest her. "You're here because of the poachers. Don't worry, I won't tell anyone your secret. That would spoil the excitement, though I don't suppose it is exciting for you. You must do this sort of thing all the time. Everyone else is making such a tremendous fuss about it."

"His Lordship is anxious that the killer is apprehended. He and Castle were close."

"I'm sure Castle liked to think so."

"You didn't like him?"

"I had no feelings about the man. He was a gamekeeper. A low, presuming fellow."

A strong reaction for someone who had no feelings. Dan wondered what form Castle's presumption had taken. Had he tried to flatter the lady? Or – what might be worse – had he failed to admire her?

There was a quick footstep at the front door, and Lord Oldfield came in, his dogs pattering at his heels. He ignored Dan's "Good morning, My Lord" and hurried to his lady's side.

"Good morning, my dear," he said. "You must excuse me.

I have business with this fellow."

She smiled. "Of course. But don't forget we are going riding later."

She sauntered off. Lord Oldfield's urbane smile vanished when he looked at Dan.

"Come with me."

Dan, who had anticipated His Lordship's anger, fell in behind him and his dogs and followed him downstairs to his office, which was on the kitchen corridor. The dogs curled up on a worn rug thick with their hairs. The den was littered with nets and guns, fishing rods and muddy boots, stained coats and sporting magazines. Prints of race horses and hunting hounds hung on the walls, one of which was taken up by a map of the estate.

There was hardly time to take all this in before Lord Oldfield, standing behind his desk and fiddling irritably with his gold watch chain, said, "I am not used to waiting on the pleasure of those in my employ."

"I am sorry we did not continue our discussion last evening," Dan said. "And I assure you it was not at my pleasure."

"If it was not for Dr Russell, I would suspect you of deliberate malingering. As it was, he said that you should be left to rest, that it might even be dangerous to wake you. And we did try. Now, I will have those names, Foster, and be quick about it."

"You stand by your agreement to offer King's Evidence in return for information about Castle's murder?"

Lord Oldfield brought his fist down on the desk, causing the dogs' heads to jerk up. "The names!"

"The agreement."

"Yes, damn you, I have given you my word."

"Dunnage heads the gang."

His Lordship sank into his seat and the dogs settled down again. "His family have been tenants on the estate for three generations. He and his shall never set foot on my land again."

"There's Travell, the village shopkeeper."

"I might have known that Jacobin swine was at the heart of

it. That's how it started in France, with the wretches claiming the right to hunt. I should have dealt with him years ago."

"Bob Singleton."

"But he's had my estate business for years, the ungrateful scoundrel!"

"There's also Abe Wicklow, one of Dunnage's labourers. The dealer is Luke Warneford, the travelling animal doctor. Buller at the Fox and Badger receives the game and sends it to Warneford in Bristol by the carrier, Sam Bryer. Whether or not Bryer knows what he's carrying I don't know, and won't be able to prove unless they peach on him."

Lord Oldfield opened a drawer in his desk and drew out a sheaf of pre-printed arrest warrants. "Damn it all, Foster, these men might already be in custody."

"No they couldn't, and can't be a while yet, not until I have some men from Bow Street to make the arrests."

"For a handful of villagers?"

"For a handful of desperate men surrounded by people who will do their utmost to protect them."

"I have men. Mudge, Witt and Potter will be glad to help."

"And I'll be glad to have them along when the time comes, but they won't be enough."

"I have others."

"Servants and stable boys? Even if they succeeded in bringing them in, where would you put them? The way feeling is in Barcombe, they wouldn't be in that lock-up for long. No, My Lord, this is not a job for amateurs. It's what you brought us in for, and we're the best ones to do it. And on that, I think even Sir William would agree with me."

"Hell and damnation! When can I be rid of this vermin?"

"Warneford's the problem. He'll be gone tomorrow or the day after, so there's no time to bring men up from London. We'll have to wait until his next visit."

"How long will that be?"

"He doesn't keep to a regular schedule, though he doesn't seem to be in Barcombe less than every two or three weeks. As soon as I know when he next plans to visit, I'll get word to you and you can write to Sir William."

"Two or three weeks?"

"I have an idea that might bring Warneford back sooner. I will try at any rate."

A maid brought a tray of coffee and rolls. When she had gone, Lord Oldfield said, "So. Tell me how you intend to handle the arrests."

"They will be at night, at each man's home, timed to take place together. It's an operation my men are skilled in. Since the village lock-up is not secure, I plan to take the prisoners to the nearest gaol as soon as I have them in custody, before daybreak and news of the arrests gets abroad. I think I am right in saying that Shepton Mallet is fifteen miles?"

"Yes."

"I will need a covered cart."

"Mudge will arrange that."

"Can you suggest a safe rendezvous?"

"What about Cottom's old place?"

It was about half a mile out of the village on a lonely stretch of road. "Perfect."

Ackland came in with a message for Lord Oldfield.

"Mr Sutter has sent to ask if you would step down to the stables, My Lord, and tell him if it is right that Wicker is to be saddled for Lady Helen."

"Wicker? What is the man thinking of? He's not a lady's mount."

"Apparently Lady Helen requested the horse, My Lord."

"I see." He swept the blank warrant forms back into the drawer and stood up. "That will be all, Fielding."

His Lordship hurried out, and Ackland rolled his eyes at Dan before following him. It was not hard to guess what was going on at the stables. Lady Helen thought she had waited long enough for Lord Oldfield's attention and had found the perfect way to get it by insisting that the stableman provide her with an unsuitable horse. Only His Lordship could countermand her orders, so he must abandon his business and go to his future wife.

Dan went back up to the room he had slept in and changed into the clothes Lord Oldfield had provided. He made a bundle of his own and carried them away.

A more than Sunday silence hung over the village, and he got back to the forge without meeting anyone. Mrs Singleton was back from church, clattering about in the kitchen amid the aroma of bacon and mushrooms. In the hope of getting a second breakfast, Dan knocked on the open door.

"Dan! Will you look at your face? What a state for Christian men to get themselves into! You'd better come in and sit down. He's just getting up."

The floorboards creaked overhead, then Singleton's heavy tread fell on the stairs. His eyes were bloodshot and his face grey. He moved as if he, not Dan, had been the one to take the pounding. He looked better after he had staggered out to the yard and ducked his head under the pump, but not by much.

"Well, ain't he looking sparkish!" he croaked when his eyes were open enough to see Dan's new outfit.

His wife banged food in front of them and disappeared upstairs to pummel the bed back into shape.

"Where did you get to last night?"

"I was at the Hall. I fell asleep and the doctor said to leave me."

"You had Dr Russell out to you? Wined and dined at His Lordship's expense too, I hope."

Dan stroked his sleeve. "I've not done badly out of him. What about you? Did you stay in Kingswood or come back to the Fox?"

Singleton smiled ruefully. "Both. We had a few at the fair before setting off."

That explained the deathly hush of the village. The men were sleeping it off, the women and children tiptoeing carefully around them.

The gate from the road swung open. Singleton squinted out into the sunlight. Warneford came into the yard leading his horse, which was saddled ready for his journey.

"I was supposed to tell you Warneford's coming with your money this morning. I did offer to bring it for you, but he wanted to do it himself."

Wise of Warneford not to trust the cash to a bunch of drunken men. He tethered his horse by the forge and strolled into the kitchen, his heavy boots ringing on the flagged floor. He put his hat and gloves on the table.

"Morning, Singleton. Dan. Let's take a look at you." He grabbed Dan's chin and tilted his head. "Nairy a mark on you."

"He had His Lordship's doctor out to him," Singleton said.

Warneford lowered his bulk onto one of the chairs. "Did you now? Enjoy your taste of the high life?"

"Not really. I slept through it."

Warneford laughed. "Well, now. To business. Bit dry, though, ain't it? Morning, Missus."

Mrs Singleton appeared at the foot of the stairs, a handful of laundry in her arms. "Humph!" she said, and stalked out to the wash house.

Singleton took the hint and poured himself and Warneford a glass of beer. Dan shook his head. Warneford took a bulging purse out of his pocket and tipped the contents onto the table.

"Here it is, less ten per cent to the loser."

"No man deserves it more than Hen Pearce," Dan said.

Warneford counted the coins, swept them back into the purse, tied the strings, and handed it to Dan. He took a long swig at his drink, took out his pipe and baccy pouch, and began to tamp in the weed.

Dan weighed the purse in his hand. "You asked me once if I wanted to make a living out of boxing."

Warneford stood up and helped himself to a spill from the jar on the mantelpiece. "And do you?"

"I'm thinking about it."

The tobacco glowed red. Warneford threw the light away

and stood with his back to the fire, puffing at his pipe and looking at Dan through narrowed eyes. "You ask me, you don't need to think too hard. There's no reason you shouldn't be champion of England one day."

"You think I could challenge Jackson?"

"I do."

"I heard Mendoza is itching for a rematch," Dan said.

"Jackson won't make no rematch with the Jew. He only beat him after grabbing on to his hair in the fifth and forcing him down. Mendoza had no chance to recover from the beating, and that's the only reason he fell in the ninth. It was a clear foul and should never have been allowed. Jackson couldn't beat him if he fought fair."

Easy to tell who Warneford had put his money on.

"What if Jackson won't fight? He hasn't fought since becoming champion last year, and the word is he won't fight again."

"Then challenge Mendoza. By rights, the championship still belongs to him in any case, and I'm not the only one who thinks it."

"You really think I could beat Daniel Mendoza?"

"The Barcombe Bruiser, Champion of England?" Singleton cried. "That would be something, Dan!"

Warneford ignored the blacksmith's interruption. "Not straight off, no. You need to get a few more victories under your belt first. I could get you those."

"But His Lordship says I'm ready to fight now. He says he'll back me."

"You don't want to let him turn your head. You take on something before you're ready for it and your career'll be over before it's begun. His Lordship will drop you like a hot coal."

Dan pretended to think about this, then said reluctantly, "Who would I have to fight?"

"Couldn't say offhand, but I dare say I could scratch something up in a few days."

Warneford finished his pipe and emptied the ashes into

the grate. "There are plenty of good Bristol men, and you could beat any one of 'em all hollow and make a name for yourself into the bargain. Then you'll have your pick of lords for backers. Maybe Prince George himself. Look, I've got some business over there this week. Why don't I ask around and see what's doing? When I come back, I'll let you know the form and then you can decide. How does that sound?"

This was the tricky bit. Warneford did not like giving out advance notice of his movements, but Dan was banking on his desire to get his hooks into him before Lord Oldfield did. He looked sulky and said, "But when will you be back?"

Warneford seemed to hesitate for an age before admitting, "Wednesday week."

"All right," said Dan. "I'll wait until then, but no longer, mind."

When Warneford had gone, Dan laughingly shook his head. "Champion of England. It doesn't sound like me."

"Sounds right to me," Singleton said, pouring himself another drink. "I'll drink to your success."

Mrs Singleton bustled back in. "What sounds right? Nothing connected with that man, I'll be bound. I don't know why you allow him in the house. He's never up to any good." Grumbling, she passed through the room and went upstairs again.

"I'm going for a walk," Dan said. "Don't want to seize up. What about you?"

"Nah."

Singleton heaved himself from the table and got as far as one of the chairs by the fire. He put his head back and closed his eyes. He was snoring by the time Dan reached the door, which was just what Dan had hoped he would do.

The church clock struck twelve, the sound lingering sweetly in the still atmosphere. The day was sunny with a cool edge to it, very pleasant for walking. Wisps of woodsmoke hung on the haze. Occasionally the faint sound of a cow lowing or sheep bleating drifted down from the fields. Dan sauntered through the village, but when he had left the houses behind, he broke into a run. His muscles did not like it at first, but as they warmed up they benefited from the loosening and stretching.

The doctor's front door stood open on to an untidy porch filled with walking sticks, coats, gaiters and boots. Dan did not go in that way; he wanted to speak to the doctor without being seen by anyone else. He skirted the house until he came to the consulting room at the back. It had glass doors opening into the garden. Dan peered inside. It was a large room with armchairs dotted about, small tables piled with books and magazines, and a desk with papers and inkstand neatly arranged upon it. The walls were lined with glass cases containing jars of varying sizes, but he could not see what was in them. A fire had been laid in the hearth, but not yet lit.

Dan tried the handle. The door was not locked and he stepped inside. As his eyes adjusted to leaving the sunshine, he realised his mistake. The room was not empty. There was a woman in a pale gown standing in a corner. She turned slowly towards him, and his heart, still hammering from his exercise, all but broke out of his chest. It was not a woman at all. Or perhaps it once had been. He had no way of knowing.

Not for the first time, the image of Girtin's gore-soaked Bloodie Bones flashed into his mind. Barcombe superstition was infectious, but his senses and mind were too used to working in unison for the contagion to last more than a few seconds. Of course a doctor would have a skeleton in his study, as he would also have models of feet and stomachs and hearts, jars of pickled limbs, cases of dissected frogs and birds and mice. The skeleton, wired together and suspended on a stand, swung softly in the draught.

Dan was congratulating himself on not being ridiculous enough to flee when the inner door opened and in came Dr Russell.

"I thought I saw someone coming round the house. I suppose I should be glad it's the police and not a housebreaker."

Very cool, for a man who thought he might have a burglar in his study!

The doctor laughed. "Actually, I recognised you. What seems to be the problem? Your injuries didn't seem too serious when I examined you last night."

"No, they aren't, but if anyone has seen me coming here, you can say you treated a sprained wrist. I've a message for Lord Oldfield."

"What is it this time? Is he to break down his own fences or throw stones through his own greenhouses?"

"He'll be pleased with this one, and with getting it so soon. Tell him he can write to Sir William Addington at Bow Street and ask him to send ten or a dozen men, to be here the Wednesday after this, to rendezvous after dark at the location His Lordship and I discussed this morning."

"Then you are making the arrests at last. Is His Lordship allowed to know who the men are yet?"

"He already knows."

"And?"

"I'll leave it to him to tell you himself, if he wishes it. Do you think – "

"I could go up to the Hall at once? Of course. What will you be doing in the meantime?"

"I'll carry on at the forge as normal."

"Good luck then, Foster."

They shook hands, and Dan left the way he had come.

Chapter Eighteen

Dan was not attracted by the prospect of watching Singleton snore off last night's excesses. He had not seen Anna Halling since giving her the lace. Now it was his turn to acknowledge a gift.

"I came to thank you for the salve you sent me," he said when she opened the door.

She eyed his cuts and bruises. "You don't look too bad for it. But look at your knuckles! Didn't you put anything on them?"

"I forgot."

She clicked her tongue and pointed to the bench by the door.

"Sit down."

She went inside and came back with a cloth and a jar of ointment.

"Hold out your hands."

"It stings!"

"Don't be a baby."

He watched her dab gently at his broken skin. "So you don't mind me fighting?"

She put the lid on the jar and wiped her hands on the cloth. "I'm a healer. I can't see the point of deliberately seeking harm."

"That's not why I do it. It's a discipline."

"Are you so undisciplined without it?"

"I was until I learned the rules of boxing."

"There are rules? I thought it was just two men punching one another."

"At its worse, that's all it is. At its best, it's a sport. An art even."

"You do make it sound grand. Walter thought it was. He couldn't stop talking about you last night."

"What did he say?"

She shot him a sideways glance. Yes, he was fishing for compliments.

"He said you were brave, that you fought fair, that you didn't gloat when you won."

"He said all that, did he? And what do you say?"

"I say – what do you care what I say?"

"I do. Truly. I would like to know."

"Then I say it's a shame you should get involved in such a low business."

"There's good money in it, honestly earned." He grinned. "More or less."

They could not, after all, make criminals of the Prince of Wales and pugilism's other aristocratic supporters. Dan had often been called upon to police a fight, but only if the crowd threatened to be disorderly, or to keep a lookout for thieves. Unless a magistrate had a special reason for preventing it, most turned a blind eye to the fight itself.

"I don't call betting on the outcome of a brawl an honest way to earn a living. I don't see the wisdom of risking your life for a new suit of clothes either."

"They do look handsome, though, don't they?"

She laughed in spite of herself. "Perhaps."

The bench was a pleasant spot to sit in the afternoon sun. Soothed by the trilling of small birds, the rustling leaves, Anna's gentle presence, he leaned back, stretched out his legs, and shut his eyes. Something brushed lightly across his cheekbone. His eyes shot open. She pulled her hand away.

"You should put something on that bruise."

He clasped her fingers and put them back on his face. "Have you got anything?"

*

185

It was late afternoon when he left. He would rather have stayed in the warmth and peace of her bed, but Walter would soon be back for his dinner. The air was cool and shadows were gathering under the trees. He walked back to the forge, still half asleep, lulled by the sound of the church bells ringing for evening service.

He had become the adulterer Caroline had long and groundlessly accused him of being, and the only thing he regretted was that he could not tell her. If he did, she might leave him and he would be free of her for good. But it would not make any difference. As Caroline delighted in reminding him, even her death would not do that, not while the church said a man could not marry his wife's sister. Caroline knew no word of love had passed between him and Eleanor, but far from respecting his restraint, she looked on it as a pose, accusing him of playing the hard-done-by husband still loyally protective of his difficult wife. She twisted even his efforts to do the decent thing, and Anna would be one gift she would accept with real gratitude. She would take great delight in telling her sister, "This is the man you think so noble and long-suffering..."

Yet he had never set himself up to be either of those things. Even so, Eleanor's good opinion was all he would ever have any right to, and he could not face the thought of losing it. So he would not tell Caroline, and she would not leave him, and everything was back where it was.

He had not made any promises to Anna, and she had not seemed to want any. He had started to tell her that he was not sure he was going to stay in Barcombe, but she had hushed him and said they would talk later. They had not talked later. Even if they had, there was not much he could say. She would find out who he was and why he had come to Barcombe soon enough. He would be able to explain everything. Then, of course, she would understand, and no harm done.

*

Sir William sent a six man patrol under Captain Sam Ellis, a carpenter by day and a patrolman by night. Dan had paired with him when he worked the turnpike roads. They had been together the night Dan shot and killed the highwayman, Jack Williams, a vicious piece who had crowned a violent career the day before by stopping a coach with two women in it and beating the mother half to death in front of her daughter. The rest of his gang gave themselves up when he fell. Perhaps it was the shock of realising the Devil had not granted their leader immortality.

Dan got to Cottom's place and whistled softly. Patrolman Thomas stepped out of the shadows, recognised Dan with a grin, and let him pass. Dan warned him to be on the lookout for the keepers, who were due at midnight.

The bare room was dimly lit by two shuttered lanterns, easy to snap shut if someone should pass by. Dan was not surprised to see Rawlinson, who usually partnered with the Welshman. Thomas and Rawlinson were experienced officers, older than Dan, but they did not envy his promotion. There were only six Principal Officers at Bow Street; not everyone made the rank, or wanted to.

Sibbetts was sitting cross-legged on a heap of old sacks, sharpening his blade. Tickner, a burly, genial-looking young man who could be far from genial when up against low life, was having a quiet smoke. Robbins lolled on the floor with his back against the wall and his eyes shut, which meant he was alert to everything going on around him – a ploy that had fooled many a villain. There was one Dan did not know, a young recruit called Jones. They were all armed with cutlasses as usual, and had also been issued with pistols.

Dan and Captain Ellis shook hands. "You're looking well, Dan. Country life seems to agree with you."

"I'd rather be back in London. I feel safer there."

Ellis laughed. "What's the plan?"

"Simple enough. Gather round, men."

Dan had drawn a map of the village and marked on it

the forge, Travell's shop, Dunnage's farm, Abe's cottage, and the Fox and Badger, where Warneford was sleeping. Dan had been in the Fox with him and Singleton earlier, discussing Warneford's proposed match against Bill Ward. Ward lived in London, but would be happy to come back to his native Bristol for the fight. He had been defeated twice by Mendoza. He had also served three months in Newgate for the manslaughter of a blacksmith in a brawl in a coaching inn yard. Dan said he did not see how beating such a man would win him much praise. He knew all the time that Ward was a skilled fighter, but he grumbled all evening until seeming to give in at last and telling Warneford to go ahead and arrange it.

Sam Ellis held up one of the lanterns so the men could study the drawing.

"The keepers are bringing the warrants with them," Dan said. "They'll be your guides. You can also rely on them to help with the arrests. Remember to keep it quiet, we don't want to rouse the village. Singleton is likely to be the most trouble, so I'll go for him myself with Tickner." He reeled off the other assignments.

Ellis pulled an enormous ancient watch out of his pocket. "It's nearly midnight."

"Sounds like someone coming, sir," piped up Tickner.

The door opened and Thomas put his head in. "Here's the keepers."

Instead of the three Dan expected – Mudge, Witt and Potter – four men crowded into the room. At their head was a dashing figure in boots and dark cloak, a pair of pistols at his belt.

"Lord Oldfield!" Dan exclaimed. "What are you doing here?"

"What do you think? I've brought the warrants as you asked, and here's your pistol."

"I did not mean that you should bring them yourself. This is a dangerous operation, My Lord. You'd best leave it to us."

He laughed. "Not likely, Foster. I want to be in on this. I'm coming with you."

There was no point telling him it would not be as much of an adventure as he seemed to think. Something about taking a sleeping man unawares took any glamour out of the thing. There was nothing for it: Dan had to adjust his plans. Though as head of the operation he should take the most hazardous assignment, he would send Ellis for Singleton. The captain would understand the need to keep Lord Oldfield out of danger.

Mudge shifted uncomfortably, conscious of the rough treatment he had given Dan on the night of the fire. Dan held out his hand. "No offence taken, Mudge."

"And I suppose I should thank you for that sock on the jaw," Witt said.

"Saved getting you killed."

"How do you do it?" asked Potter. "I could never have stuck it out without giving the game away."

Dan shook his head. "Sometimes I'm not sure myself. Now, to business. Captain Ellis and Tickner, you will go for Singleton. Witt, you can take Rawlinson to the farm and pick up Dunnage."

Witt sized up Rawlinson and nodded his satisfaction.

"Potter, you can take Sibbetts and pick up Abe."

Potter, eager to avenge Ford's injuries and his own beating at the hands of Abe and Dunnage, cradled his cudgel in his arms and smirked.

"Robbins, Jones, Thomas and Mudge, you're to the Fox and Badger for Buller and Warneford. Be careful of Warneford. I wouldn't be surprised if he sleeps with a pistol nearby."

Mudge looked a bit green at this. Ellis noticed and said, "Robbins and Thomas should do Warneford."

That left Jones with Mudge to go after Buller. Dan decided that if Ellis trusted the young man in a situation where he might be as good as single-handed, that was good enough. In any case, he did not think the landlord would put up much of a fight.

"His Lordship and I will go for Travell. Mudge, have you got the covered wagon ready?"

"It's in the farmyard ready to go."

"Good. Get the prisoners down there as quickly and quietly as you can. Only use your pistols if you have to. I don't want to wake the village. I want the prisoners out of Barcombe before anyone realises what's happening. Sibbetts and Potter, Rawlinson and Witt – you have further to go so you had better set off now. We'll meet you at the home farm."

Lord Oldfield handed around the warrants and the four men jogged off into the darkness. The rest loosened their cutlasses in their belts, muttered "Good luck" to one another, and waited tensely. Good men never took their prowess for granted. True, they were well-armed, experienced, and taking the criminals unawares, but things could always go wrong, and a man could end up injured or dead if he weighed his advantages too much in the balance.

Dan hustled Travell up to the wagon and pulled the hood off his head. The shopkeeper clambered in and collapsed, whimpering, in the corner. He had been whimpering ever since he and his wife had woken to find Lord Oldfield and Dan standing over their bed. They had got him dressed and down into the shop with a tail of weeping women and boys straggling after: his wife, the serving girl, and three pupils who lodged with him. Here, in a patch of moonlight, Mrs Travell recognised Lord Oldfield and was struck dumb with fright.

Dan showed her the warrant. "We're taking him to Shepton Mallet prison. There's a watch on the house. No one is to leave until morning. Do you understand?"

It was the girl who gabbled, "No, sir, we won't, sir, we'll stay here, sir."

If Travell had not been quaking so much, he might have pointed out that they had no right to place the women under house arrest, real or imaginary. As it was, all his legal knowledge had deserted him, and they left the women safely shut indoors. The maid shooed the boys back to their beds and ushered her mistress into the parlour, where they left her plying the stricken woman with Bristol Cream.

Dan had just got Travell settled when Tickner and Ellis arrived, Singleton's bulky shape stumbling along between them with Ellis's pistol in his back. In spite of being cuffed and gagged, he went for Dan. It took the three of them to manhandle him into the wagon, where he bucked and kicked until Ellis knocked him out with the butt of his pistol. Tickner tied his legs.

"What about Mrs Singleton?" Dan asked. "Not too alarmed, I hope?"

Ellis laughed. "Alarmed? She held the door open for us when we left. You should have seen his face. We'd got the gag on him by then, but I don't think he could have said anything if he'd been free to speak…I'll see if I can rustle up something for the men." He wandered off to the house, where Lord Oldfield and Mudge stood talking in the patch of light from the open door.

The party from the Fox and Badger came in with Buller and Warneford. The landlord took his place calmly, Warneford with a swagger and a wink. Buller's daughter was locked in the cellar. No one would hear her banging and shouting until the morning drinkers turned up.

Rawlinson and Witt arrived with Dunnage. The farmer had a bloodied head, and Witt looked pleased with himself. Sibbetts, Potter and Abe completed the party. The sullen youth shook off Sibbetts's steadying hand as he struggled into the wagon. Robbins and Thomas got in with the prisoners and checked that cuffs were tight and gags snug. They sat down near the tailgate with their pistols at half-cock, trained on the prisoners.

Mrs Mudge appeared with a bottle of brandy and tumblers on a tray. Dan shook his head. "No thanks, but give the men some. And if there's anything to eat…"

"Nancy's bringing some meat and bread fresh out the oven."

Ellis came up. "Mudge is saddling a horse for me. What about you?"

Dan said, "Gamekeeper Potter's volunteered to drive the wagon. I'll sit up with him."

He followed Mrs Mudge with her tray of used glasses to the house. Lord Oldfield and Mudge had been joined by Witt.

"A good night's work, men," Lord Oldfield was saying as Dan came up. "Come up to the Hall in the morning and I'll reward you properly for your service. The same goes for you, Foster, and I'll be writing a letter of commendation for you and your officers."

"Thank you, My Lord, but I shan't be here in the morning. I'm leading the prison escort and I won't be back until the day after tomorrow."

"Garvey will be here by then to hear your full report. You will stay at the Hall."

It was a command, not an invitation, but Dan said it would be an honour. Which it was, as the looks on the other men's faces showed. It was not an honour he wanted, but he could not go back to the forge.

Chapter Nineteen

"I'll kill you for this, Fielding!"

Singleton flung himself across the cell and scrabbled at Dan's throat with his manacled hands. One of the prison officers cracked his stick across the back of the blacksmith's knee and he went down. The two gaolers dragged him back to his chair and held him there.

"Believe me," Dan said, "this is the part of my job I like least. But you have broken the law, Singleton."

"I'll kill you. However long I have to wait, I'll kill you."

"So you've said. Could you put it aside for a moment? I've something to say to you."

"I've got nothing to say to you. Fucking scum."

They had reached Shepton Mallet soon after dawn, roused the gaolers, shown them the warrants, and got the prisoners inside. Dan had commandeered a room for the interrogations and had been given a bare, windowless chamber. When they'd opened the door and shone in a light, beetles and spiders scuttled for cover. The rats were still scratching behind the walls. A drain from a necessary house ran under the cell, the damp stink oozing through the floor. Dan wondered how many men had died of gaol fever in here.

The prison had two centuries of miserable history behind it. All the rooms were poky and dark, the ceilings too low, and the damp, bulging walls had not seen a lick of whitewash for years. A recently built extension meant that male and female prisoners could be separated at night, which had at least resulted in a drop in the number of children born to live and die in the squalid atmosphere. It was lucky for Singleton and his friends that they could afford better accommodation than the other inmates, who were mostly impoverished petty offenders and one sheep stealer.

"It's about Walter."

Understanding flickered across Singleton's face. "You and him were very pally, weren't you? And now the little bastard's turned us in."

"Walter didn't turn you in. He didn't have to. I've got enough on you without asking him to speak up."

"So you're going to arrest the lad too?"

"No. I want to keep him out of this. He's young and – "

"Ah, you've got a heart of gold. Then I'll be a rich man when I've ripped it out."

" – he's got a life ahead of him. I want your promise that you won't mention Walter and that you'll make sure the others don't either."

"Why should I promise you anything?"

"It's not for me. You know he only stole from Lord Oldfield because he was upset about his dog, and he'd given it up before this. What's the point of ruining him now he's gone straight?"

"I won't mention him and nor will any of the others, without you having to tell us. We're not the kind who rat on our friends."

"There's one more thing."

Dan dragged a rickety chair across the slimy stones and sat down close to the prisoner. The gaolers tightened their grip on his shoulders, but Singleton had gone quiet and was staring moodily at the floor.

"You know you'll be up on capital charges. They'll probably dissect you as well."

Singleton flinched, but said nothing.

"If it was just the offences under the Black Act, I'd say your chances of avoiding the gallows were good. Juries don't like it. But there's Castle's murder as well."

"That had nothing to do with me."

"The problem is we've got no one else to blame. You were

all in the wood that night, you all had a reason to want the gamekeeper out of the way. You were in it together, but you needn't hang together. Lord Oldfield is willing to drop the hanging charges and just bring you up on deer stealing. You'd be facing transportation. All you have to do is tell me who killed Josh Castle."

"Is that what this is all about? It is, isn't it? That's why you came to Barcombe. That's why Lord Oldfield sent for you – to find out who killed his precious high-and-mighty Josh Castle. Damn the pair of you. I hope you join the gamekeeper in hell. I wouldn't tell you if I knew."

"Why is that, Singleton? Don't want to peach on yourself? You're strong enough for the job. Did you sneak off from the others, smash his skull, and break his bones? Because if it was you, there's only one decent thing left for you to do now, if you don't want the lives of your mates on your conscience."

"It's not me who should be worrying about that, Fielding."

"Whose idea was it? Who struck him? Did you all have a go? Whether you were in on it or not, your only chance of escaping the rope is to tell me who killed Josh Castle."

"Fuck yourself."

And that, with small variations, was all Dan got out of them when, one by one, they were brought in for questioning. Travell would have told him if he had known, and if anyone deserved consideration for a lesser sentence it was Travell, who had always hung back when the fighting started. Unluckily for him, he did not know, though Dan saw from the look of desperate cunning on his face that he contemplated accusing one of the others anyway. Dan soon put that idea out of his mind.

He thought if anyone was going to turn in Walter it would be Abe after their quarrel, but he had underestimated the loyalty bred in villages where every house harbours a poacher. Apart from cursing, Dunnage said very little; he was still dazed from the fight with Witt. As for Buller and Warneford, since the most they faced was a fine or three months in prison for illegal sale of game, they could not be intimidated. Buller was silent and sullen, and Warneford silent and sneering.

When Dan had finished with the prisoners, he sorted out the paperwork with the prison clerk. The gang would be brought up at the quarter sessions in January and tried at Taunton April Assizes. That done, he hurried over to The Red Lion. The men had wolfed down a hot breakfast and were sitting around a bowl of punch, sharing tales of their exploits of the previous night. Captain Ellis sat alone at a small table.

"Anything?" the captain asked when Dan joined him.

"No. I told Lord Oldfield I didn't think they were responsible for the gamekeeper's murder, and I still think it." He signalled to the maid that he would take a plate of the ham and eggs. "Have you sorted out any transport yet?"

"I'm sending Jones to hire a post-chaise when he's finished his drink."

"I'll sort out your rewards and expenses when I'm back in London. Just keep a note of everything you spend. Ah, here's my food. I'll have a cup of coffee with it, miss."

"What about you?"

"Potter says we'll have to rest the horses, so I told him to sort out some rooms here for us. I could do with a good night's sleep."

"Do you want one of the lads to go back with you?"

"No, thanks. I've got Potter."

"I wasn't thinking only of the journey back."

"I'll be fine."

"If you're sure. But be careful, Dan."

"I intend to."

In the morning, Potter tied Ellis's mount to the back of the wagon. Though he looked a well-mannered beast, Dan preferred to sit up with the gamekeeper again. They made good time now the vehicle was empty. It was early afternoon when they reached Barcombe. They did not see anyone in the road, but Dan knew word of his return would quickly circulate.

Potter dropped him off at the back of the Hall and ambled on to the farm with the wagon. Dan went to the kitchen, where the cook and her staff were busy preparing dinner, which Lady Oldfield insisted on taking at the unfashionably early hour of three – one of the arrangements he imagined Lady Helen would change as soon as she was in charge.

While he was drinking a cup of water, a red-eyed girl emerged from the scullery carrying a stack of copper pans. She caught sight of him and let go of the pans. Cook was so startled she dropped a mixing bowl, and the girl at the range almost knocked over a pan of boiling water. As the clash and clang of the heavy pans echoed around the high stone ceiling, the cook bustled over to the stricken girl and gave her a sharp clip around the ear.

"You'd better not have dented any of those pans, else you'll be paying for it out of your wages for a very long time! Pick them up and wash them all again. Mary, go and help her."

"Is that Sal?" Dan asked as the girls scuttled off with their arms full.

"Yes, and she's been useless ever since you took Abe away. Though good riddance to him if you ask me, sly young devil. And if you're going to set the girls a-screaming, go and do it elsewhere."

Ackland came in just then with orders that Dan was to join Lord Oldfield when he was ready. He would find his portmanteau and hot water waiting for him in the room he had previously occupied. Dan bathed quickly this time, washing off the stench of the forge and the gaol. Then he put away Dan Fielding's rough boots, soiled linen and corduroy trousers.

Resuming his own clothes was a part of the job he always relished. It was as if he was reliving his rise from the brickfields: the transition from dirt and want to prosperity and comfort. This moment, standing in front of the mirror in his long coat, smart breeches, tall boots and striped waistcoat, all in muted colours but of decent cut and cloth, was a moment of triumph. His disguise had worked – and it had only been a disguise.

He retrieved the Bloodie Bones notes from their hidden compartment in his bag and put them in his pocketbook. It was safer to keep them with him now the bag was not under lock and key.

He knocked at the door of the green drawing room and went in. Lord Oldfield sat in an armchair with a glass of wine in his hand, regaling the company with an account of the arrests. Garvey, who had arrived an hour ago and to whom the details were new, listened with quiet, professional attention. Lady Oldfield looked bored and disapproving. To her it was a low tale that did not improve with repeating. The adventure had not lost its charm for Lady Helen, who was a most appreciative audience with her starts, gasps and exclamations. Dan thought Lady Oldfield was nearer the mark.

"And that was when the captain and Tickner arrived with the blacksmith. I wouldn't have believed two such ordinary-looking men could have brought the brute in, but he crept along between them like a beaten cur. I tell you, in a fight I'd rather have one Bow Street man with a cutlass than a whole regiment of dragoons with muskets and sabres...And here is the man who deserves our gratitude. Come in, come in, Foster. Have a glass of wine."

"Really, Oldfield!" his mother snapped.

It seemed that Dan was fated to set the girls a-screaming today. Lady Helen uttered a cry, as if she thought, or perhaps hoped, that he was going to rattle his cutlass, which of course he did not have on him.

Garvey nodded a cool greeting over his sherry. "Whatever congratulations are due for the capture of a gang of village poachers I do indeed accord you, Officer."

"Thank you," Dan answered. "I wish I could tell you how much your congratulations mean to me."

Lady Helen listened delightedly to the barbed exchange. "But really, Mr Garvey," she said with a malicious smile, "don't you think Mr Foster's done a splendid job?"

"Of course, My Lady. It cannot have been easy to defeat such formidable adversaries."

She laughed.

"Well, Foster, tell us how it went at Shepton Mallet," said Lord Oldfield, oblivious to his betrothed's mischief-making.

Dan, who did not think it suitable for the ladies' ears, did not know how to answer. Luckily Lady Oldfield had the same thought.

"I believe we have heard enough of this for one day. Come, Lady Helen. We will leave the men to their business."

Lady Helen pouted, but having no choice, she followed her future mother-in-law out of the room.

Garvey and Lord Oldfield sat down, and His Lordship waved Dan to a chair. He told them the outcome of the prison interviews. When he had finished, Lord Oldfield gave a satisfied sigh.

"You've done marvellous work, Foster. You will have no need to doubt my gratitude, I promise you."

"Thank you, My Lord, but I do not feel I have yet earned your thanks. I told you before I arrested the poachers I did not think they killed Castle. Now I've questioned them I'm convinced of it."

"Because no one confessed? I know these men, Foster. They're defiant and unmanageable, and their silence proves nothing."

"Then you know that if any of them would have spoken, it was Travell. But even he couldn't name the murderer to save his skin."

"What they will or won't say doesn't alter the fact," Lord Oldfield said. "They murdered Josh."

"I admit appearances are against them, but without a confession or other conclusive evidence, there is good cause to doubt that they killed Castle."

"You are the only one who doubts it," Garvey said, "which is neither here nor there."

"It might be if I put my doubts to the jury."

The lawyer smiled. "A jury can easily be persuaded that not all testimonies need to be given equal weight."

"Discredit your witness, you mean? I'd like to see you try."

This was mere bravado. There were plenty of people willing to believe that Bow Street officers were incompetent and corrupt. There was the money he had taken off Warneford for one thing. It was all above board as far as the office was concerned. Any profits the officers made were considered fair recompense for the discomforts and dangers of their work, which no man would undertake solely for his salary of a guinea a week. But it would not be hard to hiss "Bribery" in a jury's ears.

"No one is going to be discredited," Lord Oldfield said. "Come, Foster, you have already told me there is no case against anyone else. This is the right result."

"As we told you it would be," Garvey said.

Dan had to acknowledge the truth of Lord Oldfield's words. He had a result, he had a generous reward coming, His Lordship was happy. What else did he want? Maybe the problem was simply that he could not bear to have Garvey proved right.

Ackland announced dinner and the gentlemen joined the ladies in the dining room. Dan went down to the kitchen and asked one of the maids to bring him something on a tray and some writing materials. He went to his room and settled down to write his report. After half an hour staring out of the window, he gave up and decided to go into the village, partly to see how Mrs Singleton was bearing up, but also to gauge the mood in Barcombe.

The long shadows of late afternoon lay across the fields, but it was still light when he walked past the Fox and Badger. No smoke curled from the chimney and all the windows were dark. He walked on, jumped over the locked gate into the forge yard. The furnace was cold, the house silent, and no one answered his knocks. As he climbed back into the road he saw Louisa Ruscombe standing in the graveyard holding a cluster of bright yellow chrysanthemums.

The door from the rectory garden opened and Mrs Poole hurried out, drawing a shawl about her. She had seen Louisa from an upstairs window. Louisa had not seen her, nor did she hear the lychgate open and her friend's rapid steps on the path, so was startled when Mrs Poole slipped her arm through hers. She let her head droop on the older woman's shoulder. They stood silently looking down at the grave, then Louisa wiped her eyes, stooped and placed her flowers on the mound. The women exchanged a few more words before Louisa started slowly down the path. She was weeping, and did not see Dan by the forge gate.

Mrs Poole lingered in the graveyard. Dan thought she might know where Mrs Singleton had gone, and crossed the road.

She turned at the sound of his footsteps. "Can I help you?"

He took off his hat. "It's Foster, ma'am. Dan Foster, Principal Officer of Bow Street."

"Of course. You called yourself Fielding, didn't you? And you've just arrested the poachers."

"An unpleasant business, like all these operations, but it has to be done."

"The law must be upheld."

She smiled as she uttered these pontifical words. Dan suspected they were not her own.

"I came to let Mrs Singleton know her husband is safe and well, but she's not there. Do you know where she's gone?"

"That was kind of you. She's with her family in Mells."

"I thought as much. Well, I'll get a message to her."

He turned to leave. The bright flowers on the grave caught his eye and he glanced at the headstone. The name engraved on it was not Frederick Ruscombe. It was Josh Castle.

"I put them there," Mrs Poole said quickly. "I do from time to time. There aren't many to leave flowers for him, poor man."

He let her think he believed her. "I'm sorry. I didn't know you and Mr Castle were close."

201

"I would not say we were close. He was a decent man, though."

"You call him a decent man, but many in the village accuse him of fathering – and perhaps worse – the babe that's buried on the other side of the wall."

"No. The poor thing wasn't his."

"But it was he who asked Mr Poole to bury it."

"It was. When Mr Castle brought that wretched bundle of bones to us, my husband very rightly..." she stressed very "... pointed out that the Office for the Dead cannot be used for any that die unbaptised. Castle said it was not seemly to bury the child in a common hole, and I think he was right. It was a living infant once and ought to be put to rest near its own kind, not left alone in the dark. In the end Mr Poole agreed to let it lie by the wall. Mr Castle dug the grave himself."

"He must have been very persuasive."

"He was Lord Oldfield's gamekeeper and friend," she said drily.

"Does the Reverend Poole hunt?"

"No. He doesn't approve of parsons who shoot, particularly those who side with their parishioners on the question of the unfairness of the gaming laws."

"Why do you think Castle went to so much trouble if the child wasn't his?"

She hesitated. "I believe he had a special sympathy for the child."

"Because his own father was illegitimate?"

"Yes. Here is Mr Poole."

"There you are, Laura," Poole said, flapping towards them in his robes. "It's nearly time for evening prayers and the ringers have not turned up yet. I suppose I will have to do it myself again...I don't believe I know you, Mr..."

"This is Mr Foster, the Bow Street officer," she said.

Poole held out the hand he would never have offered to Dan Fielding. "I have heard of you from Lord Oldfield. Well done, sir, well done! You've done this village a good turn, ridding it of murderers and thieves. Let us hope their fate will be a warning to the rest of them."

"They haven't met their fate yet," Dan said.

"No, no, of course not. We must pray for their judges, who have a difficult and painful task ahead of them."

Dan thought Singleton and the rest were more in need of prayers, but kept it to himself and said, "It would be useful if you could let me have the Bloodie Bones note that was thrown through your window."

"Of course; it is important evidence. And if I am called upon to testify – "

"I don't think that will be necessary," Dan said, and wished them a hasty good day.

A few minutes after he left the churchyard the bell began to ring.

He could think of only one reason for Mrs Poole to lie: she was protecting her friend's reputation. A single woman leaving flowers on a man's grave was bound to cause speculation, and speculate he did. Why should Miss Louisa Ruscombe mourn the death of the gamekeeper? There was an obvious answer and it explained much that had puzzled him about Josh Castle. The self-improving books and fancy clothes, the scented soap and silver hairbrush, the faded posy in the bedroom. Josh was no ordinary gamekeeper. He had noble blood in him. But if Louisa and Josh had been lovers, did it have any connection with the murder?

Darkness already filled the space between the tall hedges along the lane to Oldfield Hall. He heard something rustling in the shadowy foliage on his right and turned towards the sound. A stone arced towards him and hit him full in the chest.

Chapter Twenty

The next stone knocked off Dan's hat and skimmed a trickle of blood from his scalp. Three men brandishing cudgels burst through a gap in the hedge, their faces covered with scarves.

Dan had his flintlock raised and cocked. "Who wants to die?"

They faltered to a halt but did not retreat. Too late he realised there was someone behind him. There was a loud crack, pain shot up his arm, and he let go of the gun. Another blow across his hamstrings sent him to his knees. He reached for the pistol, but it was kicked away from his scrabbling fingers. A boot in his ribs shoved him sprawling to the ground.

He knew he would die if he stayed down. He tried to get up, but they thrust him back. Through a blur of dust and pain, he noticed one of them had thin, bandy legs. A weak spot. He grabbed the man's ankle and tipped him up. The manoeuvre broke their ranks, distracting them long enough for him to get to his feet, shake the blood out of his eyes, and get his fists up. A quick one-two and the nearest man staggered. Dan danced and lunged, getting in beneath their weapons with stinging blows to ears, stomachs, heads – though sometimes he took a thwack too. They fell back, wary of his fists, but Bandy Legs was up and they were able to reform their circle.

A fifth man armed with a crook loomed out of the darkness. Dan thought he was done for then, but he was not going down without leaving his mark on his assassins. He singled out a man who was momentarily off guard, clutching at his jaw and muttering, "Bloody son of a bitch!" Dan aimed a punch at him, but before his knuckles made contact the crook came down on the man's head and he crumpled.

"That's enough!" the newcomer cried.

"Stay out of it, Drake," shouted one of the gang. "It's none of your business."

"It's my business when I see murder committed," the field officer retorted. "Leave off. Now."

"Fuck you!" the man snapped. "You get out of it and leave this to us."

"I know you, Pip Higgs. I know you all. Kill this man, and I'll have your names before the justice before you can blink. Unless you want to kill me too."

"Then we'll do that," said Higgs.

Bandy Legs shifted uneasily. "Just a minute – "

"Shut your face!" Higgs snapped.

But they had not reckoned on reinforcements, especially one as tough as Drake. The man he had knocked down staggered to his feet, croaked, "I'm out of this!" and fled. Bandy Legs set off after him at an ungainly run, and the third was not long in following. Higgs hesitated, swore, aimed a last blow at Dan which was easily dodged, and fled too.

Dan snatched his pistol, and from a half-kneeling position sent a ball after him. He missed, and the fugitive had forced his way through the hedge before Dan could reach for his powder flask.

Drake helped him up. "Are you all right?"

Dan winced when he put his weight on his left foot. "My knee's buggered...So that was Higgs? I thought I recognised the stink. And the others?"

"When I said I knew them all I was only trying to put the wind up them. The bow-legged fellow is Thomas, one of Dunnage's men. I couldn't swear to the other two."

"Shouldn't be hard to find them. If Higgs and Thomas don't turn them in, I have only to look for men with torn clothes and scratched faces."

"And a black eye or two, judging from what I saw. Were you

going to the Hall? I'll see you back."

Drake found Dan's hat and knocked the dirt off it. Dan covered his throbbing head, then reloaded his pistol. He doubted the men would have another go, but there was no harm in being ready. He leaned on Drake and limped alongside him.

They were met at the Hall gates by Lord Oldfield, Caleb Witt, Mudge and Potter, all armed with guns and followed by a posse of stable boys and servants equipped with sticks and pitchforks. His Lordship's dogs streaked towards them, barking wildly.

Lord Oldfield called them off. "Back, Captain, Trusty... Foster! We heard a shot. What happened? Are you hurt?"

"No, My Lord. A few cuts and bruises, that's all. Drake came up before they'd time to do any real damage. There were four men, two Drake recognised as Higgs and Thomas."

Lord Oldfield looked at Witt, who said, "I know them. I'll be after them now, if it please you."

"Do that. Call on Ayres on the way. Better have the constable with you, useless though the fellow is. Bring them back here and lock them in one of the cellars. I'll take their statements tomorrow before sending them over to Shepton Mallet. I'll allow no bail."

Witt nodded, jerked his head at Potter, and with the underkeeper and half a dozen of the toughest-looking stable boys and gardeners, the hue-and-cry set off.

Dan moved off after them.

"Where do you think you're going?" Lord Oldfield said. "You can hardly stand. You'd better come inside. You too, Drake," he added, though with less warmth. "You're owed a reward for this."

"I don't want no reward, thanking you, My Lord," Drake answered. "And I'd best be off. The missus has the care of my mother all day. She doesn't like being left with her all the evening too. So you'll excuse me, My Lord."

"I'll need to take depositions from you and Foster tomorrow

to send to the court with the prisoners' statements. Can you attend in the morning at nine, Drake?"

"Yes, My Lord."

"Do you want some men to go back with you?" Dan asked the field officer.

"No."

Dan had not expected any other answer. They shook hands. Drake tipped his hat, turned, and walked back into the dark lane. Lord Oldfield took Dan's arm and steered him towards the house. Dan turned his head, hiding a wry smile: he had never expected to find himself arm in arm with a lord.

Lady Helen had come out to the doorway to enjoy the spectacle. Lord Oldfield said a few reassuring words to his betrothed, who did not seem to need them, and sent her back to his mother in the drawing room. They went down to his den. Garvey was bending over a large map spread over the clutter on the desk. It showed the Oldfield estate, Barcombe Heath, and the neighbouring villages. Garvey was making pencil marks on it.

"Is everything in order?" the lawyer asked.

"Some ruffians set upon Foster."

"Yes, you look as if you have been in a scuffle," said Garvey, looking Dan up and down with distaste.

Dan's clothes were filthy, and there was dried blood and dirt on his face and hands.

"Perhaps I should go and clean myself up."

"Have some brandy first," Lord Oldfield said. "You look as if you need it. Sit down. Do the honours, Garvey."

The lawyer put down his pencil and went to the side table with its bottles and glasses. He handed Dan his brandy with no very good grace and refilled two wine glasses for himself and His Lordship. Dan took a sip just to be polite and put the stuff aside.

"There's one good thing about all this," Lord Oldfield said. "It'll get rid of another batch of troublemakers, and that will smooth my way considerably."

Garvey gave a discreet cough. Dan had heard that tickle in Garvey's throat before, on the night he had first met Lord Oldfield. His Lordship had spoken of removing troublemakers then. They had been looking at maps that time, too.

"Smooth your way for what?" Dan asked.

Garvey coughed again.

"Stop humming and hawing," His Lordship snapped. "The notices are going up tomorrow, so it's not going to be a secret much longer...I'm going to enclose Barcombe Heath." He waved his hand over the map. "By rationalising my estate and those of the neighbouring farms, we'll all make substantial savings in improved roads and reduced tithes, as well as benefit from increased crop yields."

"We?"

"I have the agreement of all the neighbouring landowners. We've been negotiating with them for months. There's still a long-winded legal process to go through: notices and hearings, and the Bill to get through Parliament. Then we have to appoint commissioners to oversee the process. Garvey, of course, and two other men. Tedious stuff."

"You didn't do that for the wood."

"I didn't need to. The woodland belongs to the manor outright. The common land is different. Enclosing the wood first was Garvey's idea."

"With the aim of drawing out the protesters before we present the Bill for the heath," Garvey said. Now the stratagem was in the open he did not want to miss taking the credit for his part in it.

"Very clever," Dan said. "When does this enclosure take place?"

"It will be several months yet," Garvey answered.

Dan remembered what Singleton had said to him a couple of days before Drift Day: *Don't think we could stomach Lord Oldfield interfering in the heath after what he's done in the forest*. The announcement could not be more ill-timed.

"Then I suggest that you wait before putting up your

notices. The village is unsettled. It isn't wise to stir up any more strong feeling."

"You think Lord Oldfield should change his plans because you have been in a brawl?" Garvey said.

"Only delay them for a few days, until things have calmed down."

"I'll not wait on their moods," Lord Oldfield declared. "There's been enough delay. This estate needs bringing up to date."

"Indeed," said Garvey, "you cannot seriously think His Lordship's plans should depend on the whims of a few clodhoppers?"

Dan shook his head and immediately regretted it. "I think it best to avoid trouble."

But there was no arguing with them, so he made his excuses and left. They were poring over the map before he reached the door.

In the morning, Dan snatched a quick breakfast in the kitchen, which was like eating in the middle of a whirlwind. His Lordship had company that afternoon, and the cook and her staff were busy. He was limping across the hall – his knee had swollen in the night – when the library door opened and Lord Oldfield emerged with Garvey and Mr Poole. The rector had a roll of papers under his arm.

"So you'll put up the notices immediately?" His Lordship asked.

Poole nodded. "Of course, My Lord. And on the question of the provisions for the poor of the parish, I am at your disposal whenever you are ready to discuss it further."

"Oh, yes, of course. I'll be in touch, Mr Poole."

"Good day, My Lord."

It was a wonder Poole's forehead did not sweep the ground when he bowed. He hauled himself up and stalked to the front door. Ackland showed him out with flattering ceremony.

"Do we really have to bother with all that, Garvey?" His

Lordship said as soon as Poole had gone. "I don't see why I should give the ungrateful beggars a damned thing."

"It is for the sake of appearance only," Garvey answered. "Let it seem that you are eager to make provision for the poor when you enclose the common land and you will make friends, or at least avoid making enemies, of meddling philanthropists and politicians."

"So I have to compensate the rabble for helping themselves to my wood and game?"

"You will be in control of the dispensations. Those who prove themselves undeserving will have no claim on your beneficence."

Which was a long-winded way of saying that anyone who did not toe the line could shiver and starve. Dan wondered how long men like Girtin and Tom Taylor would survive in Barcombe after His Lordship's 'improvements'.

"If you say so...Ah, Foster, come along. Drake should be here any moment. Show him into my office when he arrives, Ackland."

Garvey gathered up his papers and they trooped downstairs. Garvey sat at one end of the desk with pens at the ready. He was going to act as clerk for the justice and take down the depositions.

"You seem to be in pain, Foster. I'll send for Dr Russell."

"Please don't trouble yourself. A bit of ice will do the trick, if I could have some later."

Lord Oldfield said there was no need to wait, rang the bell, and ordered Ackland to bring some ice. A chunk covered in a towel appeared a few moments later, and Dan sat down and wrapped it around his knee. His Lordship and he chatted about the relative merits of cold and heat for the treatment of sprains and bruises, and were debating the use of smelling salts as revivers during a fight when Drake arrived. He was a few minutes into his account of the attack when there was another knock on the door. Ackland ushered in Caleb Witt.

A downhearted Witt reported that he and his men had

failed to arrest Higgs and Thomas. They had waited all night outside their homes, but the pair had not come back. Nor, they discovered, had the labourer Creswick and Jem Cox. Two angry wives were on the warpath looking for them.

"Can't say I'm surprised they've gone," Dan said. "I'll get their descriptions to Bow Street and into the *Hue and Cry* journal. It would also help if you could write to your fellow justices in the county," he suggested to His Lordship.

"Of course. I'll offer a reward."

"That will help even more."

Garvey sniffed. "There's not much chance of catching them now."

"You'd be surprised. Men like this have a habit of turning up again. Chances are they don't have much money, they've no spare clothes, no food, no transport, and no skill at dodging the law. I can't promise we'll catch them, but I wouldn't say we never will either."

"I'm very sorry, My Lord," Witt said glumly.

"Can't be helped now," Lord Oldfield answered. "You may go."

"Well," said Garvey when the keeper had clumped off, "we'd better finish these depositions. You were saying that the man you called Higgs threatened to kill you."

Drake nodded. "The others weren't up for it and ran. Higgs didn't hang around after that. Foster grabbed his pistol and fired after him, but he got away."

Garvey read the statement back and Drake added his signature to it. Dan gave his statement and signed it. When Drake had gone, Lord Oldfield stood up and stretched. "I'm going for a ride."

The lawyer took his work upstairs to the library.

As for Dan, there was a woman he had to see.

Chapter Twenty-One

Thanks to the ice pack, Dan was able to walk without too much discomfort. He did not expect trouble in broad daylight, but he kept his pistol handy. The Fox and Badger and the forge were still shut up. He walked past them and on along the Bath Road until he came to Dr Russell's house. The gate stood open and the stable was empty: the doctor was out on his rounds. Dan continued along the lane, past the house belonging to the Wests, the theatrical couple. He turned into the gateway of the end house, which was overshadowed by the yew tree after which it was named.

A maid let him in and left him in the hall. A moment later she returned and took him into a drawing room overlooking a well-kept garden. It gave on to a view of meadows and woodland with glimpses down to the twists and turns of the Stony River. Mrs Hale snored softly in an armchair by the fire, an ugly old cat purring wheezily on her lap. Her niece sat at a table near the window, working over a pile of books.

She rose to meet him. "If I had known I had a visitor coming, I would have put them away. Barcombe does not think Latin a suitable study for women. My brother was more enlightened."

Dan could not see what use it was to a young lady like Miss Ruscombe to pucker her brows over Latin. He knew there were females who enjoyed such things, but they were usually aged crones in dowdy dresses.

"You're Lord Oldfield's Runner," she said, inviting him to sit on a sofa. She took the other armchair and folded her ink-stained hands in her lap.

Dan glanced at her aunt.

"Aunt Joanna won't wake up yet. What business can you possibly have with me, Mr Foster?"

"You know that I'm in Barcombe to investigate Josh Castle's murder?"

"Yes. I do not see how I can help."

"Don't you?"

She tapped her foot and stared out of the window.

"You put flowers on his grave yesterday."

Her foot stopped moving. "You are mistaken."

"I saw you. Afterwards I spoke to Mrs Poole. She said she put the flowers there, but I know she was lying. She was protecting you. Why, I ask myself, does a young lady like Miss Ruscombe need protecting?"

The old lady snorted, mumbled into her moustache, and lapsed back into a deep slumber. Louisa seemed to lose herself in contemplation of her aunt's red, wrinkled face. It was a puzzling complexion to be sure, more suited to an outdoor life than a drawing-room existence.

"Do you want to wake her?"

"No," Louisa said quickly.

"Then will you answer my question?"

"There is nothing to answer."

"Do you want me to find Mr Castle's murderer?"

"Of course I do. That is – I – the murder of any man is a terrible crime."

"And the loss of a man you cared about is a very terrible thing."

"I did not..."

But she could not tell that lie. She gazed down at her entwined fingers.

"If you want me to catch his killer, you must talk to me."

There was a long silence. "Mr Castle," she managed after a moment, "Mr Castle was...he and I..." She raised her head defiantly. "We were going to be married."

Dan was not shocked, or even very surprised. "And you kept

the engagement secret. You knew that it would seem improper to many people given the difference in your stations."

"As if I should care for that!"

"Your family might care."

"My mother was a farmer's daughter. My father met her while he was on a walking holiday when he was at Oxford University. Aunt Joanna is her sister."

Dan wondered how far the sisters had resembled one another. Louisa must have guessed his thoughts, for she said, "My father used to say Mother fitted into her family like a princess stolen by the gypsies. She died when I was young, but I remember her well. She was a gentlewoman by nature if not by birth, with a natural delicacy and refinement."

So that was how this genteel young woman came to have an aunt who looked like a dairy maid. He admired Miss Ruscombe for defending her family, but he still had questions to ask.

"And Mr Castle was a gentleman?"

"He was. He had as much right to marry me as Lord Oldfield himself."

"But Mr Castle's descent was not..." he hesitated.

She supplied the word. "Legitimate? But it was. Josh's grandparents were married in London before they went to Oldfield Hall."

"An invalid marriage carried out by an excommunicated clergyman called Alexander Keith of the Fleet Prison."

"That was what the Oldfields wanted people to think. Josh grew up thinking it, and would never have thought of questioning it until we made our plans. It made no difference to me, but Josh went over and over it in his mind and started to put together things he'd heard as a child. He was only a boy when his grandmother died, but he remembered they sent for a priest for her. Josh had never seen a priest before. It was a condition of the allowance the Oldfields had given her that her son should be brought up in the Church of England, and she was scrupulous about it. When the priest came out of his grandmother's room, he said she wanted to talk to Josh's father. He took Josh in with him and sat the boy on his lap."

Dan remembered Elena's story as he had learned it from Mrs Singleton and Lord Oldfield. Francis Oldfield, defying his father, ran away and joined the army. He fought in America, where he met Elena Castillo, the daughter of Spanish parents. There had been a dispute with Spain in the colonies, a war that started when a sea captain had his ear cut off by Spanish coast guards. The only part of the story Dan had been interested in as a schoolboy was that the captain brought back his ear and displayed it whenever he told his tale.

Francis brought Elena back to England and they married – or so they thought – in London. They travelled on to Oldfield Hall, where the young man died of a fever, leaving his wife pregnant with John Castle, Josh's father.

These were the facts so far as Dan knew them. But now, as he listened to Louisa tell the story, the scenes she recounted, informed by her love for Josh and her interest in the outcome, rose vividly to Dan's mind...

A sweet smell hung about the priest's black robes. He was a tall, gaunt man. Josh thought he looked stern, and wondered how Grandmother found any comfort in him. The man made a gesture with his hand and rustled out of the room, leaving him and Father alone with Grandmother. At first Josh fidgeted on his father's lap. There was a fire in the hearth and the sickroom was brightly lit with real wax candles in honour of the priest's visit. Gradually the heat made Josh drowsy and he settled into his father's arms.

Grandmother was propped into a half-sitting position on a pile of cushions. Her hair, which still had some black left in its thin grey strands, was neatly tucked away under a nightcap. She breathed shallowly, and there were long gaps between one breath and the next when her chest did not lift at all. Her face was sunken and lined, her eyes pink-rimmed, milky, bulging slightly as she struggled to focus on her son's face. She clutched feebly at his fingers.

"Johnny, Johnny, I have done you wrong!" Her voice was faded and indistinct. It was as if she was seeping away, dwindling to nothing.

"Hush, Mother," he said. "You'll be all right in a bit."

"It all goes back to the day I was married. Ever since I first set foot in a Protestant church all has gone ill with me. *Dios mío, ten misericordia de mí!*" *God, have mercy.* "I told myself there was no harm, because the church was dedicated to St George and he was a soldier, like your father."

Josh gasped as his father's grip on his shoulder tightened. He looked up into his father's face, which suddenly had a clenched look to it. "What are you saying?" he said through tight lips. "What church?"

"I don't know. We walked in Hyde Park afterwards." She raised her head from her pillow, her watery eyes bright. "It was so pretty, with all the carriages and I in my new dress, and Francis so handsome! I was carrying the flowers he bought me."

"But the church, Mother. The church you married in. Which was it?"

Her head sank back, and for what seemed a long time her chest did not move. Then she shuddered and sucked in a breath. "*Hijo mío, perdóname,*" she whispered. *Forgive me, my son.*

Grandmother had not spoken again, though Father sat there for hours, leaving her side only to carry Josh to bed. When Josh woke the next day he was told she had died in the night. Mrs Jackson from the village had already been to wash her and lay her out. His father took Josh in to kiss her. She lay on her back beneath a clean sheet, her hands folded across her chest. She wore the white shroud she had made many years ago. Josh had not liked the feel of the cold, dead skin beneath his lips, nor the empty look of her face.

The day after the funeral, Father said that he was going to the Hall to see Lord Oldfield, the present Lord Adam's father, who had inherited the estate from his father, Francis's brother.

He whistled as he put on his best hat and jacket. When he was ready, he sat down and pulled Josh to his side. He looked around the room as if he did not recognise the old sideboard and the scrubbed table, the smoke-blackened rafters, the wooden chairs.

"Think of something special you'd like," he said.

Josh did not have to think very hard. "A bow and some arrows."

Father laughed and ruffled his hair. "They will be yours."

He put the boy aside and left the cottage. Josh went out to roam the heath, as he usually did when he got the chance. When he got back, Father was home. He was not smiling or laughing any more. He sat by the cold hearth, his face grim and dark. Josh asked what was for tea, and he snapped, "Get yourself some bread and cheese." In the morning when he went out to work, he slammed the door. He did not come home till after dark, when the first and only thing he said to Josh was "Get to bed." There was little left in the house to eat, but that did not seem to bother him: he who had always come in and fallen on his supper with the hunger of a man who had spent hours at hard, outdoor work.

So it went on for several weeks, his father brooding and bad-tempered, the house more and more neglected. Josh lived on bread and water, did not wash, ran wild about the village. Then one day he went home to a fire in the hearth, the floor swept, and the beds made, soup on the table, and a cold scrubbing in a tub in the scullery.

Everything went back to normal, except that there was no Grandmother any more. Father and son grew close. Josh absorbed all his father could teach him as he went about his work in Barcombe Wood and the surrounding estate. He did not mind that the other village boys regarded him warily as the son of the gamekeeper. He had a friend in Adam Oldfield, whom Lord Oldfield sent to learn to hunt, shoot and fish. Sometimes he caught Father looking at them with a strange, angry look in his eye. When he met Josh's gaze he would shake his head and shrug, as if casting off some uncomfortable thought.

Josh never got his bow and arrows.

"Then it wasn't a Fleet wedding," said Dan when Louisa had finished speaking.

"No, it was a church ceremony."

"So John Castle learned that his mother was married in church, but he didn't declare himself legitimate. Presumably that was because he couldn't. There was still something about the wedding that wasn't right."

"That's how it seemed to Josh and I, but it was all so mysterious. How could Mr Castle be illegitimate if there was a church wedding? And what did Alexander Keith have to do with it if he was a Fleet parson? Josh decided to look for the church and try to find out the truth about his grandmother's marriage."

"Did he, now? Well, that's not an impossible undertaking. St George's Church in Hanover Square is close to the Park, and St George's Chapel of Ease is practically on Hyde Park Corner."

"What a pity you were not here to tell us that a few months ago! It took Josh a little longer to make the discovery, and of course he could only get up to London when the Oldfields were away. Eventually he found St George's parish church in Hanover Square, looked at the register, and found nothing. He was about to leave when the churchwarden, who was used to people trying to prove their ancestors were properly married, said didn't he want to look at the registers for St George's Chapel? Josh had no idea there was a St George's Chapel, or that its records were kept in Hanover Square. In them he found a note of the marriage of Francis Oldfield and Elena Castillo on 17 June 1742, in a ceremony carried out by Dr Alexander Keith."

"So all Josh Castle succeeded in doing was proving the Oldfields right. Keith was not qualified to perform weddings."

"That's what Josh thought. The churchwarden saw how

upset he was and said he was sorry he hadn't found what he was looking for. Josh said he had, but it had Alexander Keith's name against it. The churchwarden said yes, Dr Keith had been the incumbent of St George's Chapel when it had been a popular place for run-away marriages among the fashionable. 'In fact,' the man said, 'it's a history we're very proud of, for our church played a large part in the doctor's downfall.' Josh asked him to explain, and the churchwarden told him that the then rector at Hanover Square had taken exception to Dr Keith's practice and insisted that all marriages in the parish should take place in the parish church. He ordered Dr Keith to stop performing marriages in St George's Chapel. The doctor refused to give up his profitable business, so the rector took him to the Ecclesiastical Court. Keith was excommunicated in October 1742. Six months later he was sent to prison, from where he continued to run a marriage business, employing his own curates in a private chapel he established within yards of St George's Chapel."

"That's a clever bit of work! Josh found out that Francis and Elena were married four months before Dr Keith was excommunicated, and nearly a year before he went to prison."

"Yes. The marriage was valid."

"But if the proof was there all the time, why did Mrs Castle consent to be passed off as the mother of a child born on the wrong side of the blanket?"

"She was a young girl, alone in a foreign country and ignorant of the law. The Oldfields told her the marriage was illegal, and she had no wedding certificate to prove it otherwise. I do not know if she was ever given one, or if Francis Oldfield had it in his possession when he died and his father destroyed it. I would not put it past him – all I have heard of him suggests he was a ruthless man. He did not want the blood of a foreign Papist tainting his family. But it was more than that. Her family refused to take her back when she was widowed, because in their eyes and the eyes of the Catholic church she was an unmarried mother. Dr Keith could have been the Archbishop of Canterbury and it would have made no difference: a Protestant marriage was as good as no marriage to them. Her upbringing convinced her that they were right."

"What did Josh do? Did he tell Lord Adam?"

"I persuaded him to let me consult our family solicitor first, Mr Langhorne of Bath. Unfortunately, Mr Langhorne was not optimistic about our chances of proving the marriage, in spite of the register entry. He said that while it was true many of Dr Keith's weddings had gone unchallenged, in a case where so much property was at stake he did not doubt that a clever lawyer could easily find reasons to challenge it. These old registers are notorious for falsification and forgery. It would also be difficult to prove that all the legal requirements had been complied with, such as the reading of the banns. What was more, Elena was a minor and she did not have parental consent. And while it was true that the ceremony was carried out before Dr Keith's excommunication, all this, taken with what was known of his character, could mean that an ecclesiastical court could easily refuse to uphold a marriage performed by a clergyman of such dubious qualifications."

Garvey was an extremely clever lawyer. Dan thought Mr Langhorne had been wise to advise caution.

"What did you do?"

"I told Josh what Mr Langhorne had said. We quarrelled. I said that since I did not care about such considerations I preferred to drop the whole thing rather than become involved in an undignified and costly dispute. Josh said that Lord Oldfield was as ignorant of the truth of it as we were; like us, he had only believed what his elders told him. Once he knew the truth he would not hesitate to put matters right. I did not share Josh's faith in His Lordship."

"But he spoke to Lord Oldfield?"

"No. I made him promise to think it over for a few more days before he did anything. That was the last time I saw him. Two days later he was dead."

Louisa had trusted Castle's promise, but Dan did not. He

may have spoken to Lord Oldfield in spite of it.

Aunt Joanna stirred and woke. "What are you young people talking about?"

"Nothing, Auntie," Louisa said. "Shall I ring for tea?"

Mrs Hale gave Dan a roguish look. "Will you stay for a cup, Mister…"

"Foster, ma'am," he said. "No, thank you."

The aunt had jumped to romantic conclusions, and Dan imagined she was not one to keep her suspicions to herself. He pitied Louisa having to put up with such teasing when she was heartsore, but could think of nothing more sympathetic to say to her than, "Thank you, Miss Ruscombe. You have been most helpful."

He was heartsore himself. There may not have been much to like about Lord Oldfield, but Dan had given His Lordship credit for much less snobbery than he had met in men of lesser rank. That was when Dan believed Lord Oldfield's gamekeeper had been one of his closest friends. Now it was impossible not to conclude that he had murdered that friend.

If Lord Oldfield had been anyone else, Dan would have confronted him at once, and none too gently, but he could not make accusations against a lord until he was sure of the facts. He needed proof.

Chapter Twenty-Two

Reverend Poole had been busy, and Lord Oldfield's notice of enclosure was already pinned to the church door. Drake stood in the porch reading it aloud to the men clustered about him, among them Sukie Tolley's father, grimacing stupidly, and three or four smocked labourers Dan recognised from the Fox and Badger. They listened with bent heads, holding their hats in their hands out of respect for the place.

Men can quickly lose respect for the most hallowed ground if provoked enough, and if they caught sight of Dan it might be sufficient. He decided to retrace his steps before they saw him and go a long way round to Oldfield Hall. Before he moved, however, Drake finished reading and, turning away from the door, caught sight of him. The others followed the field officer's gaze. Silence fell, broken only by Girtin, who sat on a gravestone rocking back and forth, moaning. Cursing the officious rector, Dan put his hand in his pocket for his flintlock.

"Stay back, lads," Drake said, pushing his way through.

The men muttered, one or two clenched their fists, and someone spat, but they did as Drake said. They were still too stunned to think of doing anything else.

Drake took Dan's arm and drew him out of earshot. "Did you know anything about this?"

"Not until last night. I asked Lord Oldfield to wait until the fuss about the arrests had died down, but he wouldn't."

"No, I don't suppose he would. It's clear he's been planning it for months. That's why he's been buying up properties like Cottom's, not renewing farm tenancies, and clearing the parish of squatters. If the properties are empty, no one's exercising the common rights that go with them. That makes it easier to do away with them for good when the Parliament men step in."

"Is it very bad for Barcombe?"

"I should say so. First the wood, now this."

"He said he was going to make provision for the poor." Dan did not say how grudging that intention was. He wanted to offer some comfort.

Drake was no fool. "The workhouse and poor rate? They're only slow ways to starve a man who's never had need to go seeking charity before. It's not just the ones who are poor now, but the new poor it will make: the smallholders who won't have anywhere to graze their one cow or pig, and the farmers who've always relied on being able to pasture their herds on the heath."

"But won't they get a share of the enclosed land?"

"The parcels they'll be entitled to will be so small they won't be worth the expense of fencing them. They'll sell them to Lord Oldfield and the other big men. It'll be the best they can do. It's the end of the Barcombe we were born to."

"What about you?"

"They won't need a field officer."

Dan could think of nothing to say to this.

"His Lordship is storing up a deal of trouble," Drake said after a moment. "You know that, don't you? They're angry enough as it is. Bloodie Bones will walk."

"There must be no more Bloodie Bones. You must tell them, Drake."

"I don't know if they'll listen to me. And I don't think I'd blame them."

"If they break the law, they'll suffer for it."

"Aren't they going to suffer anyway on account of that law? And whose law is it? The old laws, the field laws, are done for. You can keep your law."

"It's not my law. I have nothing to do with fields and woods. I came to Barcombe to catch a killer and I have to do it, without fear or favour. The same goes for them. If they make trouble while I'm here, I can't let it go. You have to stop them."

"And what could I do to stop trouble, if it comes? No, I tell you what. It's already here."

Drake turned on his heels and went back to the church. The others closed around him, asking questions, trying to understand the blow that smote them, bewildered, anguished. Seeing their pain, Dan understood that it was not just about their livelihoods, though that was vital enough. It was love of the land they had roamed for generations. Of the old trees whose shade they had grown up in, shortly to be cut down. Of the native copses to be cleared and replaced with straight-rowed plantations of foreign species. Of ancient paths unknown to outsiders, their course dictated by ditch and stream, to be closed, and the people driven along straight roads that had no sympathy with the land.

Dan did not like it. He liked even less the feeling that he had been tricked into helping to bring it about.

The kitchen was hot and hectic. Everyone was busy, which was good for Dan's purposes. He slipped into Lord Oldfield's den, closed the door, took the Bloodie Bones notes out of his pocketbook, and selected the *Tirant* note he had taken from the scarecrow left near Castle's body. It was on expensive paper, the kind a lord would use, and he would not buy a sheet at a time either. There had to be more to match it.

If Lord Oldfield was a cold-blooded killer, he was a careless one. Estate papers lay scattered on the desk, along with a dismantled gun, a bottle of cleaning fluid, and a greasy broken girth. The desk drawers were not locked, but did not contain anything of any interest: magistracy forms, broken and blunted pens and penknives, cartridge cases, seals – all the odd little things he had thrown in anyhow. There were a few sheets of letter paper with the Oldfield coat of arms embossed on them, grimy and crumpled and only fit for lining pie dishes. There was nothing matching the Bloodie Bones note.

Dan was careful to leave everything as he'd found it: some

untidy people have a knack of knowing exactly where they have put things. He went upstairs. The sound of voices and the plink-plink of a harpsichord came from the large drawing room. He had never been in there, but had seen it through the windows. It was a spacious room opening on to the rear lawn, overlooking the lake and temple. It was furnished with groupings of chairs, card tables, musical instruments, and scatterings of books and magazines.

He went into the small drawing room. He could not imagine His Lordship spending much time at the tiny desk with its thin legs and fancy green leather top. It was a piece designed for a lady to write her notes at, not a man to do business. There were a few sheets of letter paper and an inkstand on top of it, and in the only shallow drawer a few more bits of paper, pens, and sealing wax. He was closing it when Lord Oldfield came in.

"There you are, Foster! What are you doing?"

"Looking for a piece of paper, My Lord."

"Don't you fellows carry memorandum books?"

"I might have one upstairs."

"Never mind that now." He reached into his pocket and handed Dan a silver note case and pencil attached by a slender chain. "Keep it. I've plenty more. Come along. My guests want to meet you."

"Meet me? Why?"

"They have never met a Bow Street Runner."

"But I do not – "

"I said come along, Foster."

The afternoon was drawing on, and the drawing room was already brightly lit. The party was gathered around the marble fireplace playing some sort of writing game. They had pencils and paper in their hands, and a large vase stood on a low table between them. Scattered around this were folded sheets on which lines had been scribbled in a number of hands.

Lady Helen put her hand in front of her mouth and whispered loudly to the long-faced girl sitting next to her,

"I wonder what verse we could make of *runner – mystery – Newgate – hue-and-cry – magistrate – prisoner.*"

The girl tittered, probably on principle, but when the words had sunk in, she said doubtfully, "But they aren't very good rhymes."

Her voice was so high Dan had to look again to be sure it came from a human throat. Dr Russell, who sat on her other side, gave her an admiring look, though neither her beauty nor her brains warranted it. A doctor has to be polite to build up his practice. Or was he aiming higher – at a good marriage perhaps?

Garvey murmured, "Perhaps it should end with a couplet: *clueless – fruitless.*"

Lady Helen laughed.

"But that doesn't rhyme properly either," the girl screeched.

Dan let Garvey and Lady Helen have their fun. They had a shock coming to them soon enough. Dan hoped for Lord Oldfield's sake that his lawyer was as good at criminal as he was at civil law.

A fat man in a tight silk jacket put a glass to his eye and looked Dan up and down. He was squeezed into a wooden armchair next to his stout wife, who shared a sofa with Garvey. She fluttered a handkerchief in front of her bosom and said, "Are you sure he doesn't have gaol fever?"

"I can assure you that he does not, Mrs West," Dr Russell said. "It is not Mr Foster who has to spend time in prison but the villains he apprehends. Isn't that true, Foster?"

"It is," Dan answered, bowing to the lady.

Mr West, meanwhile, had finished examining him. "I think I could do him!" he cried. He leapt to his feet, put up his podgy fists, and pranced about on the hearth rug.

"My husband has been compared to David Garrick for his ability to portray king and commoner with equal veracity," his wife complaisantly announced, while the rest 'bravo'd' and applauded.

The little man put down his mitts. "You have no doubt

heard of me, Mr Foster. Nathaniel West. I always take people from the life, it is my particular method. My Hamlet is still spoken of. I am no longer on the boards," he added. "Private performance only."

The long-faced girl piped, "Oldfield says you have single-handedly captured a desperate gang."

"Not single-handed, ma'am. I had the help of a number of officers sent from London for the purpose."

She lapsed into disappointed silence and sucked her bottom lip.

A middle-aged woman with bulging eyes said, "It is interesting that the protesters used a mythical figure to justify their violent campaign. The Bloodie Bones legend is an ancient and potent one. There are many similar figures associated with rebellion and protest: Jack Straw, Robin Hood, the Earl of the Plough. Some of them are based on historical figures like Wat Tyler, and – "

Her lecture was interrupted by a young, goggle-eyed man Dan took to be her son. "Protest! Seems more like a case of simple thieving to me."

"As it was," Lady Helen said. "Thieving and vandalism. You can hardly believe what Lord Oldfield has had to endure."

"Such depredations are only too inevitable when the ignorant babble about the rights of the poor," Mr West said. "If they are entitled to anything – though it is unlikely – why do they not take the wise course and go to law?"

"I should think it very unlikely that they can afford it," Dr Russell remarked.

"It is just as well," said Garvey. "They'd only be wasting their money if they could."

"Of course they would. Lord Oldfield has every right to do as he wishes with his property," Lady Helen declared.

The lady with the frog-eyes launched into an explanation of manorial rights, which was again interrupted by her son. "Let us play another round. Whose turn is it to provide the rhyme scheme?"

"I believe Lady Helen has already suggested one," Garvey said.

Attentive Dr Russell handed his companion her paper and pencil, Lady Helen gathered up the used sheets on the table and pushed them to one side, and the learned lady assumed a learned pose. Mrs West dithered about for her notebook.

"Here," said Lady Helen, thrusting one of the used sheets at her, "the other side is clean."

"Oh – yes – of course – I don't know where mine could have got to."

"Shall we begin?" Lady Helen said.

Mrs West unfolded the sheet and spread it out on her lap. Dan was standing behind the sofa next to Lord Oldfield and saw it clearly. It was cream with a deckled edge – an exact match to the paper used for the *Tirant* message.

Before he could think of a way of getting it off Mrs West, the door opened and Ackland walked in at something quicker than his customary stately pace.

"May I have a word outside, My Lord?" he whispered. "And perhaps Mr Foster might accompany us?"

Lord Oldfield looked surprised, but only said, "Of course. If you will excuse us."

Garvey was already dropping his verse into the vase, and the others were too busy scribbling to notice.

Drake stood in the hall, mopping his face with a hand-kerchief. With a perfunctory nod at Lord Oldfield, he said, "There's a mob building up in the village, and they'll be heading this way soon. May already be halfway here for all I know."

"A mob?" Lord Oldfield repeated. "What do you mean?"

Drake dismissed the confused Lord with a withering glance and turned to Dan. "I warned you, Foster. There's no containing them. You had best make plans to defend yourself."

"Hell and damnation…How many?" Dan demanded.

"A score, but there's more joining every minute, with a few come in from Stonyton to lend support."

"Are they armed?"

"Yes, with sticks, scythes, knives. I didn't see any guns."

"But who are they?" Lord Oldfield again.

"I don't know. They're masked."

Drake probably did know, but he would not betray his neighbours by name, and Dan would not ask him to. He said, "Ackland, summon the male servants to the servants' hall. Send to the home farm for Mudge, and send someone to find Caleb Witt and Potter. Get word to Sutter in the stables that he and his lads will have to protect the yard and the rear access to the house. And tell the housekeeper and any women you can trust to do the job properly to lock all the doors and shutter the windows."

The butler, who was no fool in a crisis, did not wait for Lord Oldfield to approve the orders. He hurried off.

"Lord Oldfield, how many guns do you have in the house?"

His Lordship had stopped asking questions and was beginning to grasp the situation. "A dozen or so in the gun room."

"Good. We'll distribute them to anyone who can use them. We need to get the ladies upstairs. Do you think Lady Helen can do that?"

"Of course. I'll have them join Mother in her sitting room."

"Drake," Dan continued, "you'd better go before they know you're here."

He shook his head. "I'll stand with you. Don't matter the wrong, I'll break no law."

"Then follow Ackland to the servants' hall. Find out what weapons they can gather. I'll be down soon. And now, My Lord, we'd better tell your guests."

Dr Russell came out of the drawing room and carefully shut the door behind him.

"I came to see what's wrong," he said in a low voice.

"We've a riot on our hands," Dan said.

"I can shoot. Give me a gun."

"Fine…Let's get the women out of the way."

The ladies in the drawing room had already been made uneasy by the sound of shutters and doors slamming, the running footsteps, the whispering in the hall. Mr West tried to calm his wife, who had her handkerchief to her eyes. Dr Russell's lady-love sat with her hands crammed over her mouth, her eyes wide. The scholarly woman was pale. Lady Helen, however, was nonchalantly tidying away the game, while Garvey calmly sipped his sherry.

"I must ask the ladies to join Lady Oldfield upstairs," Lord Oldfield announced. "Lady Helen will take you. Nothing to worry about. There's a gang of low fellows on their way here and I don't want you exposed to any unpleasantness while we see them off."

Mrs West screamed at the darkening windows as if she could already see a line of murderous faces pressed against the glass. The doctor produced a phial of smelling salts and wafted it under her nose.

Lady Helen rose. "I don't wish to hear any unpleasantness, do you, Lady Felicity? Dear Mrs West, do come with us and tell us some more about Mr West's Hamlet. And Mrs Cotterell, perhaps you would read us another of your poems?"

Dan had thought Lady Helen bold, but he had not imagined she would see the thing through in such style. Mrs Cotterell, thrilled by her hostess's sudden interest in her blue-stocking jottings, followed without a glance at her son, who was shortly to be exposed to danger. Mr West supported his wife out of the room, and Dr Russell gave Lady Felicity his arm to the foot of the stairs. The doctor rejoined the rest of them in the hall, but West went up with the women, gabbling something about not being able to leave his frightened spouse.

"Where do you want us, Oldfield?" Garvey asked.

"Get the guns," Dan said. "I'll go and organise the servants. Join me back here."

The gentlemen clattered off after His Lordship to the gun room. Dan hurried through the door to the kitchen. He waited at the top of the stairs, and when the others were out of sight slipped back to the drawing room.

The paper was not on or under Mrs West's chair, nor in the vase. He rifled through the sheets Lady Helen had left neatly stacked on the table. It was not there either.

If he had been able to see it, then so had Lord Oldfield. Dan had to award him the belt for coolness: he had shown not so much as a twitch or a flicker. Somehow he had managed to remove it in the confusion, though Dan could have sworn he had had him in view the whole time. There was nothing he could do about it. The paper had been consumed in the fire by now.

Chapter Twenty-Three

Dan sent a boy down the drive to keep a lookout. By the time they had armed themselves with guns, knives, and whatever else would make do as a weapon, he was back with the breathless news that torches were visible in the lane.

"And they're making rough music," the boy added.

They did not need him to tell them. They could hear the din of the rattles, bells and horns.

Dan stationed men at the downstairs windows, concentrating the guns at the front. Ackland and the footmen were in the hall, and Cotterell, Garvey, Mudge and Potter in the dining room. Dan took the library with Drake, Dr Russell and Lord Oldfield. Caleb Witt was with them too. He had frightened the life out of one of the scullery maids when he had pounded on the back door a few moments earlier. He had seen the torches from the wood and run cross-country to reach the Hall.

Dan did not intend to let Lord Oldfield out of his sight. No man, murderer or no, should meet his death at the hands of a lawless mob, but Dan did not want His Lordship giving him the slip either. Though he must know Dan had seen the paper, nothing in his attitude suggested that he viewed him as a threat. Was he so confident that without it Dan could prove nothing against him? Which was, damnably, the case. But knowing the identity of the murderer was a good starting point.

They had had no time to close the gate, and it would not have held the mob back if they had. They passed through it, torches smoking over their heads. Their faces were blacked and hidden by scarves. Some were dressed in the mummers' costumes worn at the Fence Fair to remind the lord of the manor of their rights to Barcombe Wood. One man had antlers on his head; another was astride a hobby horse; one wore a skirt over his breeches.

As far as Dan could tell, their weapons were the tools of their trades: billhooks, cleavers, hammers, axes and mattocks, with a few cudgels, staffs and swingels. Above the racket was the marrow-chilling chant: "Bloodie Bones – Bloodie Bones!" True to the rough music tradition, they had an effigy with them: a skeleton jiggling at the end of a long pole.

Lord Oldfield cursed. "They've raided the mausoleum again."

"No," said Dr Russell. "The skeleton is wired."

"Then where did they get it?" His Lordship asked.

"From my house. My poor old housekeeper! They'll have frightened her half to death."

The skeleton had given Dan a turn when he'd seen it at Dr Russell's house. Seeing it prancing in the air above two score desperate men was much more unsettling.

They straggled to a halt and fell into a semi-circle around their leader. He was a tall man, all bone and muscle, with the carriage of someone aware of his physical strength. A build very similar to Singleton's.

"Oldfield!" he bellowed, and his voice was so like the blacksmith's that Dan exclaimed, "Singleton? How did he get here?"

"It's his brother, Silas," Witt said.

From Peasedown. Dan should have guessed. A brother out for vengeance.

"What should I do?" His Lordship asked.

"Wait here," Dan said.

He went to the hall, handed his gun to Ackland, and ordered him to open the door. When it was wide enough he squeezed through, and the butler locked it behind him. He walked towards the crowd, his hands held out to show he was unarmed. Hard eyes glinted from the muffled faces. Stars glittered above the twisting flames. Dan's breath smoked on the cold air.

"What do you want with Lord Oldfield?" he demanded.

"It's the Runner," someone cried. He felt their hatred surge towards him. They edged closer.

"What do you want with Lord Oldfield?" he repeated.

"To talk," said Silas Singleton. "If he's man enough."

"Why should he talk to men who come armed and masked to his home at night?"

"We mean him no harm. We want him to hear our petition."

"Petitions should not be delivered at the point of a sword."

Silas laughed. "None of us have swords, pig."

"If I tell him what you want, will you go home quietly?"

"We'll tell him to his face."

"He's listening now."

"We'll tell him and no one else."

Dan heard the door open behind him, then His Lordship's voice. "It's all right, Foster. I'll hear them."

"No!" Dan said, keeping his eyes on the crowd. "It won't do any good. Go back inside."

Lord Oldfield took no notice. Drake, Witt and Russell followed him out of the house, though he had not asked them to. Drake took advantage of the shadows to hand Dan his gun, and he pocketed it while all eyes were fixed on Lord Oldfield. He signalled Witt and Drake to keep close to His Lordship, nodded at Russell to take a wide left flank, while he himself moved out to the right. Between them and the guns at the windows, they would be able to produce a raking volley of shots if need be.

"What is your petition?" asked His Lordship.

The crowd shuffled and murmured. They had not expected it to be this easy.

Singleton silenced them with a chopping motion of his hand. "First, we demand the release of the men you have cast in prison to satisfy your bloody laws: Bob Singleton, Martin Travell, Jonathan Dunnage, Abe Wicklow, George Buller and Luke Warneford. Second, we demand that you give back the rights to Barcombe Wood. And third, we demand that you leave the heath open."

Dan willed His Lordship to answer carefully. After a moment, he did.

"Very well. I will consider your petition. Now, do as the law officer says and go home."

Oaths and protests filled the air. Silas gestured again, reducing the outcry to angry muttering.

"We want your answer now," he said.

Lord Oldfield's self-control snapped. "I am not going to give my answer now. Not while you and this rabble – "

Dan saw the first stone coming, grabbed Lord Oldfield's arm, and shoved him back towards the house, Witt and Drake guarding his back. The protesters rushed forward, the skeleton gibbering above them. The sound of breaking glass came from the library. A stone struck Witt on the shoulder. Others thudded against the door. It shot open, and Ackland pulled his master inside. Witt and Drake tumbled in after.

As Dan yelled at the doctor to go back, someone grabbed his arm. He spun round and smashed his left fist into a face, at the same time trying to reach for his gun. But there was another man coming at him from the other side, and he had to let his right hand swing too. There was more breaking glass and a shot rang out from one of the library windows. It came from Drake's station and passed over their heads. A sensible aim. If any of them had gone down, the rest would have torn Dan apart. The rioters faltered, Dan dived through the door, and Ackland slammed and bolted it. From upstairs came a scream, quickly stifled.

"Are you hurt, My Lord?" Russell asked.

"No...I'm going to read the Riot Act."

"There's no point," said the doctor. "We've no militia to enforce it."

"But we are armed," Dan said. "And we should give them due warning before we aim at them. I think His Lordship should read it. But not from here, from an upstairs window. Doctor, you and I will stand guard beside him. It doesn't look as if any of them have firearms, but if anyone does pull a gun, don't hesitate. Shoot them."

Russell nodded, and they ran up to one of the front bedrooms. Dan and the doctor opened the shutters.

"You are breaking the law by being here like this," Dan yelled at the upturned faces. "Don't make it any worse for yourselves. Go home now."

The only response was curses. He cocked his gun and held it so they could see it. The doctor did the same.

"Go on," he said to Lord Oldfield. "But stay back."

"I am about to read the Riot Act," His Lordship announced. "Once I've read the proclamation, you are required to leave within the hour. If you do not, we will take whatever measures are necessary to disperse you."

They took no notice of the warning. He took a scroll from his pocket and unrolled it, though he only glanced at it. The words were few and he knew them well. What magistrate didn't?

"I order silence," he cried.

"Come down here and shut us up!"

"Our sovereign Lord the King chargeth and commandeth all persons, being assembled, immediately to disperse themselves, and peaceably to depart –"

"Death to magistrates!"

" – to their habitations, or to their lawful business, upon the pains contained in the act – "

"Give us back our forest!"

" – made in the first year of King George, for preventing tumults and riotous assemblies. God save the King."

"God save King Bloodie Bones!"

Stones flew at them from every hand. Dan pushed Lord Oldfield out of the way as a flint gouged the polished wooden floor where he had been standing. All at once the bombardment stopped. Something else had caught the mob's attention and they were running back towards the gate. A cart careered down the lane, the horses sweating under the whip and shying at the sight and smell of the torches. Some of the men seized the harness, others gathered around the tailgate, while the driver and his mate clambered into the back of the vehicle and distributed the contents of a large crate. Wisps of straw fluttered in the air and the torchlight glinted on glass. One of the men lowered his brand and his neighbour thrust a bottle into it. A fuse flared. Bottle in hand, the man twisted round and took a running aim at the Hall. A streak of flame smashed through a dining room window, immediately followed by half a dozen more.

Ackland yelled at the footmen to get the fire buckets from the kitchen corridor. They clattered up and down stairs, dashed sand over the flames, flung the empty buckets aside, pelted back for more. When the sand ran out, they stamped and beat out the fires with rugs, cushions, books – whatever came to hand. Still the incendiary bombs kept coming. With the tumult, the fires, and the capering skeleton, the crowd was reaching frenzy pitch.

"It's no use," Dan said. "We'll have to fire."

"I'm ready," said Dr Russell.

"Ackland!" Dan shouted. "Witt – Garvey! Fire over their heads – now!"

Lord Oldfield pulled out his gun and knelt by the sill to take aim. Russell and Dan stood over him, and they fired together. The crowd had exhausted the bottles by now, and the salvo from the downstairs and upstairs windows made an impressive show. The fumes of powder and the echoes of the retorts hung heavy on the night air.

Now the attackers had to weigh up the chances of men armed with sticks against men with guns. The driver leapt into his cart and whipped the frightened horses out of the gates. His mate shouted "Oi!" and ran after him. Silas Singleton yelled,

"Stand your ground!" but some of the others had already had the same idea.

They reloaded the guns, and Dan gave the order to fire again. Another clutch of Singleton's men flung their torches into the mud and bolted.

"Next time we shoot to kill!" Dan warned.

The man carrying the skeleton flung it to the ground. Singleton, stunned by the speedy collapse of his army, had to be dragged away by his friends. One lone straggler faced the Hall and shook his fist up at the window, dislodging his scarf from his face as he did so. Lord Oldfield was already on his way to his mother's room to tell the ladies the danger had passed and did not see him. Nor did Dr Russell, who was fiddling with his gun. But Dan got a clear view. It was Walter.

"Damn him, damn him, damn him!"

"What's the matter?" said Dr Russell.

"Nothing. I'm going to check outside. Stay here and look after His Lordship. Don't let him leave the house. It isn't safe yet."

On his way out, Dan saw Ackland and repeated the order to keep Lord Oldfield inside. "Get the windows boarded up. Serve brandy and wine, food for them that want it. Post sentries outside, two front and back. Lock this door behind me."

The scuffed gravel was littered with hissing torches, broken glass and shattered bones. Dan sprinted around the side of the Hall and saw Walter running across the lawn, his figure silhouetted against the scaffolding around the half-built temple. He made for the nearest entry point into the forest and slipped into the trees.

Dan plunged in after him. Branches whacked his head and arms, brambles snatched his ankles and legs. He stumbled into a pile of fence posts and put out a hand to save himself. A coil of wire cut into his fingers. Pain shot through his left knee. And he had lost Walter.

No. It was too sudden. He was younger than Dan, but he

was no fitter. Dan might not know the sounds of the wood, but he knew the sound of a winded man trying to catch his breath. The lad was somewhere to his right.

"Walter, I know you're there. I'm not going to arrest you. I just want to talk."

Leaves rustled. A twig broke. Dan twisted round, but could see nothing except darkness under the trees.

"I'm not going to arrest you," he said again.

"No, you're bloody not!"

Walter flew at him, swinging a thick branch in a two-handed grip. An easy target. Dan ducked and brought his fist up under the lad's chin. He staggered, doubled up against a tree, the branch still in his grasp, trailing on the ground.

"Stay back," he gasped, "or I'll kill you."

"Don't be stupid. Put that down. I've come to send you home."

"So you can arrest me in the morning? No fear. I'm off. I'm leaving Barcombe tonight."

"And turning yourself into an outlaw? You'll be on the run for the rest of your life – which will be short. Do as I tell you and no one need know you were here tonight. Go home and stay there. Keep away from the village, away from the forest, away from Singleton and the rest."

"I'm not going to do anything you tell me. You lied to me. You put my friends in prison. You pretended you were one of us and you put them in prison. And that's where I'd rather be, with other good men."

"Hanging with your other good men, you mean? First a poacher, now a rioter...There'll be no mercy for you if you stay mixed up in tonight's work, despite your youth."

"Why should you care?"

"You know why."

"The poor orphan boy made good. Lies. All lies. Well, fuck you, you Bow Street bastard."

Walter shifted his weight and raised the branch. He was young, inexperienced and angry, and his clumsy attack gave

239

Dan the upper hand. He stood his ground and let Walter come on.

There was a bang and a flash of light. Walter screamed and skidded to a halt. Dan turned round. Dr Russell stood behind him, one pistol held out, still smoking, another at his side.

"What the hell did you do that for?" Dan yelled.

"He was going to kill you. And I want to do that."

Dan was so taken up with Walter he thought he had misheard. The doctor had missed, and Walter, realising he was unhurt, had disappeared into the trees. Dan started after him, but Russell pointed the second gun at him.

"Stay where you are or I'll shoot."

"What the hell are you doing?"

"I'm killing you and blaming your little friend for it."

Russell stooped and picked up the branch Walter had thrown away. He weighed it in his hand. "Nice and heavy. Should break a few bones. Don't worry, you'll be out cold. Turn round and kneel."

The way Josh Castle had been killed: knocked down and beaten to a pulp, only then it had been an iron bar, wielded by a man who knew exactly where to strike. All the time Dan had been wondering when Lord Oldfield had had the chance to get rid of the notepaper from the parlour game, and it had been Russell who had seen Dan notice the paper, Russell who had thrown it on the fire. The realisation that he was looking into the face of Josh's killer was not likely to do him much good now.

"No. You'll have to shoot me. Pin that on Walter if you can."

"Then I'll shoot you. An unfortunate accident. The boy was attacking you – I fired in the dark – you got in the way – the boy fled. I'll be grief-stricken, and you'll be dead."

"And when they find Walter and he tells them what really happened, what then?"

"Who will believe him?"

"What about the shot you've already fired? Someone's bound to have heard it."

"Now you're getting desperate. Obviously I fired at the boy in an effort to bring him down during the chase. Then I fell behind and he cornered you. I ran up to find you struggling with him, etcetera, etcetera."

"I've already told Lord Oldfield it was you who killed Josh. Killing me won't save you."

"No, you haven't. If you had, do you think Lord Oldfield would have let me stand beside him tonight? 'We were like brothers,' he said, as he stood blubbering over the body in the ice house. Like brothers – a lord and a gamekeeper! It's his fault Castle thought so much of himself and got ideas so far above what he deserved. The man was a peasant."

"A peasant in love with a lady, isn't that right? I remember now, Doctor. You in the churchyard with Miss Ruscombe on the day of Castle's funeral, offering her comfort and sympathy over her brother's grave. You knew she wasn't weeping for her brother, didn't you? And you thought all you had to do was wait. She couldn't mourn a peasant forever."

Russell had had enough talk. He raised the gun and took aim. There was not much an unarmed man could do save make a desperate attempt to get out of the way. Dan flung himself to the ground. As he went down he thought he saw something move behind the doctor. There was a loud *crack*. Russell crumpled.

Dan struggled to his feet and limped over to Walter. The youth dropped a fence post and gazed at the fallen man in horror. "Have I killed him?"

"No," Dan answered, though he could see why Walter might think so. Russell's face was covered in blood and his eyes stared sightlessly into the darkness. He groaned when Dan snatched the gun out of his hand.

"Why did you do that? You were going to kill me yourself a few moments ago."

Walter shrugged. "What would Mother have said?"

"Help me get him up. We need to get him back to the Hall."

"What about Lord Oldfield and the riot?"

"Say you'd come out to gawp at it and it was lucky for me you did...I'll back you up."

"But what if the doctor says something?"

Dan hauled Russell to his feet. "Who'll believe him now?"

Chapter Twenty-Four

The doctor was fully conscious by the time Dan and Walter got him back to Oldfield Hall. Crossing the lawn, they saw Mudge and Potter moving around the house with lanterns, checking all was clear. Some of the servants were hammering boards over the broken windows. Inside, others were taking down tattered curtains, shifting scorched furniture, rolling up singed rugs.

Cotterell, Ackland, Witt and Drake were in the hall, checking the firearms.

Cotterell, his eyes bulging with indignation, flew to the doctor's side. "Dr Russell! This is a fine return for all your charity in the village!"

"Was it an ambush?" asked Witt.

Drake wanted to know if Dan had seen the attackers, and Ackland asked how many there were. Dan ignored their questions.

"Ackland, fetch Lord Oldfield. Witt, Drake, help me get him into the parlour."

Cotterell, not wanting to miss the excitement, came too. So did Walter, who kept close to Dan. For him, coming into a magistrate's house was like sticking his head in a lion's mouth. He withdrew to a corner of the room.

Drake kicked the fire back into life, Ackland brought hot water and dressings, and Witt stood by, cracking his knuckles. Dan was bandaging Russell's head when Lord Oldfield hurried in.

"Dr Russell, my dear fellow! If I find who did this I – "

"Walter did it," Dan interrupted. "And lucky for me he did.

This, Lord Oldfield, is Josh Castle's murderer."

"Dr Russell? What nonsense is this? Russell, what is this about?"

Russell's eyes glittered from beneath the bandage and a horrible half-smile, half-sneer twisted his face. "Pity I missed."

Lord Oldfield turned so white it was hard to tell which of them looked the sicker.

"It was you who shot at me? But why?"

Dan gave the doctor a shove in the back. "Why don't you tell him, Russell? Tell him it wasn't for game or money or revenge, but for a woman."

Lord Oldfield sank into a chair. "What woman?"

"Miss Louisa Ruscombe," Dan answered.

That drew a response from Russell. "If you were a gentleman, I'd call you out for speaking of a lady in male company."

"But I'm not a gentleman. Neither was Josh. That's what rankled, wasn't it? That she could pass you over for – what was it you called him – a peasant?…Miss Ruscombe and Castle were planning to get married. They thought they'd kept it secret, but the doctor had his eye on Miss Ruscombe, probably followed her to one of their meetings. She knew nothing of his passion for her, nor his villainy. And he blamed you, Lord Oldfield, for raising Castle above his station."

Ackland appeared at Lord Oldfield's elbow with a glass of brandy. He took it and gulped it down. "When did you know, Foster?"

"Not until tonight, when I saw Mrs West take a piece of paper from the vase." Dan took out his pocketbook and unfolded the three Bloodie Bones notes. "It was the same as the one that was pinned to the scarecrow: *'Tirants Bwar Bloodie Bones.'* Look at how different it is from the other two. It's written on expensive paper, thick and watermarked, not the sort of thing you'd expect to find in a poacher's cottage. The other two are genuine, this was written by Dr Russell."

"That sheet of paper?" Cotterell said. "I was using it. I found it in a book when I was browsing." He turned and waved vaguely towards one of the tables, where lay a number of volumes of prints. "I didn't know it was important."

Russell laughed. "There goes your proof, Foster. The paper belongs to Lord Oldfield."

"Let me see it," said Lord Oldfield. "It is yours, Russell. It's the sort you use for Lady Oldfield's prescriptions."

"But I left it here and you used it, Lord Oldfield. Or should I say Lord Bloodie Bones? You killed Josh Castle."

Dan clouted him. "Shut it."

Russell lay back on the sofa and closed his eyes, smiling to himself at some private joke.

Lord Oldfield handed the note back to Dan. "Strange that a sheet of paper can bring a man to the gallows."

"I'm not relying on that alone. I may find more of it when I search his house, though I doubt it. He saw me looking at the note when we viewed the body and probably rushed home and destroyed his entire supply. But it doesn't matter. I have his confession, that and his attempt on my life, which failed thanks to Walter."

"Who is Walter?"

Dan beckoned to the boy, who stood in the shadows biting his fingernails.

"Walter Halling, apprentice to his uncle, a shoemaker in Stonyton. He came out to look at the riot."

"What, found it entertaining, did he?" Lord Oldfield snapped.

"As people find fires, floods and brawls entertaining. You can't blame the lad for that. And you have him to thank for the doctor's capture."

"Do I?" Lord Oldfield eyed the boy shrewdly, then with a sharp glance in Dan's direction wisely decided to stifle his suspicions. "Then you have earned a reward, my lad. I'll speak to Mudge about it."

Walter scowled. Dan was afraid he was about to scorn the offer and tax Lord Oldfield with dog-murder, but Cotterell exclaimed, "Good Lord, what now?"

They had been so busy with the doctor they had not noticed the sound of hoof beats drawing near to the house, nor the growing mayhem beyond the drawing room door: running feet, yelling, windows and doors banged shut.

"Keep an eye on him," Dan said to Witt and Drake.

He ran out of the room, Walter and the others following. He knew it was not the rioters coming back – they would not be on horseback. By the time they'd got outside so did everyone else, and the panic had died down. The door the footmen had been frantically trying to close was flung open. Through it Dan saw half a dozen horsemen riding out of the grey dawn. They clattered smartly down the drive and reined to a halt.

"Where is Lord Oldfield?" cried their captain.

His face was bright with excitement – and what handsome young man wouldn't enjoy wearing gleaming boots and epaulettes, and galloping about the country on a splendid, snorting horse with a sword at his side and a clutch of like-minded fellows at his back? Lord Oldfield stepped forward. The captain took off his hat and, with an elegant flourish, bowed low in the saddle.

"Captain Ffox-Harrington of the Bath Loyal Association at your service, My Lord."

"You are very welcome," His Lordship answered. "Who sent for you?"

"Your rector. Don't know his name. Turned up in town with some fool of a constable. As soon as he told me you were under siege, I mustered my troop and here we are – volunteers pledged to protect King and Country."

"Now the fighting's over," Ackland muttered.

But Dan was glad to see them. If the rioters did have thoughts of coming back, armed volunteers would put them off. In the meantime, Ffox-Harrington's men could guard the prisoner while the rest of them got some breakfast.

Reverend Poole and Ayres turned up while they were eating. The rector lapped up Lord Oldfield's expressions of gratitude for his prompt action, but Ayres kept out of the way. He was glad that no one paid him much attention, though Dan did not hold it against him that he had not the nerve to join the defenders. It was not easy for a man to turn the law on his neighbours, especially so feeble a creature as Ayres.

Dan did not find any paper in the doctor's house and did not waste a lot of time on the search. He was more concerned about seeing the prisoner safe to Shepton Mallet. This time they travelled in Lord Oldfield's coach and had the Loyalist militia as an escort.

On their return, Ffox-Harrington and his men were entertained to a splendid luncheon by His Lordship and a sparkling Lady Helen. Even old Lady Oldfield smiled upon them with a faraway, reminiscent look in her eye, thinking, Dan supposed, of the gay young officers she had flirted with in her own girlhood. He slipped away as soon as he could. He had one last duty to perform.

The cottage door was open, and from inside came the slosh of water. Dan stopped on the threshold, casting a shadow across the room. Anna looked up from her work. A spasm of anger shot across her face, quickly controlled.

"So you've come then," she said, putting aside her mop. She did not take off her apron or smooth her hair.

Dan took off his hat and ducked inside. The chairs stood on top of the table, the hearth was swept and a fire laid, but not lit. The windows were wide open to dry the damp floor. Anna did not offer him a drink or invite him to lift down the chairs.

"I'm leaving tomorrow."

"I know. In His Lordship's carriage. I heard it at the village shop this morning. Mrs Travell's cousin has come over from Bath to help her run the place. I think they'll get on very well. They're both women who like a gossip, and you are the talk of the village."

He tried a smile. "I'm glad I don't know what they're saying about me."

She did not smile back. "I could tell you, if you like."

"I'm not interested in them. It's your opinion – "

"You made clear to me how much you value my opinion when you lied to me."

"I wanted to tell you. It wasn't safe. I know Singleton and the rest are neighbours of yours, but to me they were dangerous, violent men, and it was my job to bring them to justice."

"They were no friends of mine. You know that. I didn't want Walter running with them. I'm glad they're in prison."

"He isn't."

"He will be when he's got his own home and family and can look back on his narrow escape. I don't forget that was your doing. I'm grateful to you for that."

"I wish the boy well."

"I expect you do. Is there anything else you lied about?"

"Like what?" Dan asked cautiously.

"Is there a wife back in London?"

"Yes. But it isn't simple. It's – "

"I know. It's a loveless marriage. You were forced into it. She's gone off with your best friend. She's barren, frigid, cold, and a man has his needs. Which is it?"

"It's none of them. It's – "

"Spare me your tale of a wife who is no wife. Do you think that makes it right to lie and cheat and trick people?"

"Anna, I didn't want – "

"But you had no choice. Very well, Dan Fielding – I'm sorry, I mean Foster. Your life was in danger, I can see that. But you could have said something without putting yourself at risk. Dan Fielding might have mentioned a Mrs Fielding he'd left behind somewhere. Then at least I'd have made my choice with my eyes open."

"Would you have made the same choice?"

"Don't ask me that. Don't try to trap me into saying it would have made no difference."

"You still don't know everything."

"What is there to know?" She made a dismissive gesture and turned away from him. He grabbed her wrist and twisted her round to face him. She struggled, but he hung on, let her spit and scratch and kick until her hair was loose and she was sobbing and flushed with anger.

"Her name's Caroline. She's a drunk. She's mad with it. It makes her low, cunning and vicious, fills her with venom, with self-loathing, makes her a fury one minute, a pathetic creature the next. And she hates me, she blames me…and maybe it is my fault. I stopped loving her a long time ago."

Anna had stopped fighting but he still clung on to her. He let go. When he saw that his fingers had left red marks on her wrist he was filled with self-disgust. He had not only lied to this woman, he had tried to win her sympathy with a whining, self-pitying tale.

"I'm sorry, Anna. That's all I can say."

He turned away, had reached the door by the time she caught up to him and clutched his arm. "No, wait! Dan!"

He did not look at her. He could not have seen her if he had for the film across his eyes. Foolish and weak, he told himself, you are foolish and weak. You should keep moving, keep walking, leave it like this. But he did not.

"I'm sorry for you, Dan, I truly am, but you must see that it's no good for me, or for Walter. The boy needs a father and I need a husband. I hoped you would be that man, though you never spoke any promises. But there's more to promises than words, isn't that so?"

"I meant what I said. I wish you and Walter well. If you ever need anything, if there's anything I can do…"

She laid her finger on his lips. "I don't want your promises now. I know you don't think you're lying, but you are. You're in a habit of lying. You tell yourself it's because of your job, and maybe it is to start with. But before you know it, it's reached into every bit of you until it's who you are. It'll be your ruin, you'll see that one day." She lowered her hand. "Goodbye, Dan."

Chapter Twenty-Five

In the morning, Dan breakfasted with His Lordship in his office. Garvey, who was staying on to deal with the enclosure business, ate with the ladies in the dining room.

Lord Oldfield handed Dan a full purse. "You've earned this, though I'd rather give you one earned in the ring."

"Thank you, My Lord. I prefer to get my rewards this way."

"All the same, if ever you change your mind my offer is still open. You could choose whoever you liked as your trainer. We'd have a rare time, Foster. I'd have you fighting at Newmarket – Brighton – Epsom…No, don't naysay me. Just promise me you will at least think about it."

Dan hesitated. It was unwise to turn good offers down with too much finality. "Very well, I will think about it. I'll promise nothing more. But in return, may I ask you something?"

Lord Oldfield flicked a gracious hand.

"I know the lands are yours: Barcombe Wood, the heath, the farms, the village. But in a manner of speaking they belong to the people too. Their families have lived here for generations, like yours. They've depended on the country for firewood and food, just as yours has for revenue and rents. Taking it away from them will make them poor, and that will make them desperate. You've seen yourself what that leads to."

"You think that I should give in to mob rule as the nobles of France have done? That I should reward the villains who terrified my household, damaged and stole my property, and even desecrated my family tomb?"

"No, I don't think you should give in to mob rule. I do think that if you'd been a little more careful, none of it would have happened."

"You think I'm to blame?"

"I think as a law officer. I see the peace broken and I see that it could have been avoided, that further outbreaks can still be avoided. You're a rich man, Lord Oldfield. You don't know what it's like to rely on a few sticks of wood or a handful of berries just to survive. Don't drive them to destitution. Open the wood to them, at least some of the time. Let them take kindling in due season, let them forage, turn a blind eye to the loss of the occasional rabbit, hare, or fish, as your father did."

"I have deer in those woods and I plan to increase my herd. I can't have them racketing through the place, disturbing the does and butchering the stags."

"No, and I agree such acts should be punished. But if you fix the times they may come in to gather a few logs or acorns, you can manage it. If your fear of the disturbance they might make is so great, cut the wood yourself and distribute it. Gather the food and herbs and hand them out."

"I don't intend to give them a thing, not after the ungrateful way they've behaved."

"You've given them nothing to be grateful about. You've robbed them. That's how they see it. They see that you can afford to be generous, and they see that you refuse. How can you expect their gratitude?"

"They are worthless dogs. I will give them nothing, I tell you!"

"Not every object of charity is deserving, but some can change. Look at me."

He did, surprised.

"I was once a thief. I broke the law because I was starving. Then a generous man saved me. You can let Barcombe turn into a nest of sullen, hopeless criminals, aye, and nurture revolution on your own doorstep. Or you can treat them with kindness and reap the benefits of peace."

"Well," Lord Oldfield said after a moment, "I wasn't expecting that from you. A law officer who defends the lawless."

"I defend the peace."

"I won't deny that you've given me something to think about. So I'll promise you the same as you promised me. I'll think about it."

"Then you will soon see that my way is the wisest." Dan smiled. "Speaking as a law officer. Until Taunton Assizes, Lord Oldfield."

They rose and shook hands. "Until then."

In the stableyard, Dan asked Lord Oldfield's driver if it was possible to avoid driving through Barcombe. Since the riot a brooding peace had hung over the village, and he did not want to provoke a renewal of hostilities or rub the people's noses in their defeat by bowling through the streets in His Lordship's carriage.

"It'll mean going a deal out of the way," the man said, "and tire the horses more than usual, without His Lordship's permission too." But Dan was popular with the servants at Oldfield Hall, and the driver agreed to his request. The young groom who was to accompany them said he was game, so instead of turning left on the Bath Road and following it through the village, they went in the opposite direction then turned off to strike the road circling Barcombe Heath. Eventually they came out on the Bath Road with the spire of Barcombe church behind them. Above them was a long wooded ridge like the one Dan had gazed upon on that first morning when he had woken under the hedge. Idly, he looked along the hedgerow as they passed, wondering if he was near the spot.

A man in a shapeless coat rose suddenly from the side of the road. He stood swaying at the roadside and watched the carriage pass. His eyes, yellow in his grey face, met Dan's through the glass. At their mutual recognition his mouth fell open and he uttered a cry of panic which was drowned out by

252

the noise of the vehicle. Stumbling, he fled.

Why should Girtin flee from Dan? Spit at the carriage as it went by, yes, but run as if Bloodie Bones himself was at his heels? Or a Bow Street Runner...

Dan pulled down the window. "Stop!"

The driver pulled up, but Dan was out of the carriage before the wheels had stopped turning and running back along the lane. He came to the place where Girtin had been standing and looked about him. A movement in the opposite field caught his eye. He sprang forward, leaped over the fence and pelted up the hill. The old man was no match for him: in a few strides Dan was close enough to hear his laboured breath, smell the spirits on it.

"Girtin," he said.

Girtin shuddered to a halt and faced him. Dan, a few feet below him on the slope, looked up into the terrified face.

"The Tolleys lost their daughter. You lost your sons. Was it justice, Girtin?"

Girtin trembled and his skin shone with perspiration but he did not answer.

"You killed Sukie and the child you'd fathered on her, didn't you? That's why you started drinking – before your sons went away and your wife died; before you lost everything. You started drinking because of what you'd done. And you hang around the churchyard because all that's left to you is graves."

Girtin's gaze slewed over Dan's shoulder. "And now Lord Oldfield is changing everything, I won't even have that. There's no place in Barcombe for me any more. I might as well hang."

He moved towards Dan, who stepped away, his hands at his sides. "No. I won't take you. But before you go from Barcombe, you should tell the Tolleys that Sukie won't be coming back."

Girtin's knees buckled and he sank to the ground. Dan did not offer to lift him up. He knew Girtin would not tell;

he'd been a coward when he slew the girl and a coward when he admitted it. It did not matter. When he was back in London, Dan would write to Mrs Poole with the information; she would know what to do, and be kindly about it too. He turned on his heel and walked back to the lane.

Lord Oldfield's carriage dropped Dan at The Lamb in Bath, where he took an inside place in the London mail coach. He got out at the Gloucester Coffee House at around eight the next morning, and walked along Piccadilly and through Leicester Square towards Covent Garden. He stopped at Old Slaughter's Coffee House for breakfast, which was served by a waiter whose company was too cheery for a man who had spent a sleepless night in a coach.

He still had his report to finish, as well as the descriptions of the men who had attacked him in the lane to circulate and file. Silas Singleton was on the run too, but most of the rioters remained unidentified. Dan was happy to leave it at that, and even Lord Oldfield saw there was nothing to be gained from transporting every last man in Barcombe and throwing all their families onto the poor rate.

Instead of going to the office, Dan went to Cecil Street. Noah was overseeing a sparring match between two boys who were much the age Dan had been when he'd met Noah at Blackheath. Noah called his assistant, Paul, to take over. The old soldier hurried up, his ready smile on his face. Unfortunately for him, it was not a smile that won friends, not until they got to know him and could see beyond the fearsome spectacle of his jagged teeth. It was the result, he said, of a French rifle butt in the mouth at Quebec in '59. His looks had never bothered Dan. He had seen uglier faces in the brickfields, some ravaged by syphilis, some by gin, others badly put together after backstreet fighting contests that were as far removed from Broughton's Rules as war from peace.

It was the parlour where Dan and Noah sat and talked. 'Parlour' was too grand a word for the dark little alcove with its battered furniture and threadbare rug. Only a curtain separated it from the gymnasium, so the sounds of glove on flesh, grunts, and Paul's shouts – "Elbows out", "Arms up", "Bear on the right heel" – echoing off the stone walls were an ever-present background.

The chamber smelt of liniment and spirits. These last were not for drinking – Noah never drank intoxicating liquors – but for boxers to soak their fists in to toughen the skin. The table, floor and chairs were cluttered with old newspapers and yellowing notices of fights, rolls of bandages, odd gloves that had burst and awaited repair when Paul had a moment, ropes, weights, buckets, and a copy of Mendoza's book *The Art of Boxing* that looked as if it had stood up to forty rounds in the ring. They had eaten their meals in here when Dan was a boy; the food came straight off the fire, hot and fresh, so the room also smelt of fried beef and onions.

Dan sipped soda water while Noah looked at his injuries.

"You'll do," he said, "but I wouldn't move around on that knee too much for a few days. We'll focus on some upper body work and weights."

"Fine. I'll be in tomorrow as usual."

Noah sat down. "You look down, son. Was it a bad one?"

"Not pleasant. When are these things ever?"

"You've maybe had enough of it?"

Dan laughed. "If I had, I've had another offer." He told Noah about Lord Oldfield's plan to make him a professional pugilist.

"You could do worse. You've some good years left in you."

"And I've been trained by the best."

They both smiled at the old catchphrase. Noah sat back in his chair and watched Dan thoughtfully. Dan caught his eye and shrugged.

"It's nothing. I'm tired. I was travelling all night."

"Have you been home yet?"

"No. Is all well?"

"Same as ever."

Same as ever, and Dan could not put it off much longer.

He said goodbye, and waved at Paul and one or two men he recognised as he went out. In the street he thought again about the work waiting for him at the office, but he still could not face it.

It had never been easy going through the door after a day's or night's work, not knowing what he would find. When he let himself in and the first thing he heard was the rattle and clash of dishes, he tensed. Then he noticed a savoury smell. Someone was cooking. It would not be Caroline.

He put down his bag and went into the kitchen. Eleanor was bending over the hearth, stirring a pot of stew. Startled, she looked up.

"Dan! You're home...You're limping. And your face is bruised. Captain Ellis said you were all right."

Somehow they were standing close together, their hands almost touching. "It's nothing. Ellis called, did he?"

"Yes, so I – we knew you'd be back soon."

"I would have been sooner, only – "

The back door opened and a stout little woman bustled into the room.

"Don't block the way like that, Nell. It's brass monkeys in that privy." She shut the door. "Keep the heat in...Heavens, it's Dan, and we never heard him come in. Well, put the kettle on, girl. The man's fair worn out." She still had a Yorkshire accent: a warm, homely sound.

Footsteps sounded overhead, and a voice croaked, "Is it him?"

Mrs Harper went to the foot of the stairs. "Are you awake, love? Yes, it's Dan. We didn't hear him come in...I'll come and help you get dressed."

Dan and Eleanor listened to her footsteps pass overhead, the murmur of voices – Caroline's peevish, her mother's soothing.

Dan wondered why Ellis had called. He had not asked him to; had not sent him with any message. "Has Ellis visited before when I've been away?"

"Once or twice. He's always very polite."

"I bet he is."

She smiled. "He's always very polite to Mother. I don't always see him."

He knew he had no right to be pleased, but he was. Ellis was a good man; he ought to tell her that, he ought to encourage her to think kindly of him. Ellis was a good-looking man too. They would be a handsome couple.

The thought was like a cut to the eye, a crimson, blinding agony. A fighter reacted to pain by instinct, protected himself from it without thinking, so his brain had to catch up with his body. Before he knew he was going to do it, Dan had seized her hand, swooped over her, pressed his lips on hers. Her arms went around his neck; her mouth responded to his; their pent-up passion cried for release.

Someone blundered against the door and they leapt apart. Mrs Harper ushered Caroline into the room. "Here she is, here she is, all better now you're home, Dan."

No need for anyone to tell him what was wrong with Caroline. Her face was puffy and her eyes bloodshot, but she was neatly dressed with a shawl about her shoulders. Her hair was loose but had been brushed.

"So it's you, Puritan."

"I've asked you not to call me that."

She laughed, slouched towards the armchair by the fire, and sat down as if exhausted by the effort. She closed her eyes for a moment and swallowed. She was still feeling sick.

"Been in the wars, Dan?" she said.

"A little. It was a tough job."

"And you're the toughest man they could find to do it. Don't you think he's a tough man, Nell? So brave. Such a hero." She yawned. "What's that you're cooking? A feast for the hero? Smells disgusting. It's turning my stomach."

"It's not that that's turning your stomach," Dan said.

"What did you say? Did you speak to me? Well, I am

honoured by your attention, I'm sure. You must have mistaken me for my sister."

"Now, now, Caro," said Mrs Harper. "Let's not bicker. We'll have a cup of tea. It will do you good. You must be hungry, Dan. I'll cut you some bread."

"Do you want a cup, Dan?"

Eleanor was busy with teapot and caddy, her hands shaking, her face turned away from him. He could see a red spot on her cheek that was not put there by the heat from the fire. Her eyes glinted with tears she would not shed in front of Caroline, who would seize on them and revel in them as she always did, watching Dan for any sign of emotion as she taunted her sister. Nothing Dan did or said could turn her spite away from Eleanor. His presence only fed her rage.

He snatched up his hat. "I haven't got time. I have to get back to Bow Street."

THE END

Notes

Beat all hollow A man who is "beaten all hollow" in a fight never stood a chance of winning.

Black Act In the early eighteenth century, a bitter conflict broke out between local people and government-appointed officials in royal parks and forests. The dispute was over rights to the produce of the land – the game, wood and so on. Armed protesters, known as Blacks because of their blacked-up faces, went on poaching raids, set fire to hayricks, cut down trees, and sent threatening letters to local landowners. The government response was the Black Act of 1723 (also known as the Waltham Black Act) which made it a capital offence to go out 'armed in disguise', or to take game, or to damage property, or commit a range of other offences (some fifty offences were listed as capital). Thus going 'armed in disguise' without committing any of the other crimes could in itself be enough to attract the death penalty.

Broughton's Rules Champion pugilist Jack Broughton (c. 1703–1789), who ran a boxing academy for the gentry in London (the ampitheatre on Oxford Road), formulated the first set of rules for the sport in 1743. They included the requirement for the chalking of a square in the centre of the ring where the fighters were placed on the lines opposite one another at the start of a round or after a fall. Defeat was signalled by a fighter failing to come up to the mark within the allotted time (thirty seconds), or if his second declared him beaten. The rules also banned hitting a man when he was down, and a man on his knees was counted as down. Originally intended only for use in his academy, Broughton's Rules were widely adopted, and were not replaced until the introduction of the 'New Rules' in 1838.

Buggybow A bogeyman (such as Bloodie Bones).

Doubler A blow causing someone to double up.

Fleet marriage A clandestine marriage performed by an unscrupulous or unqualified person which did not conform with the legal requirements for a valid marriage. Clandestine marriages were available at a number of locations, most notoriously in and around the Fleet Prison in London. The Marriage Act of 1753 (known as Lord Hardwicke's Marriage Act after the then lord chancellor, Philip Yorke, First Earl of Hardwicke (1690–1764)) regularised the legal requirements for a valid marriage, stipulating, among other things, that marriage was only legal if banns had been read or if a special licence had been obtained, and that a marriage of minors (individuals under twenty-one) without parental consent was void.

Gabey A foolish fellow.

Game Laws A series of statutes stretching back to the Middle Ages to control the hunting of wild animals, which based the right to hunt on a property qualification. Amongst other things, the various statutes define types of game and hunting seasons, and regulate the sale of game.

Hell-Fire Club A secret eighteenth-century organisation whose male, aristocratic members indulged in orgies, pagan rituals and heavy drinking.

Humbugging To impose upon or trick someone, or (as here) to delay or avoid getting on with the business in hand.

Necessary house A privy or latrine.

Small beer A weak beer for everyday drinking.

The Earl of the Plough
One of many folklore figures evoked during episodes of social revolt, the Earl of the Plough was possibly associated with the rural celebration Plough Monday, when a plough was dragged around the village. Many of the figures had their origins in similar rural rituals and mummers' performances. Perhaps the most well-known was Captain Swing, who led the agricultural labourers' riots against the introduction of threshing machines which deprived them of their jobs in the 1820s and 1830s. Similar folklore figures which represented a challenge to repressive authority (and which are mentioned in *Bloodie Bones*) were Robin Hood, who needs no explanation, and Jack Straw, who was a rebel leader during the 1381 rebellion. The fictitious Bloodie Bones of Barcombe is one such figure, intended to strike fear into the hearts of the enemies of the people, and also disguise the protesters' identities.

The Fancy
Followers of boxing. (Also used of other sports, e.g. pigeon fanciers.)

The London Corresponding Society
A radical men's organisation founded by shoemaker Thomas Hardy (1752–1832) in 1792. The LCS called for universal male suffrage and annual parliaments, and welcomed the French Revolution. As its name suggests, it was in constant contact with radicals in other parts of the country. However, the government took increasingly repressive measures against it, finally outlawing it in 1799. (Dan Foster will meet the LCS again in the second Dan Foster novel.)

The Riot Act
The Riot Act of 1714 made it a capital offence if more than a dozen people refused to disperse within one hour of being ordered to do so by a magistrate, who read out the relevant section of the Act and was empowered to call troops to his assistance. Today we still talk of 'reading someone the riot act'.

Tipstaff
A staff carried by certain officials as a badge of office. The one carried by Bow Street officers was six–seven inches long with a crown-shaped top, and could be of wood, brass, or even silver. Some were hollow with a top that unscrewed so that the officer could place a magistrate's warrant inside it.

Acknowledgements

I would like to thank all the people who have given me help and support in the writing of this book. Special thanks go to Sanjida O'Connell and Ali Reynolds of ARC Editorial; to my 'beta readers', Debbie Young and Martine Bailey; to my sister, Glynis van Uden; to Catherine Hunt and Antonio Moreno for the Spanish; and to Helen Hart and the wonderful team at SilverWood Books. And a very special thank you to my husband, Gerard, who has been at my side in sickness and health; who tracked down the most obscure books when I needed them for research; and who knows a thing or two about colons and semi-colons.

Bow Street Runners and bare-knuckle fighters, radicals and pickpockets, resurrection men and bluestockings...

Find out more about Dan Foster's world at
lucienneboyce.com/DanFosterBSR

Lightning Source UK Ltd.
Milton Keynes UK
UKHW011327121118
332199UK00002B/449/P